# The
# Bartholomew
# Fair
# Murders

Other books by Leonard Tourney

*Familiar Spirits*
*Low Treason*
*The Players' Boy Is Dead*

# The Bartholomew Fair Murders

by
Leonard Tourney

A
Joan
Kahn
BOOK

St. Martin's Press
New York

*Design by Doris Borowsky*

Copy Editor: Eva Galan Salmieri

Library of Congress Cataloging in Publication Data

Tourney, Leonard Γ
    The Bartholmew Fair murders.

    "A Joan Kahn book."
    I. Title.
PS3570.0784B3    1986        813'.54        86-3700
ISBN 0-312-06710-0

First Edition

10 9 8 7 6 5 4 3 2 1

"Thou art the seat of the Beast,
O Smithfield . . ."

Ben Jonson,
*Bartholomew Fair*

# The
# Bartholomew
# Fair
# Murders

# • *Prologue* •

On the eleventh of June, the Eve of the Feast of St. Barnabas the Apostle, the old woman who had ruled England longer than most of her subjects could remember strolled amid the floral blazonry of the royal garden at her father's palace of Whitehall, contemplating the very thing it was most distasteful for her to contemplate, her own death.

She had just come from the chapel, where a certain Reverend Bishop of the Realm—a foolish, prattling knave without the sense of a radish—had preached learnedly and long on the demise of the body. Not only on its demise but its putrefaction! Hardly music for the royal ears that could better endure the rude minstrelsy of a country wedding or the clamor of Thames fishmongers than a tedious sermon on the theme of decay, worms, and dust.

As if she needed that bitter pill in her age and condition, when every creak and rattle in her old bones played herald to eternity.

The Bishop's sermon had put her in a mortal frame of mind. It had dropped her like a stone into a pool of sullen melancholy. She walked now in the most beautiful of gardens, a triumph of art, a wedding of nature and human cunning unparalleled. Yet no birdsong nor gardener's skill gave her delight. The sun of this most blessed month provided no warmth for the mortal chill at the bone. Even the efflorescence around her seemed to mock her waning vitality. Why, she might as well have gazed upon a chapless death's-head for all the joy the garden gave her.

Her maids, guards, and sundry other attendants waited her pleasure at the foot of the garden. Waited at her command. A flick of her little finger would have brought the whole fawning pack running. But that gave her no pleasure either. She ignored them all, walking erect of back and high of head as though she needed none of them, insisting upon her privacy for a change, a respite from the constant obsequiousness she both demanded and despised. Her sole companion and confidant at the moment—he whose arm she used for support, not that she could not have done without it if she wished—was he whom she trusted more than any other in her old age. Sir Robert Cecil. Son of the great Lord Burghley. The same Lord Burghley she had trusted more than any other man in her youth.

Cecil, small of stature, misshapen in body—the result of a fall as a babe—appearing older than his forty winters (what, after all, were forty winters to her nearly three score ten?), listened unfailingly, like an heir awaiting mention of his name in a will. That, she had concluded long ago, was the best of Cecil's virtues. That and most careful discretion. Cecil knew when to listen, when to speak. And at the moment, he at least was pleasing her by playing chorus to her meditations, reproving her gloom without too much insistence (God's blood! If she wished to be gloomy she would be!) nor adding to it with depressing observations of his own.

"My body will rot. It will rot and occupy no greater room than will hold the meanest of my subjects," she said.

"Ay, Majesty," Cecil replied. "It's a sad truth, but please, give over this talk of rotting corpses."

"For Queen and clown—life's but the same span," she went on obstinately. "Does it not seem contrary to reason, good Robin, that a Queen should not live twice or even thrice as long as the elderly fishwife of Billingsgate who they say lived to be a hundred and five?"

"Reason *would* dictate that a Queen's life be longer," Cecil said, "since she is the very font of civic virtue and the vice-regent of God on earth. Unfortunately, reason does not prevail in the matter. God has set man's span—yea, and woman's too."

"Oh, I am weary of this world, Robin. Weary of my crown."

Cecil chuckled. "I doubt you are weary of either. Come now, Majesty. Put yourself in a better mood. Give over this melancholy. The air is fair, the garden fragrant and goodly to look at. Your recent indisposition is past. You have great cause to be joyous."

She gave assent with a nod but spoke no more; Cecil did not interrupt her silent contemplation. They followed another path through the garden, out of sight now of her attendants. She began to think about the Bishop again. How she hoped her scowl of disapproval was plain enough when he had finally said *amen*. Ridiculous, presumptuous fellow. Like the lot of them. Was not the truth of Our Lord's Gospel verified in its survival—despite its rankling churchmen and theologians who gave her more trouble than consolation and kept the nation in an uproar with their disputes over discipline and doctrine?

Then she thought of St. Barnabas, whose feast day the morrow was. Good St. Barnabas. A simple man, like the apostles. An obscure fellow, Barnabas, no preening prelate, but a simple servant of God and man. She had always confused Barnabas with the other one whose name began with the same letter. Bartholomew. Yes, he of the great massacre at Paris wherein all those French Protestants were murdered. The booksellers at Paul's churchyard ever placed stacks of Bibles in their stalls on Bartholomew's Day to commemorate the event and tweak the noses of the Papists, who sought to keep God's Holy Word the private preserve of priests and monks. St. Bartholomew's Day. The twenty-fourth day of August. Bartholomew also of the greatest fair in England. The fair she had taken great pleasure in when a child and young girl. Bartholomew Fair. What a joy it would be to see it one more time. Perhaps the last time. Dusty, dirty, vulgar Bartholomew Fair, but what of that?

The idea leaped into her brain like a nimble dancer full of japes and tricks. Her mood suddenly lightened. At once she gave voice to her wish.

"Should God grant me till August, Robin, I would gladly go to Bartholomew Fair," she said, contemplating an expanse of flowers so arranged as to form the initials of her name and title, *Elizabeth Regina.*

"A royal progress in Smithfield!" Cecil replied, obviously surprised at the suggestion. "If it rains, you will be surely mired in the mud. If dry, dust and the stench of horse dung will be the death of us all. A most scurvy resort of the rout of beggars, country bumpkins, and common citizenry."

"I don't dispute it," she said, holding her chin even higher. "Come fair time, half of England will be there."

"And must you therefore parade before them with your train so that they may feast their eyes on Your Majesty while their mouths drool with Bartholomew pig and barrel ale?"

She laughed, and although it was his arm she leaned on she managed all the same to steer him into the path she chose. "It's my pleasure to see the fair once more before—"

"Do not say it, Your Majesty," Cecil pleaded. "May God grant you twenty more years to rule—"

"Twenty more! Why, if it's a tithe of that 'twill be a miracle, Robin. You haven't started lying to me like the others, have you?" She searched his face for dissemblance and found nothing in his eyes but that upon his lips. And by the Mass, regret too! And devotion unfeigned! A good and faithful servant, her little Pygmy, as she called Cecil in her playful mood. She smiled thinly and with her bejeweled hand took in the garden in a sweeping gesture.

"All this glory must fade and pass. Its wintry state I well remember, its iron grip of frost. That winter will come again, for all the garden's present luster. Nonetheless, I tell you, Robin, it is my pleasure to see the fair again before death takes me. I long to see the jugglers, the dancers, the garish shows, to hear the beating of drums and blaring of bugles. Just thinking upon it makes me young again. Don't worry yourself about the dirt and stench. I won't. I am an Englishwoman born and bred, noble Henry's daughter—no French lady with her nostrils in the wind for fear of inhaling other than her own perfumes. I will taste of roasting pig and drink good English beer with my subjects. I know how gossip has had me practically dead and buried this half year. 'Twill be a marvelous resurrection, and as I say, half of England will be there. What a better way to satisfy the multitude that Elizabeth lives and rules still?"

"You have been often sick of late, yet no one believes—"

"Hush, Robin. Now I do know you lie in your teeth. I know what is said of me behind my back. Even now at the end of the garden that gaggle of maids—green girls, the lot of them—whisper of my condition. Give more attention to the state of my urine than a dozen bungling physicians and are ever after rouge to remedy the pallor of my complexion. Because I'm old, they think me deaf. But I can hear the mouse behind the wainscotting, and I have heard their whispers in the gallery."

"If you will permit me to say it, Majesty, it does not seem to me advisable," said Cecil, wording his objection to the proposed visit with proper caution.

"But it *is* *my* pleasure, Sir Robert," she replied shortly. She indicated with a toss of the head that such was her last word upon the subject. "Come now, lead me back to the geese and their cackling. They will be beside themselves to know the matter of our conversation this half-hour. God, how I weary of these court intrigues. Since before you were born, Robin, since before you were born."

They walked in silence. She had had her fill of the garden, since she could not stay its decline or her own. Yet she would go to the fair, she thought. Yes, and eat pig too. She would not be gainsaid by her meddling physicians. Let them warn against it if they dare. There *were* some compensations for being Queen.

The Queen and her Principal Secretary came to the foot of the garden. She was surrounded by attendants. She said to Cecil, "Prepare an announcement that my coming may be no surprise to Lord Rich or the Mayor. Tell him I want nothing too elaborate in the way of ceremony. On the other hand, don't invite his parsimony. Stingy fellow. I presume he will remember that I am Queen."

"I'm sure he will remember, Majesty," Cecil replied with a condescending bow.

"The officials at the fair will be overjoyed. My coming can only make them the richer. Surely my attendance will bring the crowd, will it not?"

She tossed her head and laughed heartily before Cecil could reply. Happy to see her morbid mood had passed, he bowed with the others and watched while she was led inside to supper, a train of maids following in her wake. The afternoon air had turned cool. It was feared the Queen would catch cold.

As Cecil rode homeward in his coach, he stared vacantly out the window and thought again of the Queen's desire to go to Smithfield. And what a desire it was! Why, what would she think of next in her dotage? A tour of the London fishmarket? A picnic in the slums of Southwark? If it was public exposure she wanted, what was wrong with a leisurely progress on the Strand or some other place of fashion compatible with her royal station?

It was silly; it was dangerous. He tallied the risks, not the least of which was the likelihood of contagion among such an unwashed multitude. He reckoned the cost of her personal security—especially at fair time and in an atmosphere of holiday misrule. He shook his head, frustrated.

He was in the process of methodically refuting her own reasons for going, when his own instinctive prudence began to give way to his royal mistress's native political sense. Well, there were risks beyond doubt—and they were considerable. That could not be denied. Yet she was Queen and *would* have her way. That was true too. He considered her plan again— from beginning to end; and by the time he had arrived at his own house, his opposition had tempered into something resembling mild support. Indeed, he had come around to the Queen's way of thinking—not because he was obsequious but because like all men of intelligence he could recognize a good idea even when he had not thought of it himself.

Well, he resolved, the Queen should have her day in Smithfield, since that was her wish. Stinking Smithfield. Bane of Puritans and scorn of the nobility. Sinkhole of vice and villainy. He would advance the motion for policy's sake and pray for dry weather. As for himself, he would find some excuse to stay home, claim some minor indisposition if need be.

# · 1 ·

Fate might have chosen another circumstance for such an appalling deed—say, an obscure, owl-haunted night, or driving, blinding rain, or some dismal wood remote from human habitation. But it is only in the imagination of poets that time, place, and weather necessarily conspire to make a fit setting for violence. The act in question was accomplished in the full light of day, upon a broad open road, and before at least a dozen witnesses as though the thing done were an act of corporal mercy worthy of commendation. That the witnesses did not at the time understand what they saw, or how the act itself might threaten harm to a much greater one than he who presently would be dead, does not mitigate the audacity of the killing. Nor does the fact that the deed was provoked by an impetuous gesture of the victim. There were supernatural forces at work. Whether satanic or divine, let every man judge for himself.

It was August. Not a breath of wind relieved the oppressive heat of midday along the road that led south from Norwich to London. A young man of pleasant if weary countenance, with a staff at his side and a small pack on his back, rested in the shade of a hedgerow. His long, slender legs stretched out before him to reveal much-patched hose and worn, dusty shoes. He had traveled a long distance and stared listlessly at the road, caught up in some private meditation.

Hidden within his sweaty shirt was a well-thumbed volume of quarto size, loosely bound with paper cover and thus hardly more than a pamphlet, which he had purchased from a bookseller a week before and had since studied with great interest. Its title had piqued his imagination upon first view, but upon reading the work itself he had become wholly absorbed by its message. The slender volume was in part responsible for his present deep contemplation, and its title—to abbreviate somewhat and yet keep faith with the substance—was A *Faithful Discoverie of the Sundrie Shapes in Which Satan Hath Appeared from Antiquity to Present Times.* Its author, a learned clergyman named Richard Foxworth of London, was a rigorous sort of Puritan who by diligent search of the Scriptures and collection of anecdotes from other learned authors had chronicled Satan's delusive metamorphoses and warned of his triumphs in the latter days as figured forth in the Revelation of St. John.

This bracing reading, done with care and eyestrain in the fading light of barn lofts where the youth was fortunate enough to find refuge of nights, had brought about a crisis in his thinking. Only recently had he turned from the wickedness of his earliest years and, under the tutelege of an itinerant preacher, received the blessing of saving grace. Still green in his biblical studies, he had found Foxworth's vivid description of the Beast as recorded in the thirteenth chapter of the Book of Revelation so forcefully presented, so subtly interpreted, that he wondered how the men about him could possibly carry on the normal course of living when such a titanic struggle between the forces of good and evil was not only in the offing, but presently under way, although as the book's author had said, such a struggle as could only be witnessed by "spiritual eyes."

For the youth, all life had changed. Modest ambitions were forgotten; thoughts of tomorrow suspended. What had impressed itself most on his imagination was the image of the Beast. There it stood in his mind: part leopard, part lion, the feet those of a bear. Of these beasts the youth knew little, except for the bear. One such beast he had once seen in his native place, chained and made to dance a jig to a fiddler's tune. The bear was old and quite tame, or so the bearward had assured the villagers—not like the mighty Sackerson or Harry Hunks, whom he had heard were baited on Sundays in London and that all the world flocked to see at the bear pits of Southwark. Now the youth remembered the great bear feet, furry, armed with nails like blades, their strength so much beyond that of any human member, but the rest of the Beast was the worse for his inability to see it in his mind. He stared down at his own hands, turned them palms up and contorted the fingers like claws. His hands were small and white, delicate like a girl's. But strong. Yes, strong for whatever work God should call him to.

The youth wondered how many men—yes and women too—he had known who were nothing less than the Devil in disguise—not to mention the lesser creatures his path had crossed. Because of their lesser intellect these were even more vulnerable to possession—all those black dogs, ravens, ragged goats, and even bleating lambs deceptive in their innocence but once possessed as dangerous as sullen bulls with black threatening eyes and the languid cats whose sinister regard always implied some dark knowledge.

He was disturbed in these meditations by the creaking of a cart's wheels and looked up toward the road to see a man, his cart, and the weary, sway-backed beast that pulled the load.

The fat, bearded fellow in the cart dozed and whistled by turns, trusting to the good office of the sorry nag that pulled him to maintain their course and pace. He wore a broad-brimmed hat and an old russet suit of broadcloth, and the tune he whistled he had learned in the alehouse the night before—a simple ditty about a young maid whose unrequited love drove her to an early grave. The man in the cart remembered the pretty youth who had sung the song, stopped whistling, and sighed heavily. He loved such tunes. They never ceased to bring a tear to his eye when he thought of them, and such emotions as this convinced him that by nature he was a gentle and generous soul who loved his fellow man.

He was indulging these tender thoughts when he looked up to see a lone pilgrim sitting forlornly beside the road not a hundred or more feet ahead. He drove the cart forward and, seeing that this pilgrim was a youth of pleasing appearance, he ordered his horse to stop.

"God save you, young sir! A very warm day, isn't it?"

The youth looked up but did not respond to the man's greeting. The man in the cart tried again:

"I say good morrow to you. A fine, hot day."

"Ay, it's hot," replied the youth, using his staff to get up from the rock he had been using as a stool. The youth approached the cart and the older man could see that he was lame and that the sturdy staff he bore had a very practical purpose. He could see too that the heat of the day had given a rosy blush to the features of the youth's face, which were finely chiseled. There was just a suggestion of down on the youth's firm chin and he had the clear blue, guileless eyes of one who had seen little of the seamier side of life. A handsome young man indeed, thought the older one in the cart, removing his broad hat to wipe the sweat from his forehead and expose a head of hair that time had reduced to a few lank gray hairs. The man in the cart smiled agreeably.

"Where bound, son?"

"London, if it please you," said the youth.

"London, is it? A good long walk. For the pleasure of your conversation I'll share half my seat with you and you can save your legs."

The youth seemed to consider the invitation for a moment, then answered: "Many thanks, sir. I'll accept your offer."

The man in the cart motioned to the youth to climb aboard and introduced himself as James Fitzhugh. Fitzhugh suggested his new companion remove his pack and toss it in the back of the cart with the other gear but the youth said the pack was light and caused him no discomfort where it was. Fitzhugh said he could do what he wished with the pack and nudged the horse onward with a flip of the reins.

As they traveled, Fitzhugh explained his own business. He was a puppet master, and amid the gear in the back of the cart he had both his "manikins," as he called his wee folk—not without a certain fondness for the artfully made creatures—and the little theater of wood and painted cloth they played in, all disassembled now. Fitzhugh was bound for London too; for Smithfield, more exactly.

"Bartholomew Fair, as they call it. The fair that is held every year from St. Bartholomew's Eve to the day following the saint's day itself. Three glorious days! O, it's a very great fair, I warrant. All this world's goods on display in the stalls and booths. A world too of good eating, especially for those who savor swine's flesh and good strong English beer. Jugglers, magicians, fortune-tellers, bearwards, sellers of monkey, parrots, dogs, toys, odd trinkets, gingerbread and cakes and other sweets. 'S'blood, it makes my mouth drool to think of it all. Everything to delight the eye, ear, and nose. It is said the Queen herself will grace the fair with her presence."

"The Queen, you say?" said the youth, impressed.

"The very same. Good Queen Bess herself. May God protect her in her old age. I tell you, lad, once I saw her, ten, fifteen years ago. She had come to Oxford to address the scholars. I stood in the crowd, I and my manikins, and watched with the rest. Comes this black-robed scholar and gives a fine speech in Latin. I understood not a word. Then the Queen responded. In Latin too. It was said she was a better scholar than he who professed there. All decked out she was in lace and jewels, a scarlet gown of such workmanship that an army of seamstresses might have devoted their lives to the making of it."

"A scarlet gown, was it?"

"Oh yes, boy, it was," answered Fitzhugh, warming to his theme and pleased at the apparent interest of his passenger. "She had half the court with her—great lords, dukes, earls, I know not what. All were finely dressed and marching in her train with a dozen deafening trumpeters blowing their heads off and heralds prancing fore and aft. Oh, it was a sight, I tell you. You should have seen how they bowed and scraped before her, kissed her royal foot, made a path of their very cloaks. The crowd went wild. You would have thought her the Queen of Heaven—no mortal woman certainly, with fleas in her farthingale." Fithugh laughed. "Why, the Virgin Mary herself, she the Papists dote upon, is not so celebrated."

The remark led Fitzhugh to express his views on religion, describing himself as one who traveled a middle road between the absurdities of Rome and the ignorance of the Puritans, whom he professed to despise for their hypocrisy and cant. "Think they're better than the rest of mankind. God in heaven, I never knew one but that he chased skirts and gluttonized at table. Hypocrites all."

But the puppet master's young passenger was no longer paying attention. He studied the road ahead with a dead eye, his mind still fixed on the puppet master's description of the Queen. He had never seen the royal lady himself but he had heard her much spoken of—and much criticized, by his spiritual mentor, who blamed her for not doing more to advance the cause of reformation in England.

Fitzhugh continued his discourse. The road became heavy with traffic. Some town lay ahead; a church spire could be seen. Carts, wagons, horsemen. Some heading north, some south, navigating as best they could the ruts and holes filled with brushwood, an ineffectual repair the next heavy rain would undo. Now and then a coach rattled by, raising a cloud of dust that left Fitzhugh and the boy gagging and filthy.

They came to the town and passed through. Fitzhugh was still talking about religion, a subject on which he had strong opinions. They left the town.

Fitzhugh asked, "How old are you, son?"

"I will be nineteen come Michaelmas," said the youth, staring listlessly at the road.

"Ah, nineteen, is it?" Fitzhugh said, plowing the thick growth of his grizzled beard and shaking his head as though such an age were quite beyond his recollection. "I was once nineteen myself. Must have been." He laughed. "Lean and limber as you are now. That was a good thirty years or more gone. What's your name, son?"

"Gabriel. Gabriel Stubbs," said the youth.

"Gabriel," said Fitzhugh. He laughed. "Why, that's a most fitting name for one such as you, boy, for there is indeed something angelic in your looks. Tell me, I have confessed my journey's end, you confess yours."

The directness of the puppet master's question caused Gabriel momentary confusion. The truth was that he wasn't sure where he was going or why, London being not so much his destination as the end of the particular road upon which he had earlier set his foot. For days he had been making his way south, spurred by an undefined sense of mission, which only since reading the pamphlet had begun to take shape. Other persons he had encountered on his way had merely assumed by his silence that he was a runaway apprentice or farmboy, heading toward London to lose himself in the anonymity of the metropolis. Now the puppet master's question had forced the issue; yet Gabriel could not be honest. What could he say, after all? That he had been set apart? Commissioned of Heaven? Empowered by spiritual forces? These precious certitudes were not shared with just anyone. Not at this point; at least, not until a blinding light or a still small voice should reveal to him more particularly what his mission was. Meanwhile, the more he felt "called," the less real seemed the world around him. What he observed with the physical eyes—and how untrustworthy were they compared to those of the spirit!—were merely images of deeper realities. The road ahead, the woods at a distance, the flat fields, even his companion in the cart were not what they seemed.

Fitzhugh repeated his question and eyed his young companion curiously.

"I'm bound for the fair too—Bartholomew Fair," Gabriel said in a sudden inspiration. He was surprised himself that the lie so readily flew to his lips and sounded so convincing in his own ears.

The puppet master's surprised countenance betrayed no disbelief. The older man slapped his knee in a fit of hilarity. "Why, you young devil! And you let me talk on about Bartholomew as though you n'er heard of it before. Say, doesn't the very thought of Bartholomew pig a-roasting upon the spit make you drool like a hound an hour before the feast? Although maybe your tastes run to sweeter stuff. They say the girls of Smithfield are as hot as the weather around fair time—at least so they were when I was a young buck and had no look but to please my fancy."

Fitzhugh kept staring at Gabriel, studying his face. Then suddenly he burst into a snatch of song in the high-pitched voice the puppet masters cultivated for their little folk:

> Oh, it's rarely a lad who'll disdain a fair maid
> Nor regard aught else until she be laid,
> Save the chance him befall that the maid 'gins to breed
> Then be sure there's no pleading that young man will heed.

Fitzhugh was about to launch into the second verse of the song when Gabriel flushed with what appeared to be embarrassment, looked at him angrily, and placed his hands over his ears. "That's scurrilous talk—profane and damnable. Stop at once or I'll get down and continue my way on foot."

For a moment the puppet master seemed too startled by the outburst to speak, and seemed on the point of casting his passenger out. Then, collecting himself, he frowned and said, "If it please you, I'll be silent awhile. There's no need to walk, I'm sorry if my song offends you. It's an innocent enough thing, learned by me of a sailor in Chelsea who was wont to boast of amorous exploits. Now for me, I'm no womanizer. No, and far be it from me to offend those who forswear lechery with women. No, young sir, far be it from me."

The puppet master mumbled something else, shook his head several times as though to indicate his own disapproval at the song he had just sung, and then lapsed into a long silence. Gabriel, his heart still racing, turned stonily toward the road.

The burst of indignation had somehow fired his imagination; his surroundings had become even less real, and he began to wonder if this were the experience he had been waiting for. St. Paul, he had heard a preacher say, had been converted upon the road to Damascus; why should he not have an equally transforming experience upon the road to London? His heart continued to race with a strange excitement; he glanced sideways at the puppet master. The man's large head nodded beneath the broad-brimmed hat. Gabriel waited for a vision.

When it came, it was not what he had expected. He had evidently fallen asleep himself, totally exhausted both from the long journey and from sheer emotional excitement. While he slept he dreamed a disturbing dream full of savage beasts with monstrous bodies, bloody fangs, and massive hairy paws. They gathered about him, snarling and growling as he moved down an unfamiliar road. They assailed him on all sides but he kept walking toward a small point of light in the distance. Then the light faded and disappeared completely. He was aware of something touching him, pressing his inner thigh. He thought it was the beasts but they had vanished like the point of light and now all was a void of darkness in which he was aware of nothing but the sensation of being touched. It was not displeasing to him, the touch, only mystifying. The touch became a caress.

A sudden jolt of the cart brought the boy fully awake. He stared about him in confusion as the void of darkness gave way to the blinding light of midday. He saw that Fitzhugh's hand was resting on his knee, was moving then upward along the thigh toward the vulnerable groin. Fitzhugh was smiling strangely and crooning in his puppet voice, "Pretty young boy, pretty young boy."

"Damnable sodomite," Gabriel cried in disgust. He shoved the puppet master's hand away and seized the staff at his side. Before Fitzhugh could defend himself, his young passenger struck him with the blunt end of the staff just above the right eye. Fitzhugh groaned with pain, turned his head, and put up his hands to ward off a second blow. But the boy was quick and full of loathing. He struck Fitzhugh again, this time with full strength of arm and will, on the side of the man's skull. There was a loud, sickening crack. Fitzhugh was knocked back in his seat, then slumped forward as limply as one of his puppets.

The horse and the cart maintained their steady pace over the rough road; the sun beat down upon the man and boy in the cart. Fitzhugh made no motion of himself, although his body jostled. Presently the boy replaced the puppet master's hat on his head. It had been knocked off by the blows. He was aware of horsemen coming up from behind. Gabriel Stubbs turned to see who it was.

The two riders had evidently not seen what had happened although they could not have been more than fifty feet behind the cart when the incident occurred. They pulled apace of the cart and looked down at the man and boy. One of the men asked if the driver was sick.

The boy threw an arm protectively over the puppet master to steady him; with his free hand he took the reins. In a trembling voice, he said, "He's my father, masters. He's had more than he can bear of drink in the last town and so has turned the reins over to me. He'll be himself anon."

One of the riders, who by his dress appeared to be a man of substance, laughed out loud and nudged his companion at this spectacle of human folly. "Is it so, lad? Then may he sleep the sleep of the just 'til he's sober again. Godspeed you both."

The boy thanked the men and watched them ride ahead. The broad-brimmed hat concealed Fitzhugh's face but the boy now noticed the little trickle of dark blood that had made its way down the puppet master's cheek and was now collecting in the thicket of his beard.

The old horse plodded along as though its master were still at the reins. Another town, a market town of good size, now appeared in the distance. Gabriel could see the roofs of houses and a church steeple, long and thin like the sheathed dagger or poniard the dead man packed next to his swollen gut. Before him on the straight road were other conveyances—carts and wagons. He saw a shepherd with his flock and a lady riding a palfrey with her servant.

Gabriel knew that behind him were other travelers making for the town and that they surely must have seen what had happened. But except for the two horsemen who had paused to inquire as to Fitzhugh's health, no one else seemed to be paying attention to the fat man and the boy, riding in a rickety old cart pulled by a sway-backed horse.

His heart was still racing, but he felt no guilt at what he had done. Why should he? The puppet master's filthy speech had been prologue to a filthy act. Gabriel had struck in self-defense, saving more than his life. Saving his eternal soul. His dream had somehow revealed the puppet-master's true identity, and the man's intemperate action had confirmed the truth of it. *Satan's minion. The mark of the Beast.*

Ahead the road swerved to the right to accommodate a stone bridge. Beyond, a ragged hedge of hawthorn and oak separated the roadbed from a broad empty field. When the opportunity presented itself he steered the cart off the road through a break in the hedge, stopping where it would be concealed from the view of passersby by the thick tangle of branches and leaves. There he got down from the cart, dragging Fitzhugh's dead weight after him.

For a long while he stood contemplating the body. Where were the fat man's filthy jests now, his idle memories of the scarlet-gowned Queen, his devilish opinions of the true believers? The death had been the judgment of God.

But now Gabriel realized it had been something more. It had been a sign. He was sure now that his meeting with the fat man had been providential. Gazing down on the corpse, Gabriel felt a surge of spiritual strength, as though the puppet master's death had augmented his own life in some mysterious way.

He knelt down beside the body and found the dead man's knife, a long, thin poniard of French design with a shaft of bone. He drew the blade from its sheath and for a long time sat studying it.

Slowly an image appeared in his brain. He heard voices. The sun beat down on his head mercilessly. In a frenzy he seized the knife and obeyed the voices.

Moments later, half-delirious with the intensity of his emotions, he stood and regarded what he had done through a blur of sweat and tears.

And he was joyful for all of it, for at last he knew where he was going and what he should do once he got there.

# · 2 ·

In Matthew Stock's shop on High Street, ordinary business had been suspended. The clothier and his wife were about to embark on a journey, and around the shop and house (the Stocks lived upstairs) there was that familiar mixture of excitement and confusion that accompanies leave-taking in a busy household. Harried servants ran here and there to fetch this and that—their mistress's voice could be heard directing their efforts from upstairs. Meanwhile in the shop, the clothier's apprentices lugged bolts of cloth from the trencher tables on which they were normally displayed out the door and into the street, where they were to be loaded into wagons. The drivers were impatient to be off. They were to have set out at dawn and it was already nearly noon. Their horses stamped restlessly on the cobbles. The spectacle of leave-taking had drawn a small crowd of neighbors as observers.

In the midst of this bustle stood the clothier himself, a short, dark-complexioned man of about forty with an affable, good-natured expression—usually. A man of infinite patience, for the last hour he had been making a face to suggest his old virtue had worn as thin as a beggar's shirt. He leaned against a table, his face turned upward toward the stairs. He too was impatient to be off, but the delay—for which he now held his wife's indecision, about what and what not to take, responsible—was not his only concern. Something quite unpleasant had occurred earlier that morning and he still thought about it, as any decent man would.

One of the weavers came out of the back parts of the shop, and severed the thread of Matthew's meditations by asking him if Friday of the week would be a holiday for weavers too.

"Yes, blockhead. Of course, you and your fellows will have the saint's day. Enjoy your idleness. But mind you . . ." And at this the little clothier tempered his harshness, having seen the look of dismay in the weaver's eyes. "Don't make a Shrove Tuesday riot of the occasion or be as those foolish mice who while their master is abroad make merry in the larder. You'll be expected at your looms the morning after. And with clear heads, if you please!"

The weaver grinned sheepishly and hurried away to tell his fellows the news. Matthew watched him go, then turned his attention to the single bolt of cloth half-unrolled on the table beside him. He reached for the cloth and, taking the smooth fabric between forefinger and thumb, felt its texture with a loving care. If he were any judge at all—and who was his peer in such judging?—the bolt was as fine a sample of Coggeshall Whites as any produced in Essex. He had money in his pocket to wage with any London draper who might maintain the contrary.

An apprentice came to deliver the cloth to its place in the wagon, and Matthew walked over to the window and peered through the lozenge-shaped panes into the street. No less than three sturdy wagons stood before the shop, each drawn by a team of four horses. They seemed to take up the whole of High Street, which, narrow at the best of times, was now so full of wagon, beast, and man that a passerby not content to gawk at the proceedings would be at pains to elbow his way through the throng. Matthew regarded the splendid argosy with satisfaction and contemplated its destination: Bartholomew Fair, the great fair at Smithfield.

The clothier had hardly missed a year at the fair the past twenty, not since he became a man and his own master. But this year was different. For the first time his wife would keep him company. He was confident she would enjoy the sights of the fair and that the display of his wares would produce great profits for himself. His journey would also involve a reunion with an old boyhood friend with whom he had irregularly corresponded over the years and who had recently set up business as a bearward.

He heard his wife at the top of the stairs and turned from the window. She was giving instructions to Betty, a round, cheerful woman with a red, moist face, as to the care of the house in her absence. Betty had been long in service to the Stocks and this parting with her mistress was not without emotion. The two women embraced and blessed each other. The Stocks' daughter, Elizabeth, was to come from the farm she and her husband had outside of Chelmsford to mind the shop in their absence. Joan started down the stairs.

Like her husband, Joan Stock was rather short, with olive skin and dark, intent eyes. She had a pretty oval face that retained its youthful freshness, a melodic voice, and the confident carriage of a woman used to having her way. Following her came Peter Bench, Matthew's young assistant. Peter sweated and staggered with his burden, a heavy chest. More of Joan's things, Matthew thought, eying the chest with masculine disdain. His wife rarely traveled but when she did, she took enough clothing for half a year.

"In good time," he remarked. "It's nearly noon."

"Is it?" she answered in a tone suggesting she was not content to bear the whole blame for their tardiness. "I'faith, noon is God's time too. So whether it be dawn, or noon, or even, if prayers be said before and the beasts rested and watered and all stowed properly in the wagons, we leave betimes after all."

Joan preceded Peter out the door, not waiting for Matthew's reply. There she said good-bye to each of the apprentices, whom she was wont to mother shamefully and who looked very sad to see her go, although some of their sadness may have been regret that they were not part of the excursion. Matthew joined her in the street and looked up at the pale, sun-washed sky. Noon had lived up to the morning's promise. It would be a day too hot for the salamanders, whom, it was said, no fire could scorch. Everyone sweated, even the wagoners who had done nothing since breakfast but sit on their bums and watch the apprentices work.

But the heat put that unpleasant matter into Matthew's head again, that death's-head of his meditation. It was for that reason too his departure had been delayed and Matthew put to extra expense for the wagoners' time. While one of the apprentices helped his wife up onto the gray gelding that would carry her to London, Matthew's brain compressed the whole train of events into a few moments' recollection.

He had had no choice but to respond to the report, since he was town constable, elected yearly by his neighbors to perform such duties as policing the parish should require. Well, the truth was that he did have a choice, as Joan had reminded him between sleep and awake. He might have sent the man on to John Davidson and been done with it. Davidson, who was to serve in Matthew's place while the clothier was in London. Davidson was a good man, conscientious to a fault, sturdy of limb, no drinker or brawler. Yet this was the rub: Davidson was a novice in that thicket in which Matthew during the handful of years of his constableship had made himself a forester. The thicket of crime and lesser mischief.

It was not that Matthew was perfect in his duties. Nor that the particular crime occupying his thoughts was one that he alone could handle. But experience did account for something. And Matthew's experience had been such that now his reputation extended beyond the parish bounds. It was said, and truly, that he had done some service on the Queen's behalf and was a friend to her Principal Secretary, Sir Robert Cecil. It was said that a wise thief or coney catcher might practice his trade in another town, and this was true too; yet Matthew was a simple man, a lover of family and hearth, and he brought to his constableship no more mysterious skill than dogged determination and patient observation.

Of course it did no harm to have a clever wife. Joan had

often helped him in his official duties, being as she was a woman of great curiosity and remarkable intuition.

Then there was the dead man, spoiling the bright morning of Matthew's departure like a worm in an apple.

It was Samuel Hopkins, an unemployed carpenter, who had found the body. He had come early to the constable's house to report it, so early that Matthew had been roused out of bed by the carpenter's pounding and clamor. Matthew had dressed in the dark and awakened one of his servants to hitch the horse to the delivery cart. Then Matthew and Hopkins had driven out together to where the body was, with the first light of dawn staining the morning sky in spectacular streaks of rose and ocher.

While they drove in the jostling cart, Hopkins, a crooked little man with rheumy, slanted eyes and reddish hair, told his story. His voice was dry and cracked. "I got an early start, you see, Mr. Stock, before dawn, to avoid the heat. I had walked all the way from Witham, my only light and company the round moon. In time I felt a powerful urge to relieve myself and stepped off the road to do my business privily. When I had satisfied nature's call, I started back to the road again and then saw the cart, naught more than a shadow where it stood. I heard no voices, saw no fire about it. I thought it strange that travelers on the road would not be stirring afore light. I drew closer and saw the cart clearly, then all about the ground the forms of tiny bodies. Dead babies was the first thought that came to mind. My heart thumped so within my chest. God, it thumped! I started to turn, to be off, then a wiser thought came to me and I looked again. They was popkins, every one of 'em—little puppets like they use in the Punch and Judy shows. But one of the shapes was no puppet, I'll tell you. No, sir, Mr. Stock. It was no puppet. Then I did turn on my heels and made for the road again, jogging along the way until I came breathless to your house."

"You did the right thing, Samuel," Matthew said.

The carpenter drew the flat of his hand across his forehead as though to wipe away the memory of the scene. Matthew did not press for more details.

He knew he would soon see for himself. The two men jostled along in silence while morning established itself over the fields and meadows and the chorus of birds commenced in the woods beyond. After a while they came to the place. The carpenter indicated it with a pointed finger. "There," he said. "There, just off the road."

The road made a bend like the crook of a man's arm; at the elbow was a hawthorn hedge growing thick and green. The foliage made an effective screen for the cart, the tracks of which could still be seen pulling off the dusty road into the softer earth of a hollow.

Matthew thought it was the sort of place a weary traveler might have chosen for a midday nap, cool and private. A small stream would have made it all perfect, but the hollow was dry. Branches of trees arched overhead; the leaves were dewy, shining in the morning light. Matthew reined in his horse and dismounted. He would have told the carpenter to stay where he was had the little man showed any inclination to move. Hopkins sat bolt upright in the cart seat, his face turned away. Matthew caught the unpleasant smell too. The smell of decay. He steeled himself for the unpleasantness to come.

It was as Hopkins had said. Puppets dressed gaily in taffeta and swatches of other good cloth lay scattered in the sparse grass as though flung there by a giant in a fit of rage. Their little clay faces shone with enamel, their smiles or grimaces unperturbed by the rough treatment given them. Close at hand, Matthew saw a king and queen in crowns and scarlet. A fool in motley. A black-bearded blackamoor. A Saracen knight with his simitar. Farther off, a monk in his cowl, Punch and her mate. A puppet representing, Matthew supposed, a Spaniard by his fantastical dress, hung upside down in a bramble bush. All lay like fallen soldiers on a field, and Matthew could understand how Hopkins, by the eerie moonlight and predawn melancholy that afflicts all, might have thought them actual corpses, despite their diminutive size.

There was also a puppet theater of wood and painted buckram. Or what was left of it. It had been dragged from the cart and smashed. A chest lay on its side, lid open, contents scattered. A few shirts, one shoe, a patched blanket, an old cloak, and a broad-brimmed hat.

Against the wheel of the cart, propped up in a sitting position, was a gross fat man. His bearded chin rested on his chest, his bald pate waxy and exposed to the bright morning sun. Flies buzzed about him, crawling on his head. The flies and the noxious odor of decay were all that suggested the man's posture of repose represented more than sleep.

Matthew drew near and bent over to look more closely, feeling as he did the first assault of nausea. Only then did he see the full extent of the dead man's injuries.

He had seen many corpses in his time, both in his official capacity and in the normal course of living. Corpses dangling on the gibbet; corpses foul and almost beyond recognition in the ditch bottom; corpses bloated and sore-infested in the plague bed. More hideous forms than the imagination could conceive.

This dead man was no pretty sight, and while not the worst condition for a corpse, the full view of the dead man's face was enough for Matthew's gorge to rise. For a moment he thought he would be sick. His forehead beaded with sweat, while at a distance he could hear Hopkins mumbling the Lord's Prayer and begging for Matthew to come away anon, for the carpenter was sure the very ground they stood on was haunted by the murdered man's ghost.

Matthew recovered; his stomach settled. He wiped his brow with his handkerchief and stared again at the dead man's face.

There was a terrible wound above the man's right ear, a dent in the skull; the blood, from head to the grizzled beard, had turned brown and crusty. On the forehead, five slashes converged at a point above the brows, done clearly with cool deliberation by the assailant. Done without regard for the human decency that forbade the mutilation of a corpse. Carrion birds had savaged the eyes and left gaping sockets. The whole face was a hideous mask.

Matthew judged the man to have been dead for two days or more. The condition of the body suggested that, although given the extremity of the temperature it was difficult to tell exactly. In such weather, putrefaction would have begun at the last beat of the heart.

Matthew tried to detach himself from the scene, cast a cold eye on death. He reminded himself that the dead man, a puppeteer by all evidence, was nothing to him. He tried to pretend that the man was no more substantial now than one of his lifeless puppets. The inquiry into the death was all something that Matthew had to take care of, like taking his turn as juryman at quarter sessions or keeping his ditches free of filth. But it was useless. Somewhere, someone would mourn the passing of the poor wretch he now examined with finger and eye. The corpse, once a living soul, remained a thing of some significance, a vessel to be buried in sanctified ground, to be prayed over; a body to be avenged for what was clearly an act of murder.

The man's purse was at his side, tucked beneath the flesh of the belly. Matthew took the purse, opened it, and emptied the contents into his palm. He looked at the sprinkling of silver and copper. No fortune, certainly, but a goodly sum for the taking. Matthew noticed that the knife sheath near the purse was empty of its blade.

Matthew stuffed the dead man's purse in his own belt and began to search about the cart. A little distance away he found a long birchwood staff of the sort travelers carry to steady their walk and beat off dogs. He thought it strange that such a stout staff should be discarded. Unless it could no longer be used, its owner having now a horse to ride on. He carried the staff over to the corpse and looked at the wound again.

The blow had been delivered to a point just above the ear

and with enough force to crack the skull. He gripped the cold, hard wood and imagined it swishing through the air.

He conjectured that the missing blade might have made the marks in the dead man's forehead.

He tossed the staff aside and turned around to look at Hopkins. The carpenter had not left his place in Matthew's cart. He looked as pale as death himself and cried in a whining voice, "In God's name, Master Stock. Can we not be gone now? What more is there to see, but that the man is stone dead, his horse stolen, his goods ravaged? Oh, we are all prey to these highwaymen, every honest citizen."

But Matthew did not think the deed was done by a high-wayman. His imagination worked in another direction. He saw the puppet master atop the cart, another man seated at his side. A friend or, more likely, a passenger, given a ride for charity's sake. Charity's sake. Some way to repay charity, that—return a good deed with a whack on the head and a Godspeed to eternity!

Matthew walked around to have a closer look at the cart. It was old and weathered, a veteran of bad roads and hard times. The rear, emptied of its contents, was floored with splintery planks with cracks opening to the long, slightly yellowed blades of grass beneath. On the cart seat worn smooth by the puppet master's fat buttocks, Matthew noticed a few drops of dried blood. There were patches of dried mud and straw on the floor-board, mostly at the center. Matthew imagined how the dead man must have shifted from his customary position at midseat to give room to the passenger. It would have been a tight fit, given the dead man's bulk. Matthew decided that the passenger must have been slender, perhaps a boy, or there wouldn't have been room there for the two of them.

He imagined them, the fat puppet master and his slim passenger, riding along the dusty road. The blow delivered would have involved a clumsy movement likely to miss its mark, likely to be prevented by an upraised hand, likely in the best of circumstances to result only in a stinging ear. After which the assailant might well himself have fallen victim to the fat man's knife. But *likely* wasn't *certain*. Matthew had known a man who had drowned in his own vomit, and another who had been conked on the head with a stone no larger than a pea. The poor fellow had been buried the next day. The blow may not have been intended to be mortal but it was. Sometimes things turned out that way, plain bad luck.

Now, Matthew thought, a cold-blooded murderer would have handled things differently. He would have taken no chances on the puppet master's returning the blow. He would have used a knife, not a staff; and if a staff, he would have waited until the men were off the cart and the victim's back turned so that the blow could be delivered with full strength and at a certain target. That was the way a murderer would have done it.

Matthew concluded, therefore, that this death was not anticipated, by either party. It had come about of a sudden, taking both men by surprise. Perhaps there was a quarrel, an argument exploding into sudden fury. That was a common enough story. Perhaps the passenger had not meant to kill at all.

But how then to explain the mutilation of the corpse—the wounds radiating from the brow like the claws of a beast? That argued more than self-defense. That argued a rage beyond reason.

Matthew took a last look at the scene. It was all a great mystery. Who was the passenger? Where was he bound? What had caused the rage? Only the puppet master could tell. And he was dead.

Matthew returned to his own cart and drove the horse forward until the two carts were side by side, then he told Hopkins to get out and help him load the body.

"We'll not leave before," Matthew advised the quaking Hopkins, whose horrified expression made it clear he had no desire to touch the puppet master.

Reluctantly, the little carpenter got down. He walked gingerly through the grass around the other side of the cart where the body was. He seemed both fearful of the corpse and of the puppets, and Matthew wondered if the carpenter still thought of them as dead babies.

Matthew took the shoulders; Hopkins, the feet. The carpenter averted his eyes. With much effort they got the body into Matthew's cart, and then Matthew covered it with an old blanket he had thought to bring along for that purpose.

"What about the puppets?" Hopkins asked, eyeing the scene.

"I'll send someone back from town for it all," Matthew said. "The dead man had a name, although we don't know it, and possibly heirs. This stuff is worth something; then there's the purse and the clothing."

Hopkins shuddered and regarded the huge mound of flesh beneath the blanket. "I'd wear no murdered man's clothes. No, not if I must go as naked as Adam otherwise."

"Nor I. But someone will. It's good cloth and the boots still have wear in them."

"Was it robbery, then, Mr. Stock?" Hopkins asked as he climbed up on the seat of the cart.

"I don't think so," Matthew replied, driving the gelding forward and then turning the cart around so that it was headed for the road and Chelmsford again. The men rode on without speaking until the town came into view and the prospect of parting company with the corpse put Hopkins in a better frame of mind. He began to jabber about the weather.

"Another hot one, Mr. Stock," he observed, squinting up at the sun. "As dry a month as anyone can recall."

"Indeed," said Matthew.

"We could use rain," he said.

"Certainly."

"A good hard rain."

Matthew agreed.

Then the carpenter said, forgetting that the question had already been asked and answered, "Who was it did it, Mr. Stock, him that killed the puppet master and did his face that way?"

"God knows," said Matthew.

"God curse him with a like fate," Hopkins mumbled with an audible sob, as though the puppet master had been kin and Hopkins himself had cause to grieve.

"Amen to that."

They were on High Street now, passing between the houses. Midmorning. The town busy. The constable and his cart and its mortal cargo drawing stares.

He hailed a neighbor and asked him to go find John Davidson and bring him along to the undertaker's. Then he stopped the cart and let Hopkins off. Hopkins jumped down, took a last look at the corpse, and wished Matthew luck. Matthew watched as the carpenter dashed off toward the nearest alehouse.

Matthew proceeded down High Street, acknowledging the greetings of passersby, until he came to the undertaker's. There he helped the undertaker carry the dead man inside and then the two of them waited for nearly a half-hour until Davidson arrived.

Davidson was a big, heavily muscled man with square head and jaw, but he paled at the sight of the corpse and crossed himself twice. He had never seen a murdered man before, and his expression of revulsion and horror made it clear he thought it no pleasant sight. "Jesus God," he said, and then he said it again, in a slightly different tone as though, like his pious crossings, the holy name would ward off a similar fate for himself.

Then the coroner came and Matthew gave his report, delivering into the coroner's keeping both the dead man's purse and the staff, which Matthew thought had belonged to the murderer. The coroner examined the purse and the staff and then asked about the horse that had pulled the cart.

"Gone," said Matthew. "Stolen."

"By the murderer, doubtless," remarked the coroner, counting the dead man's money.

The coroner agreed with Matthew that there was little to be done. His verdict would be death by murder, the murderer being person or persons unknown.

Davidson helpfully offered to ask about town to see if anyone knew who the puppet master was, but Matthew said it would be of little worth. Itinerant entertainers tended to be men of shifting identities—in a month's time they might travel a hundred miles or more and not spend two nights in the same village or town. He said he thought it unlikely that the victim's name would ever be known.

With all this, the coroner agreed. "The man was not from hereabouts," he stated in a way to suggest the sentence might well serve as the dead man's epitaph. "At least he didn't die a pauper," he said, grinning. "The town will be saved the expense of his burial."

The coroner hefted the purse, then carefully counted out a sufficient sum to pay for a plot and modest headstone. The rest would go to the poor of the parish.

So having done all a responsible man could, Matthew went home.

Joan stopped her packing to hear Matthew's news. "Murder, was it?"

"No question about it."

She shook her head and closed the lid on her chest, applying pressure to make sure it was securely closed and fastened. "May God preserve his soul, poor man."

"It wasn't robbery," Matthew said.

"Not robbery? What then—a quarrel?"

"Perhaps." He described the scene and the evidence he had found, including the staff.

"The murderer rode off on the dead man's horse, casting the useless staff aside."

"So it appears."

"Headed off? Where?"

"God knows. The puppet master was doubtless heading for London. It's a good guess his passenger was traveling in the same direction, not necessarily to the same destination."

"Let's hope not," Joan exclaimed, turning to face her husband with a look of alarm. "For is it not likely the puppet master was headed as we, for Bartholomew Fair?"

Matthew considered this, then said, "Well, that might be. On the other hand, the fair isn't the only resort of the populace where such a fellow can do right by himself. As for the murderer, he might have set his course no more distantly than the next town."

"Chelmsford?"

"Or anywhere beyond. He might be in London by now, sold the horse. He's the worst sort of murderer. There's not one chance in a thousand we'll find him."

"Well, all I can say is that it's a great pity this should befall the town just as we are leaving it a week. Is the miller up to the business? He's had virtually no experience."

"John Davidson is a good man. I've given what evidence there is. The coroner's jury will find accordingly—murder by person or persons unknown. The poor devil will be buried—decently, his own purse will guarantee it—and that will be the end of the matter. You'll see. There's one thing, though."

"And that is?"

"The body was marked."

"How marked?" Joan asked, interested again.

Matthew described the wounds on the dead man's forehead, tracing their position with his forefinger.

Joan shuddered and made a noise of dismay. "Oh, that *is* fiendish—to mar a dead man. What can it mean?"

Matthew admitted he didn't know what it meant.

They talked no more of the matter. Matthew went downstairs and while he waited for the loading to be finished he examined a bolt of cloth that was to be one item of his wares he intended to display at the cloth fair. It had been just then that one of his weavers had come into the shop with the idiotic question about the holiday. Of course, St. Bartholomew's Day was a holiday—like any saint's day. A holiday for everyone.

# · 3 ·

It is the day before St. Bartholomew's Eve, and the several acres of low ground that stand opposite the Priory of St. Bartholomew and have given Smithfield its name—and that in wet weather are a slough of mud and in dry, merely dusty and stinking from all the cattle normally sold there—have been turned into a little city of tents, booths, and stalls with a maze of narrow lanes and alleys for the better navigation of the fairgoers to come. In one such booth, a pig seller's, a quarrel is in progress, its rancor already drawing a small audience of idle tradesmen and other passersby. The quarrel is between Ursula, mistress of the booth, and her servant, Rose, a pretty but dreamy girl somewhere between the age of thirteen and twenty. This same Rose has committed the unpardonable crime of idleness and has gawked after the bearward's helper, a young fellow named Gabriel, whom she has met only the day before and with whom she is already deeply in love—so much so that the very sight of him starts her heart to flutter like a sparrow's and her face to flush as though she had spent a long hour over her mistress's cooking fire.

But Ursula is no patroness of youthful love, although the great tun of female flesh does occasionally supplement her income from the pig booth by bawdry on a small scale, especially during fair time, and the sight of such goings on beneath her own nose is more than Ursula can endure, being the bumptious woman she is and, according to her reputation, the greatest scold in Christendom. With her red, swollen forefinger, Ursula points accusingly at the thin, quaking girl. "Up, idle stareabout! Lean polecat! Beshrew your laziness and get to work, or I'll make mincemeat of what little brain God gave you."

Rose shrinks under her employer's threats, and thinks those thoughts she fears to express, for Ursula has tremendous girth, an Amazon's strength, a sailor's vocabulary. Her unslung belly is encased in an old sweaty and saucy smock. Her huge upper arms are sunburned and quiver like jelly, nourished on the greasy succulence of swine's flesh famous throughout England as Bartholomew pig. As though it were a unique species of God's creature and not ordinary pig done to a turn over a pit of hot coals.

So Ursula, whose bulging eyes sometimes see all, sometimes nothing but her own immediate concerns, has spied Rose in the act of grievous dereliction. While the girl should have been setting up the crude tables or washing them down, unpacking the wooden cups her mistress serves her patrons tepid ale in, spreading rushes on the dirt, or occupied with some other joyless task at her mistress's behest. It was such an indiscretion that now occasions Ursula's rage and the bellowing and glowering, threatening and jabbing that have drawn the handful of idle gawkers around the pig-woman's booth—they having nothing better to do on this hot morning in August but to entertain themselves with Ursula's fulminations.

Twice that morning the young man with pale eyes, fair hair, and a face like an angel has limped past the pig-woman's booth, stripped to the waist so that his compact upper body and smooth white neck brave the sun and invite the admiring stares of the female population of Smithfield and not a few of the male. The young man's bad leg—it seems shorter than the other, hence the hobble—is more the pity. A blemish on perfection, surely.

They first met the day before when both of them had gone to the skirts of the town to dump trash in the huge fly-ridden pile of debris, garbage, and animal and human waste accumulating there. Her load is heavy, too heavy for her delicate frame, for she is no plump country wench with a boy's muscular shoulders and thighs but city-bred—a dunghill flower aptly named Rose. He offers her help in emptying her burden, having already disposed of his own, pushed there in a rickety wheelbarrow. She accepts the offer with thanks, thinking it kindly intended and not as an opportunity for some lechery, of which she has had ample experience.

They walked back from the midden heap slowly, through the narrow lanes, conversing. He told her that he was a stranger in London and that his name was Gabriel Stubbs. A lovely name, she thought. He was religious and he spoke of Christ's love and how perfect it was and of the evil days into which the world— yea and England too—had fallen.

His pale eyes shine with faith and understanding; words drop from his lips like honey. She delights in each syllable, understanding half of what he says. She longs to see him again.

Rose is unlearned and diffident, but she has an adequate knowledge of herself. And that is the beginning of wisdom. She follows his words with difficulty. But with patience and mildness of speech, Rose is made to understand.

She is aware of her comeliness, for it is often praised. Not by Ursula, however. Rose's flesh is smooth and clear of blemish; milk-white, in startling contrast to her raven hair. Her body is firm and slender; her small, high breasts make pleasing mounds in the front of her simple smock. She has small hands and feet. When she walks down the lane of booths, men's eyes follow her. She is often the subject of rude remarks, lecherous invitations, and, occasionally, assault upon her small, vulnerable person.

But she has been honored too, and that remains very much in her mind along with her thoughts of Gabriel. She has been selected by the stewards of the fair to be one of twelve Smithfield virgins to accompany the Queen in her progress on the final day of St. Bartholomew's feast. She has been promised suitable attire—a gown of white linen and bright ribbons to adorn her hair, a purse of silk full of copper, and a basket of late summer flowers to strew in the Queen's path and make sweet the air of filthy Smithfield.

What if Ursula has demanded Rose turn both gown and purse

over to her as recompense for Rose's lost time while participating in the ceremony? Rose still counts herself fortunate. After all, how many girls in England, be they virgins or no, comely or otherwise, enjoy such a distinction? To be in the Queen's train! If only for an hour!

That it *is* a distinction she has been assured by the stewards. Even Ursula has seemed impressed—at least with the prospect of the gown (which Ursula can sell) and the purse, and Ursula having done nothing herself to earn either.

Of England's mighty monarch, Rose has but the vaguest conception, and that shaped by rumor. She has never set eyes on the Great Lady, and in her mind, the Queen is like a figure in the Bible, the fairies of field and wood, or the spirits who haunt empty houses or howl at the moon from their graves. All credited on faith alone. That, therefore, the royal personage should come to Smithfield, tread upon this vulgar soil rich with martyrs' blood and beasts' dung too, and that she, Rose Dibble, the most obscure and humble of maids, should play the white-garbed virgin in her train, is almost beyond her imagining.

Yet the stewards—great men, they—have assured her that it is so. And certainly Ursula's jealousy has confirmed it. Rose has been chosen from among the maids of Smithfield. She shall have her place in the Queen's progress. And all will be for Rose's good, because the stewards have said it is so.

Rose runs afoul of her employer again that morning, when the proud sun is at the perpendicular and man and beast below are already limp with its strength, and the fetid air within the tents and booths is almost beyond endurance. Gabriel has passed by the pig booth and called out a greeting to Rose, who has just commenced scrubbing one of the trencher tables on which her mistress's patrons will feed come tomorrow. She returns the greeting, quite without thinking.

But Ursula hears the voice too. She recognizes it now, alert for the limping figure with the wheelbarrow. Sees him too, standing there impudently, in open defiance of her will.

"Damnation and hell!" she cries. She comes growling forward from beneath the shady bower that has been her resting and cooling place this half-hour, her heart full of envy at the lithe girl who does her shit work. Rage strong in her gut, she seizes Rose by the shoulder, almost ripping the smock that is more than tattered already, jerking the girl around to glower at her and scream in her face with her hot, garlicky breath and pinch Rose's shoulder until scalding tears run down the girl's cheeks.

"God Almighty, I am cursed with a curse by this skinny witless child," Ursula complains to whoever will listen.

The boy tries to intervene—a dangerous move—and is sent sprawling in the dust. Where he remains, too amazed by the sudden blow to speak or rise. Some of the neighbors notice the ruckus, grin and mind again their own business. Meanwhile Rose tries to apologize, managing a poor, pitiful excuse for herself that does no good at all. She promises she will not look in the street again, promises to keep her eyes as fixed upon the booth as though it were death to look elsewhere.

"A most likely promise with most certain outcome," Ursula snorts contemptuously. "You *will* gawk, as soon as my back is turned. Yea, and daydream too, for such is your nature. But I will be boiled in pig grease if you will do so without my revenge. Proud hussy, thinking yourself so much since you are named among the Smithfield virgins. Smithfield *virgins!* As though there was one virgin above the age of six or seven in Smithfield, let alone a dozen. Hear me now, you dishrag, you hank of hair and bone without the sense God gave a goose. If you offend again . . ."

Ursula pauses, trembling with rage. No crowd witnesses her fulminations now. Her neighbors have grown weary of her ranting and are content to ignore her. All save the wine seller, Jack Talbot, who wanders by, observes the fray. Meanwhile Rose's heart has half-stopped in her throat for terror. She knows this is only the beginning of Ursula's wrath. For Rose is accustomed to the pig-woman's rantings and ravings, batterings, slaps, pokes, and pinches. Has Rose not bruises enough to show for them, on shoulder and arm, backside and bum?

"Tomorrow the fair begins and my booth is still a shit hole, thanks to you," Ursula says, her breath finally catching up with her spleen. "I work my fingers to the bare bones while you make faces and flash your titlets at every idiot who strolls by. What? Is it the bearwarden's new whelp you lust for, he lugging the dung barrel and hobbling like an old soldier? Very fine company, I warrant! Dung for dung! You polecat! You bony-ribbed black bird!"

The observing wine seller now intervenes. A tall, lanky, good-humored fellow with a narrow, pinched face and close-set eyes, Jack is a friend of Ursula's, twenty-five or thirty years of age. One of her gossips. An old-timer at Bartholomew Fair, like Ursula herself. He has more than once interceded on Rose's behalf when Ursula's brutality became extreme.

"Now, Urse, easy on, now," Jack says, inserting himself between the pig-woman and Rose. "Contain your spleen, old smock. The girl scrubs with her hands, not her eyeballs. Remember yourself in such years. Did your eye not rove? Did you not slaver after a brawny hunk of male flesh, a well-turned thigh?"

"My eye roved for a fact," Ursula concedes, only partially calmed by the wine seller's words. "But then I had meat on my limbs, a head on my shoulders, yea, and a brain inside it too, a great novelty in these years of shame. No scrawny poultry, I, but a full-fleshed woman. Oh, the skinny birds we must pluck nowadays!"

She casts a scornful eye on Rose and shakes her head. Then she turns back to the wine seller as though to invite his sympathy. Was this not the sign of the times, this craven girl before her? The very image of the world's decay? All skin and bones, and her brain no bigger than a pea pod? Why, at home Ursula has a lapdog she swears has a bigger brain, can come when she bids and stay when she bids it and never hikes a leg within doors. "Girls nowadays have no more sense but to gape at every codpiece that passes. Let her mind her work if she wants to continue in my employ."

Ursula, winded from her diatribe and sweating as though bedrizzled by a sudden shower, now stops screaming. She grimaces and scowls, punctuating all this face-making with a snort of contempt for Rose and her ilk. She aims a heavy brow toward the wine seller too. His intercession has been a dangerous one—coming as he has between her and her wrath. Yet they are friends. And perhaps, as impossible as it must seem, lovers. For Ursula would hardly have permitted herself to be restrained by any other man, being as they are villains by nature and vilifiers by habit, so that no honest woman of trade endowed with a generous portion of flesh and smart lash of the tongue is free from their insults and taunts.

She orders Rose back to work, sees that her order is obeyed, and then returns to the back parts of the booth. Rose begins to scrub. Jack stays and watches.

"How's the arm, Rose?"

"Oh, it does hurt, I'faith it does. Like a wasp's sting."

She ceases work, glances cautiously at the booth to see if Ursula is watching. Ursula can be heard moving around inside, fussing and cursing again. But at someone or something else now, not at Rose. Rose looks at the wine seller's good-natured face. He is grinning sympathetically; his eyes are warm and moist; his body, all winey, as though he bathed in malmsey. "There shall be a great bruise, I know it," she complains.

Without thinking, she slips her loose smock from one shoulder to examine the hurt place. Gasps at the sight of reddening skin on her upper arm. In doing so, she exposes a generous share of her right breast and nipple.

"The bruise will go away," Jack says, watching the girl, the wound, the breast.

She readjusts the smock on her smooth shoulder and looks at the wine seller again, but he is already focusing his attention on the booth. "Ursula's a difficult woman, to be sure," he observes in his easygoing manner. "Her temper is that of three women, maybe four." He laughs genially. "Take my advice, stay out of trouble. Keep your eyes to yourself and your hand to your work. That's the way to avoid Ursula's wrath. Who is this boy she speaks of? He's made off, I see, a politic move on his part."

"Mr. Babcock the bearward's new helper," Rose says, forgetting about the pain in her upper arm.

"The bearward's helper, is it? He who walks with a limp?"

"That's the one," she says, proudly.

"He's a likely-looking lad, despite the limp, but I'd watch myself, Rosie," Jack says.

"Why, what do you mean?" she asks, puzzled by the sudden alteration in his expression and tone.

"Well, now, you know you're an eyeful for man or boy, girl, a juicy wench," Jack says, cocking an eye, grinning still so that she feels no apprehension at his appraisal of her body. But she is confused. What is he saying about Gabriel?

"This Gabriel of yours is a *man*, for all his handsomeness and kindly treatment."

Now she understands. Jack is saying that Gabriel is like the others. Leering and clutching and yes, more than once, pulling her to the ground and penetrating her with their things, to little pleasure for her and sometimes agonizing pain.

"Oh, he's good, not evil," she blurts in the simplicity of her heart. She begins to cry, despite herself.

"Is he good?" Jack says. "Well, maybe he is and maybe he isn't. In any case, be careful. Some men are good and some only appear so. Now, you're a very innocent creature, Rose. As sweet as your name. It's your nature to think everyone as you are—until you find out differently. But every Rose has its thorn, you know."

Every Rose? Did he mean her? Or was he talking of something else? Who was her thorn? She liked the wine seller, but sometimes his words confused her. Yet his grin was comforting, and it still lighted his face. She wiped her eyes, and the wine seller went away. She resumes scrubbing, scrubbing more energetically than before.

How she wishes she understood more. She feels confused and hurt. Jack's words have instilled doubt in her heart. But surely he is mistaken. The bearward's helper is as good as his words. She is sure of it.

She thinks of Ursula, now silent in the booth. Sleeping in the noonday shade, exhausted from her screaming—if Rose is lucky. If luckier, the woman is dead, her heart overcome by its own venom. For Rose can never please Ursula. Everything the girl does is wrong, no matter how hard she tries. Rose has no parents to look out for her. She thinks they are dead, but doesn't know where they are buried. She does know that when you are dead they put you in a box called a coffin and your soul is snatched up by God in heaven while your body remains in the box until it is like the dust in the chamber corner, mere sweepings. On the Judgment Day all bodies are quickened. The soul returns to where the body lies and scoops it up, breathes life into ragged bones, the senseless dust.

This little religion she has from sermons heard at Paul's Cross on weekdays, when great preachers address the multitude, does not answer this question for her. Yet she is a girl of great faith, and although the deeper mysteries of doctrine are unfathomable to her, the simpler pieties are well within her grasp. She is loyal to a fault. And loyal to her faith, for, in all, religion is a very pleasant thing to her—a refuge from the cruelty of her employer and the savage men who abuse her.

Gabriel, to whom her thought now turns, speaks of holy mysteries. Like the preachers at Paul's but in a milder, more engaging tone. Her image of him brings her peace.

She scrubs and scrubs and scrubs until the long tables are surely clean enough, until the strong soap makes her hands red and rough and burning. It is all futile, however. Ursula will not be pleased. She will probably make Rose do it all over again. Tomorrow, Rose thinks, half the world will be at Smithfield and these same boards she now cleans will be graced with new layers of grease and spit and other filth. Rose will take her turn sweating over the roasting pit, inhaling the pig's flesh until it sickens her; take her turn waiting on tables, pouring the cheap ale Ursula sells, slapping away the hands probing or clutching, hearing the naughty suggestions of strange men.

*No, Gabriel is not one of them.*

But then, maybe Ursula will forget about poor Rose and think only of pig and money. Pig and money, money and pig. That was the way it was with Ursula. That was all she thought about when the booth became busy—that and the other things Ursula did that were wicked and that she tried to make Rose do. But she would not, no, not for all the beatings and tongue lashings in the world.

Rose thinks of the coins Ursula keeps in the little cherry-wood box. The box is in a hole, like a little grave. A plank covers it, then rushes. All in the back parts of the booth. Ursula trusts no one. But Rose knows where the box is hidden, has seen the pig-woman secrete her earnings there. Where moth and dust corrupts, as the preacher says.

It has never entered Rose's heart to steal. God forbid she break that sacred commandment either. But she often thinks of Ursula's treasure, and it gives her some satisfaction to know what Ursula supposes her ignorant of.

Yes, Ursula's mind will be on her money and pig once the fair has begun and all the world is at Smithfield. They will come crowding out of Hosier Lane and Chick-lane and Cow-lane and Long-lane, come in droves until a wight can hardly move for all the shoulders and elbows. And in that hurly-burly Rose will be clever enough to find an opportunity to escape. Not to idleness, but to Gabriel, her heart's longing. In the meantime she yearns for another glimpse of the bearward's handsome helper.

Later Ursula emerges from the back parts of the booth, sees what Rose has done and, to Rose's surprise, grunts a few words of approval. Then she appoints another task to Rose. Some of the meat she has had from the butcher is wormy and foul, beyond use, Ursula complains. It must be hauled off, lugged in pails, brim full of globs of rotting swine's flesh. "And do you think you can find your way to the muckhill?" Ursula asks with heavy sarcasm.

"Yes," Rose says, with a little thrill in her heart, since she is already thinking of something more pleasant than wormy meat or the muckhill.

Ursula snorts with contempt. "Be about it, then. Don't just stand there. Go inside. I've tossed the bad meat in the pails, where I would gladly have tossed the butcher who sold me the meat as well. See that you're back in a quarter of an hour. No malingering, mind you, or you'll be very sorry. *Very* sorry, for a fact."

# · 4 ·

"That's good. Yes, that's well done, lad. Lay it on, lay it on. Don't stint, now. Straw's cheap as dirt and Samson loves a cheerful giver."

Francis Crisp, one of the two bearwards, was addressing his new helper, who was carrying armfuls of fresh straw from a pile in the corner to the bear's cage to replace the foul. Samson himself, an old brown bear somewhat worse for the wear and tear of many a bearbaiting, looked on, occasionally taking a swipe at the noisome flies that buzzed about his shaggy head.

· A rectangular stockade used normally for the containment of cattle or horses had been transformed into a bear garden for the fair. Benches of splintery planks of new wood rose in tiers on two sides to allow spectators a view of the pit, the sandy area in between where a tall tethering stake had been fixed like a ship's mast. At one end of the compound there was a gate to let the crowd in and a little booth where the admission was taken: tuppence for the good seats, a single penny for the common rout, some of whom could stand if they chose. At the other end was a large tent or pavilion with peaked top and closed sides. The tent was Samson's quarters and contained his cage—a sturdily built structure of iron bars and heavy oak frame—a great quantity of fresh straw, and a simple pallet in the corner for the bearward's helper.

Francis Crisp was an energetic little man in his mid-forties, with thinning hair and a long, horsey face. He watched his new helper work, with growing satisfaction, for the young man worked with a will, whistled while he worked, and didn't complain at all. Crisp thought the boy was a real godsend, given the current state of the labor market, and prided himself on

· 45 ·

finding him, although the truth was that the boy had found the bearwards. He had suddenly appeared two days before while the carpenters were still constructing the tiers of seats and everything was at sixes and sevens, with the former helper, Simon Plover, run off somewhere. The boy said he needed work, said he would do any honest thing, said his name was Gabriel Stubbs and that he hailed from the north country, as a certain lilt in his speech and innocence of expression confirmed.

"Too much drink, that's what it was," Ned Babcock had said, speculating on the cause of Simon Plover's disappearance. Ned Babcock was the other bearward, a man of strong moral convictions. "I'll bet he got soused as a dormouse and went straightway to sign up for a sailor. Mark my words, Francis. We've seen the last of Simon—and good riddance too."

Crisp had murmured his agreement and made a disapproving face. He had never liked the lazy and shiftless Plover. Gabriel Stubbs more than made up for the loss. "Overmuch wenching too," Crisp had added.

"Ay, drinking and wenching," Babcock said, sighing heavily.

"So you want to work with the bear, do you?" Crisp had asked the young man, who wore dusty clothes and had a cheerful countenance, despite the limp in his right leg.

"Yes, sir," said Stubbs.

"Bears are not to be trifled with," said Babcock, a large, round-faced man with a red, blotchy complexion and an easygoing manner. Babcock was senior partner in the bearbaiting enterprise. A man of great enthusiasm.

"One killed a child a few years past," observed Crisp matter-of-factly. "Half swallowed him. The mother was beside herself with grief. They slaughtered the bear afterward, executed him like a common criminal." Crisp glanced at Samson. The bear had given over his futile war with the flies and succumbed to the heat of the day, snoring softly.

A handsome boy, thought Babcock, finding no mark of sluggard or thief in the smooth features and assessing the contour of shoulder and arm to determine that the young man was fit for his labors. "The bear requires a steady hand," said Babcock. "Treat him well, and he will treat you likewise. But never forget. He is a beast, and he makes our living for us by breaking the backs of mastiffs and spaniels foolhardy enough to come against him."

The boy nodded and looked grateful. Wages were agreed upon. The boy was shown where he might sleep, and he was assured that in no time at all he would become accustomed to the animal's strong odor.

The boy said, "Who knows but that the world will end before Bartholomew Fair is done," apropos of nothing it seemed.

But both bearwards heard the comment and puzzled over it. Crisp said nothing but Babcock—who, although not a pious man, deeply revered philosophical sentiments in another— agreed that it was all too true. Life was short, Babcock said, and art only a little longer. Who knew what would befall any of them?

Ned Babcock liked the boy's attitude, his serious mien.

Francis Crisp showed the boy where the pitchfork was and where the wheelbarrow was in which he should haul the bear's dung and other leavings from the pit to the midden heap.

About noon of the first day of Gabriel Stubbs's employment at the Smithfield Bear Gardens, he paused in his labors to wipe the sweat from his face and ease a dull ache in his lower back. He was unused to hard physical labor and the muscles in his arms and shoulders protested the strain of lifting and pitching. His charge, Samson, ate hugely; the beast's voidings were enormous and foul. His stinking cage bottom was constantly in need of cleaning. But Gabriel did not object to his labors. He was a man with a mission, and each day its shape became better defined in his mind. When he had chance—say, at night, when the bear was asleep—he would think and pray. He would read again Foxworth's tract and feast upon its wisdom.

Gabriel noticed that Samson had awakened from his lethargy and was watching him intently. The bear was balanced upon his rump again. His short, powerful hind legs were bowed and at right angles to his midsection. His forearms were cradled in his lap, with the claws turned upward.

The beast looked all the world like a man who by some accident of nature had been cursed with a growth of fur but was, nonetheless, within the hairy excrescence a human soul who might at any moment utter a comment upon the young man's labors.

But the bear only stared. Stared at Gabriel with beady black eyes.

Gabriel felt fear in his joints and bowels. In a kind of fascination he walked toward the animal.

Gabriel stopped short when he could detect the acrid stench of animal breath, when he could see in detail the savage scars of old wounds on the beast's belly and hind legs.

For some time man and bear seemed engaged in a contest of wills to see whose eyes would drop or turn first. Samson was motionless, except for a slight flairing of his black nostrils. There was something menacing about the stare. It was the steady concentration of one who has just spied an enemy he thought dead, someone hated more than all the world and feared too. It was certainly not the menacing of an angry watchdog or bull who regards all strangers to its ground as subject to its growls, stompings, or charges. Samson's hostility (the boy saw now that *hostility* it was) was composed. It was intelligent, even logical. As though Gabriel had not only offended Samson in being unfamiliar but in being, on the contrary, *familiar* to him, as though the young man were someone with whom the bear had had a grudge of long standing.

But for all of this and as unnerving as it was, Gabriel did not look away nor once think of retreating beyond the vicious swipe of Samson's forearm should he think to attack. Gabriel was afraid and unafraid at the same time; his fear was contained in his gut, rioting there, but in his brain and legs he stood his ground. He was in control. Or *something* was in control of him.

Then, at last, Samson moved. It was a jerk of the thick neck accompanied by a low snarl of animal discontent. Samson rocked forward onto all four feet. He lumbered away, at least as far as his tether would permit.

The fear was gone; in its place Gabriel now experienced a strange sense of excitement, even triumph. And sudden illumination. This contest of wills between man and bear was not without its meaning, for under heaven's eye all things had their spiritual significance, were clues to God's intent or man's destiny, gave inklings of the order of being or were holy signs of the special providence that governed the affairs of men. All this Gabriel Stubbs believed with unwavering faith. Again he studied the bear, noting the furry body, the massive strength, the brute malice of the eyes, turned from him now but still fixed in his memory. And the claws. He realized that Samson was more than beast dragged from forest to amuse the wicked.

Was Samson not the very image of the Beast of which the Book of Revelation spoke—at least in part? Was Gabriel's encounter—a kind of duel, if rightly understood—not the same order of encounter of which the able Foxworth had written at such length?

Now Gabriel understood how good would triumph over Satan, how Samson's enslavement by chain and cage and even his torment by dog and whip were a shadow of things to come, Christ's victory over the Deceiver, Gabriel Stubbs's victory over the greatest of his sect's enemies.

In the stultifying closeness of the bear's tent, Gabriel knelt down and prayed, his heart full of thanksgiving, his brain reeling with the glory of his vision.

He took his exultant mood as a sign that he was where he was supposed to be. Even here in this sink of iniquity, this Babylon of Smithfield, where the aroma of roasting pig's flesh rose like the savory offering on a heathen altar. Where all the world was bought and sold, Mammon reigned in his glory, and Satan sent his servants whither he willed. God had delivered the evil puppeteer into Gabriel's hands, providing thereby to him a fast means of transport to London (the horse had carried him as far as Cripplegate before collapsing from sheer exhaustion). Then God had brought him into Smithfield itself, where in the same concatenation of preordained events Gabriel had met Simon Plover and then the pig-woman's girl, Rose Dibble, a plain, simple soul with whom Gabriel had shared, at least in part, the burden of his divine appointment.

He had told her what he thought prudent. For her good as well as his. And so it would be until he had put her faith to an appropriate test.

Simon Plover had been blind, stumbling drunk, smelling of bear and beer, groping his way along walls and fences—a shrunken soul already damned for its impieties in a young but wasted body.

The meeting between Gabriel and the bearward's helper had been quite accidental, or so it had seemed at the time. Gabriel had picked the poor wretch literally out of the gutter, listened to him babble about his employers and the stinking monster he had the charge of. He bragged about running off, quitting London, but was obviously, drunk or sober, too craven to do it. Unless he was given one leg up for the enterprise.

Gabriel provided the aid, finished Plover quickly. It was more an execution than otherwise, and the truth was that Gabriel felt no guilt at all and, indeed, had very little memory of the deed.

It had all been done quickly. Death, the disposing of the body—all over very quickly, like the fillip of finger and thumb. Because already Gabriel was looking beyond the death of Plover to something of more far-reaching significance.

# · 5 ·

Arrived in London, the Chelmsford constable and his wife found lodgings at the Hand and Shears, a spacious, comfortable inn convenient to the fair and much patronized by clothiers and drapers, as the inn's name suggested. Here they slept very restlessly despite their weariness from travel, for there was a continual racket on the stairs, a child wailed all night in the next chamber, and before the first light of day the hostlers in the inn yard were up and about, they and their horses, coming and going and making a great noise about it.

The Stocks rose early, therefore, since there was no quiet to be had, breakfasted, then set out for the Priory Close, where Matthew's wares had been taken upon their arrival and where they had since been put on display along with the goods of other of England's clothiers.

Although the fair would not officially begin for another day, Smithfield was already swarming with peddlers, small dealers, victuallers, showmen, tradesmen of every sort, and a good number of the general public who had been drawn there for the mere sight of it all. Along with them had come less desirable folk—rogues, vagabonds, whores, cutpurses, common thieves, roisterers, and the like—men and women and some children as well, without visible means of support but with a quick eye for opportunity and for the gullibility of the innocent and honest. These stood around in conspicuous idleness, while the reputable tradespeople put the finishing touches on booth and stall, unpacked their wares, or gossiped with neighbors and renewed old acquaintances, or complained about the high rents for stallage this particular year.

Chelmsford had of course its own fair, as did every larger

town in England, but Joan had never seen anything like this. The booths, Joan observed as she passed, were very colorful but flimsily built structures, made of poles and painted canvas, old boards, barrels, and tree limbs. Some were covered with branches or thatching to protect from sun or rain; others were roofless and amounted to no more than simple partitions with bare planks for counters and crudely lettered signs announcing to the illiterate what could be had there.

All was designed to be put up and taken down with dispatch, to fit where there was little room, and to accrue the least expense to the booth's owner, who was out to make money at Bartholomew Fair, not to waste it in costly construction. The more elaborate of the booths had insides and out. The front part of the booth displayed the goods sold there; the back parts, shielded from the front by a flap of canvas or cloth, were for storage or temporary living quarters for the tradesman, who found it wise not to leave his valuable stock unwatched during the night.

Sellers of drink and food who were in a prosperous way provided tables and benches for their patrons. Victuallers of more modest means were content to hawk from pushcart or barrel or basket. All about, showmen—and there were a great company of them—could be seen honing their skills. Jugglers, magicians, singers, acrobats—from all over England. And with the showmen were the monsters of Smithfield: the calf with five legs, the woman with beard, and a bull with a great pizzle, which had been shown in many a fair and was regarded a favorite attraction.

Joan also saw a puppeteer, entertaining a handful of children, and thought of the poor fellow that was murdered.

But the greatest impression forced on her was no sight but the stink! It was perfectly horrid, and she had not walked more than a few dozen yards into the maze of booths before she commented on it. It was indeed strong enough to cause the nostrils to burn.

"It's the cattle," Matthew explained, looking around him and obviously taking delight in what he saw. "The horse and hay market of Smithfield is famous. The stench is the price that is paid for it. Never fear, your nose will grow used to it."

But Joan doubted her nose would. Her good wife's nose, an instrument of great sensitivity and discernment, was superior to that of her husband, but she said no more about the smell. As for sights, there were almost more here than she could take in. She marveled that her husband knew where he was going. She had lost her own sense of direction completely. Did the inn lay that way or this? All was twistings and turnings. The booths had been set out in lanes, but none was straighter than the permanent alleys and streets of the neighborhood.

She also found the stares of the tradespeople disturbing. They stared boldly at her as though she were some wonder herself fit to be shown there. Was there something odd about her appearance, her dress, she wondered? Or was it simply that they were unaccustomed to the sight of a well-dressed woman of the rising middle class, astride with her husband, also of a prosperous sort, amid the booths before the fair began?

Joan decided she did not like Smithfield nor its great fair, despite its fame and dissolute glamor. She was no "Bartholomew Bird," as she had heard the denizens of Smithfield called; and she could not forgive the noxious odor of the place, no matter what her husband might say in mitigation.

In the Priory Close were permanent booths rented to the clothiers during fair time and kept in good repair. This spacious yard, surrounded on three sides by walls of good height and on the fourth by the Priory of St. Bartholomew itself, had the advantage of greater cleanliness and a measure of security during the night, for the gate was locked and the Close patrolled by the Smithfield watch. There, Matthew found his goods, already set out by his assistant, Peter Bench. Peter was reading a book and hardly noticed his master's approach.

Matthew greeted his assistant heartily.

"A very good day, Mr. Stock and Mrs. Stock!" said Peter.

"All in good order, I see," said Matthew, casting an appreciative eye over his samples.

"Oh, it's been very quiet here, sir," said Peter.

"It will be a different story, tomorrow," said Matthew.

"Let's pray it will," said Joan, "or we have all come to Smithfield for nothing."

"Hardly for nothing," Matthew said. "There's the fair. Also Ned Babcock."

Bartholomew Fair. Ned Babcock. Joan did not care at all for the first; would she like the second? She hardly remembered the man—or boy, as he was those many years before. The image of a thin boy with a round, ruddy face came to mind, then slipped away, as old memories did. Had that vanishing figure of her imagination been Ned Babcock or some other among her early acquaintances? Well, he *was* Matthew's boyhood friend, and she supposed that should be enough for her.

"We are to meet Ned at the bear pit," Matthew announced after a few more words with Peter. "Peter, you may return to your book. A collection of poems, is it?"

Peter said that it was. He had bought it at a stall near Paul's churchyard and was pleased with the contents. "Well, read on," said Matthew, in very good humor.

On their way to the bear pit, Matthew spoke warmly of Ned Babcock. "A most generous and able fellow, I tell you, Joan, despite an almost constant stream of ill luck. We were school-fellows, you know. He was an apprentice to my father's cousin, Jacob Symmington, a tailor. He forsook the craft after a time, went to London, became a bookseller, lost all in a fire, then by turns was bricklayer, carpenter, and at length, his father's heir. Was well-to-do but lost all again in foolish investments."

"And now he baits the bears in Southwark," Joan remarked, ironically.

"A recent adventure, with capital he secured from several old creditors upon promise to spend wisely and repay twice the sum he originally borrowed, with his father's land in Essex as security. His partner's name is Francis Crisp. I don't know the man, but Ned speaks well of him."

"I think I shall meet both soon," Joan said, seeing the bear pit ahead.

A large sign dangling from a newly erected post read:

Smithfield Bear Gardens, Babcock and Crisp, Proprietors. Depicted on the sign was a bear rampant, paws in the air. This, she presumed, was the legendary Samson, about whom her husband had spoken on another occasion. Already her fastidious housewife's nose could sniff the bear's acrid odor. The most unpleasant odor yet. Bear *Gardens*, indeed!

A handsome young man with a limp was standing before the bear pit entrance, watching the people pass. He told the Stocks where his employers, Babcock and Crisp, could be found. Francis Crisp was standing in the pit proper, tossing apples to a bear. The bear was catching the apples in his mouth and eating them greedily. Crisp paused when he became aware of the Stocks and said, "No baiting today, if you've come for that. Return tomorrow. The first baiting is at three o'clock."

Her husband explained that they had not come for the baiting but to see Ned Babcock, his old friend.

"So you're Matthew Stock of Chelmsford!" cried Crisp, wrinkling his face into a smile. "As I hope to be saved, Ned will be right pleased to know you've come. Now where is the man? By the Mass, he's around here someplace."

Crisp extended a sinewy, brown hand and Matthew shook it. "You're right welcome to Smithfield and its bear garden," Crisp said.

Joan stared at the bear with fascination. She had seen many bears—bears dancing, begging, decked out in funny hats or coats. The English loved them. But she had never seen a bear such as this. The shaggy creature was very large, with a massive, sloping forehead and huge snout; its paws were powerful-looking and threatening. She watched as it greedily gobbled up the last of the apples and then looked inquiringly at Crisp as though to ask if there weren't more. She noticed the bear had many an old wound on its mangy coat. He was well named, the bear. Samson, terror of dogs—and perhaps men too?

A man now came out of the tent that could be seen at the other end of the pit, shaded his eyes, and helloed.

"Ned!" cried Matthew, as the large, ruddy-faced man came toward them, his arms open in a gesture of welcome.

Had their journey been a pleasant one, Babcock wanted to know, talking very fast and with many gestures. And what did they think of Smithfield? Was it not very fine, despite the August heat, the dust, and the stink? Joan allowed Matthew to answer these questions, and felt somewhat excluded from the reunion.

"He's not Harry Hunks or Sackerson," said Babcock, referring to two of the most famous of London's fighting bears, "yet he's a stout fellow in combat, I assure you."

This stout fellow, having evidently concluded that there were no more apples to be had, was now resting his head on his forepaws and staring listlessly at his masters and their guests. In this posture, the bear resembled a large shaggy dog in the grip of unspeakable boredom, but Babcock was still going on about the bear's valor. "There's many have paid three pence or more to see Samson at work and not complained afterward of the cost. He's long in the tooth now, but he's as strong and mighty as ever he was."

Francis Crisp, Joan noticed, said little. She thought him a queer little man, shabbily dressed in contrast to his partner, and smelling of the bear. Although friendly and outgoing before, he seemed in his partner's presence to become somewhat moody and quiet, as though all the verbal energy available was used up by Babcock, whenever the larger and younger man was around. Babcock asked them if they wouldn't like a tour of the pit. It was something to see, he assured them. His enthusiasm made clear this was not an invitation to be refused.

"This hour tomorrow, the fair begun, these benches will be full," said Babcock as they walked the length of the pit and came to the tent. "In three days' time I'll be free of debt and a new man." Babcock smiled optimistically.

"Feeding Samson must be a great expense," Joan remarked as Babcock led them inside the dark, foul-smelling den. She saw the cage, taller than a man, with iron bars like a prison. Its floor was strewn with straw, atop of which could be seen the remains of the bear's last meal—a cluster of bloody bones and gristle.

Noticing that Joan had taken an interest in the cage, Babcock described Samson's diet. The bear ate great quantities of meat had from the city butchers at little cost since most of it was scrap, he said. Samson also was fond of good English beer, although the animal was provided with this treat sparingly so as not to form an expensive habit. Babcock told a story about one bear who so came to prefer the beverage that he refused thereafter to drink water.

Matthew laughed at the story. "I wonder that any hound lives who would dare fight with such a creature," he said.

Joan agreed.

"Oh, you'd be amazed," Babcock said. "A strong-hearted mastiff will sink his teeth in and hold 'til his very body is stripped raw of fur. I've seen it myself. But the most courageous dog I ever saw was a little spaniel named Twit. No bigger than a house cat. He bit half through Samson's foot before he bled to death himself. What a pity. I had to cut the spaniel's teeth off Samson. It took a month for the wound to heal properly. On your way outdoors you can see for yourself. A very ugly scar."

Joan said she would put off examining the scar for another visit.

Babcock continued on about Samson's prowess and his hopes that his new business venture would both clear his debts and make him and Crisp wealthy. "If Samson doesn't bring in the coppers this fair time, then I don't know my head from my hand. Why, every farmer and goatherd will want to match their favorite dog or bitch against him. But they will be sorely disappointed, I promise you, for Samson will send them that live whimpering home soon enough."

It was very hot inside the tent, and having viewed Samson's cage there was little else for Joan to see, except for a pile of fresh straw and, in a corner, a kind of rude pallet, with a patched blanket covering it. Babcock led them out, still jabbering about the bear, with Crisp nodding his head in wordless approval of all his partner said. Joan got the idea that Samson was only the most recent of Babcock's enthusiasms. He talked like a successful man, and had Matthew not acquainted her with the sad tale of his failures, Joan would probably have taken his boasting at face value. But what did it all amount to really, this investment in a bear that did battle with dogs? It did not seem to her an entirely honest way of life.

Matthew thanked the bearwards for the tour and promised to return the next day for the first of the baitings. Joan had earlier agreed to keep Matthew company. Matthew planned to attend for friendship's sake; Joan, for Matthew's sake. Neither cared for bearbaitings, although neither had seen one. Then Babcock invited them to take supper with him that night. "You shall meet our investors," he declared, with particular emphasis on the word *investors*. "And my daughter, Juliet."

"She that was recently widowed?" Matthew inquired.

For once the round-faced, ebullient man frowned; but it was not a face for frowning, and the stern regard soon faded. "The very one. A most unfortunate girl. Somewhat melancholy, and for very good reason. The story of her husband's untimely death is a sad one, but I'll save it for another day."

They said their farewells to the two partners and, passing out through the entrance booth, Matthew announced he would spend the afternoon in the Close, for he planned to show his wares to certain London tailors with whom he hoped eventually to do some business. He asked Joan if she would come too, but she declined. She had had enough for the morning of men and their doings and was badly in need of fresher air. If such could be had in Smithfield.

She resolved to strike out for herself, but agreed to meet Matthew at the Hand and Shears at five o'clock.

Matthew walked off toward the Priory. Joan paused, decided which way to go. Then she saw the young man she had observed upon entering, the bearward's helper. He was coming up the lane, pushing the wheelbarrow that was now empty of its odoriferous contents. He was almost to her when he stopped to talk to a slim, dark-haired girl, who had come out of one of the booths to meet him.

Joan paused to observe this pleasant view of youthful courtship. If there was ever love written upon a face, love was written upon the girl's. The young man's handsome features seemed equally affected. Joan was at too great a distance to hear their conversation, but she guessed its import. What a handsome couple they made! He with his shock of blond hair and well-formed shoulders; she with her fresh cheeks, slender form, and innocent gaze. The faces of both were bright with blushing.

Joan was in the midst of these happy reflections when suddenly a raving creature of immense girth and slovenly appearance came rushing from the booth and snatched the girl by the hair, jerking her head back with a snap. She started to beat the girl with her fists, pounding her on the shoulders and back, cursing loudly.

The bearward's helper tried to separate the two but failed. He was struck himself by the terrible woman and was sent sprawling in the dirt. Another man appeared from a neighboring booth and said something that appeased the large woman's wrath; while she scolded the girl, the boy limped off sorrowfully, nursing his jaw.

Joan felt profoundly sorry for the girl, who she now realized must be the servant of the terrible fat woman. By law, employers were allowed to beat their servants. Custom also sanctioned it. Masters could beat their servants, their apprentices, their children, even their wives. As long as the damage was within limits, no blame was attached to the beater. But Joan had her own ideas about *that*; she had never laid a hand on a servant of hers, no, nor on an apprentice or a child (although there were more than a handful of scoundrels of both sexes in Chelmsford she would have gladly pummelled, yes, and felt no guilt at it either!).

The young man came toward Joan, passing without remark. Joan thought to catch his eye, to offer some cheerful word of encouragement or consolation, but the young man's head was down, his stare fixed on the trace of muck in the wheelbarrow as though he were studying some awful revenge upon the vicious slattern who had assaulted him. And who could blame him? Joan thought, as the bearward's helper hobbled past her.

# · 6 ·

Still shaken from the violent scene she had witnessed, Joan wandered down a lane of half-erected booths, latecomers to Smithfield, steering clear of the bustle of construction. She stopped to watch a juggler keep five balls aloft while he pranced around in a circle. Paused again to survey the goods of a toy seller, wondering if her little grandson would like a toy dog or cat, a rattle or drum? The heat of noon had lived up to the promise of the morning. The aroma of roasting pork mixed with less savory smells. She felt woozy and her throat was dry. She would resist the temptation of Bartholomew pig as greasy and fattening, but how she needed something cool to drink.

"A bottle of ale to quench you in these dog days?" cried a voice at hand. A little man, as ugly as a toad, thrust the bottle at her, grinning from ear to ear.

She paid for the bottle, opened the stopple, and drank. The ale was tepid and tasteless and she would have complained of it, but when she turned around the tapster had disappeared.

Realizing that last night's sleeplessness was beginning to tell on her, she resolved to go to the inn without further delay. She looked around her to get her bearings, and was about to proceed in what she hoped was the correct direction when she saw at the end of the lane a small round tent decorated in a curious fashion. The tent was set off by itself and on its sides were painted crude representations of moon, stars, and sun. A placard set up beside the tent displayed a large open palm with short, stubby fingers, such as a child might draw. The lines of the palm were dark and wide and there were strange symbols imprinted on the fingers, the ball of the thumb, and the flat of the hand.

Joan was sure this was the habitation of an astrologer or fortune-teller. She knew that there were many in London, most Gypsies living in Cow-lane and many famous for their prognostications, horoscopes, and palm readings. Of these practitioners of hidden arts (not witches; *they* were another matter), Joan had no settled conviction. Her mind was open, for did not the Queen of England herself consult her own private sorcerer and astrologer, the illustrious Doctor Dee? And did not many lesser lights, men of breeding and education too, regard their prophesies with respect? Joan had known many a cunning-woman in her own town. Gifted women, making profit by their gifts. But she had never consulted them. She herself had gifts, *glimmerings,* as she called them, visions that came unbidden, visions that warned, consoled, informed as her need was and that she did not construe as incompatible with true religion or common sense and that had more than once saved her life—and Matthew's too. As for the influence heavenly bodies might exert on the destiny of men, who knew how some vaguely perceived constellation, twinkling weakly in the night, might mirror an inherent quality in man, disposing him to one fate rather than another?

Her curiosity was strong, and it drew her even closer to the tent. She forgot the heat and her wooziness. The tent flap was closed; and the tent seemed unoccupied. Now she observed that beneath the crudely depicted palm a word was written. *Esmera.* What did it mean? A name perhaps? She tried to imagine what manner of person Esmera might be and was still doing so when she became aware of a stirring inside the tent.

She started to move away, but then heard a voice.

"Stay, mistress, I pray you!"

The tent flap was still closed, but Joan was sure the appeal was addressed to her, and even if it had not been she would have obeyed for the words were spoken with such urgency and in such a strange voice that she felt compelled to stand where she was.

The tent flap was suddenly swept aside by a dark, bejeweled hand, and the owner of the beckoning voice showed herself.

The woman's appearance, for woman it was, was striking. She was either the homeliest woman Joan had ever seen or the most beautiful. Tall and regally thin, garbed in a long scarlet robe that stretched from shoulder to feet, Esmera had a high forehead crowned with long, straight black hair that fell to her shoulders, dark, moist eyes, the nose of a Roman empress, and very full pale lips in odd contrast to her skin color. If beauty, hers was not the English beauty of which poets had sung and courtiers raved—the damask cheeks, rosy lips, and clear blue eyes of flattering sonnets. Esmera's was an exotic beauty, born of some remote clime. Her skin was as dark as a Moor's, and for all Joan knew she might have hailed from the dark continent. She was really too tall for a woman, at least six feet, Joan estimated. And above the full upper lip was a thin patch of dark downy hair, like a little moustache. As to age, the woman was neither girl nor matron, but something in between.

Joan was utterly and helplessly fascinated.

"I am Esmera," the woman herself confirmed in a thickly accented but mellifluous voice of surprising deepness. Joan thought the accent was as strange as the woman herself.

"So you have come to speak with Esmera," said the woman. Esmera smiled and displayed perfectly formed white teeth.

"I came to look . . . at your tent," said Joan, nervously. "The signs caught my eye—as I walked abroad in the fair."

"Ah, the signs," Esmera said. "They are not without their meanings." She turned slightly to face the tent wall and with a graceful motion of her arm pointed to the symbols. "These are the governors of men's destiny," she said, indicating the heavenly bodies—the moon, sun, and stars—that surrounded the hand. "To observe their times and seasons, their positions and relations, is to know the secrets of the universe—and the destiny of man and woman."

Esmera began to speak of eclipses and constellations, planets and the signs of Zodiac, and a dozen other notions of her occult science. All these, she said, were related to another branch of knowledge, that of the human hand, which knowledge she called *cheirognomy* and *cheiromancy*. This was wisdom derived from the Chaldeans and Egyptians and other ancient peoples, and it was in this knowledge that Esmera was especially adept. "There are seven types of hands," she continued, "determined by the shape of the fingers, the smoothness of the flesh, and the proportion of fingers to palm. Hands with short, thick fingers, short thumbs, and large, thick, and hard palms betoken crass and sluggard brains. Hands that are knotty, with large thumbs and phalanges of similar length, show an equal measure of will and common sense—a philosopher's bent."

The palms of the hands were surrounded by various upraised areas Esmera called Mounts, named after the planets—of Venus, Jupiter, Saturn, Apollo, Mercury, Mars, and the moon. The center of the palm was occupied by the Plain or Triangle of Mars and was comprised of three distinct lines, the Line of Life, the Line of Head, and the Line of Heart. These various signs, along with their waviness, forked terminations, ascending and descending branches, breaks, and capillaries, were also indications of destiny.

Esmera paused in her discourse and turned to face Joan again. She asked her if she would like to have her own palm interpreted. "I see you are a woman of good sense," Esmera said, regarding Joan with interest. "Won't you come inside?"

Joan was hesitant, and yet more curious than ever. During Esmera's lecture she had gradually moved her own hands out of the cunning-woman's sight, from a kind of painful self-consciousness. She knew her own hands were small and delicate, her fingers pointed and the flesh smooth. But of this type of hand Esmera had not spoken, and now Joan wondered what these familiar mechanisms at the end of each arm might speak of her own character and destiny.

"Only for a while," Joan said.

Esmera led her inside.

The tent interior was close and redolent with an unfamiliar

but not unpleasant scent. The only furnishings were a small, round table without covering and two simple stools set on an earthen floor watered to keep the dust down. Esmera settled onto one of the stools and directed Joan to sit on the other.

"Let me have your hand, child," said Esmera in a calm, persuasive voice.

Joan did as she was told. Esmera turned Joan's hand so that the palm was turned upward. And then taking the hand firmly in her own two hands, Esmera began to look at Joan's palm with a steady gaze, as though her vision was penetrating beyond the pink flesh to the bones beneath. "A goodly temperature of the flesh," Esmera said, after a long period of silence during which Joan's self-consciousness intensified and her hand felt warm and moist. "Neither cold nor hot but in between. The color is good too. Your hand is small and delicate, a thin palm and smooth fingers, long and shapely. The joints show but a slight swelling . . . a pretty little thumb. You are a dreamer, impulsive. You desire the beautiful things of life, whether mundane or celestial. You are ruled by heart and soul."

Esmera's voice was dreamy and smooth, like syrup. Joan listened intently, much too intrigued and flattered by this concentrated attention to her own person to interrupt, for Esmera's description came very close to her own assessment. While Joan thought herself a woman of great practicality, she was aware of the other side of her personality, a side often hidden from others: airy, elusive, rooted in the world of dreams and visions, the intangible and unseen.

"But now I must turn to the lines of the palm," Esmera said decisively when her portrait of Joan's character had been drawn to its fullness and Joan's silence had implied agreement with all Esmera had spoken. "First, the line of life."

Esmera traced the well-defined crevice setting the region of the thumb off from the central plain of Joan's palm. "The Mount of Venus is very prominent. You admire beauty and melody in music and dance. You desire to please. You are a great lover of society, with a talent for friendship and loyalty. The line rising from the base of the hand is a sign of good luck. As for the life line itself, it is long and completely encircles the ball of the thumb and . . ."

Esmera paused and her eyes widened. For a long time she studied Joan's hand in silence, and Joan became nervous with expectation. Was something wrong? Was something written in the line that betokened ill?

"What is it you see?" Joan finally asked when the cunning-woman's silence was no longer bearable.

Esmera did not respond at once. She took Joan's other hand and seemed to compare the two. Then she said: "There is a break in the line of life. See, it is here." Esmera pointed to an interruption in the otherwise distinct crevice in the pale flesh. "Fortunately for you, lady, such a break appears only in the left hand, not in the right."

"What does that mean?" Joan asked urgently, her voice trembling a little. She studied her own outstretched hand and saw that the line of life was indeed broken. It ceased abruptly with a few parallel lines intersecting while the lower branch of the break turned upward toward the ball of the thumb, the wrinkled swelling of flesh Esmera had referred to as the Mount of Venus.

Esmera said: "If the break occurs in both palms, it is a sign of death. The veer of the broken line toward Venus's Mount is a warning of sudden death. Since it is only one hand that shows such a sign, however, you need fear only the danger. And soon."

"The danger of death? Soon? When?"

Joan's heart was racing now; her heart lodged in her throat so that she could hardly get the questions out.

"How old are you, lady?"

"Mrs. Stock. My name is Mrs. Stock. I will be thirty-eight come November."

Esmera bent over Joan's hand, tracing the line of life again. "The danger will be soon. This very year and season," Esmera said.

"What else do you see in my hand?" Joan asked.

Esmera shut her eyes. She seemed to go into a trance and said nothing for several minutes. Then she opened her eyes and stared at Joan's palm again. "You have a husband," Esmera said.

"I do," Joan answered.

"He makes a good living for you. A tradesman, I think."

"Yes," Joan murmured, half mesmerized by Esmera's husky drawl.

"He is also an alderman of the town."

"No," Joan corrected. "A constable."

"A man of position, of authority," Esmera went on, undaunted by the error. "I see a man of middle years, of pleasant countenance and gentle manner. A good husband for you, yes?"

"A most excellent husband," Joan said, not without pride.

Esmera's brow furrowed. She retraced the line of life. "I see misfortune, sorrow in your past."

"Oh."

"Loss, death of children."

"Only one of my children lived," Joan said, her voice trembling. "The rest were not brought alive from my womb. After a while I thought myself unable to bear living children, then—"

"Nay, let me tell you," Esmera said with quiet urgency. "Then you gave birth successfully. The child lived. And grew. She's a young woman now."

"Yes, it *was* a girl."

"And married," Esmera continued, with an expression of triumph playing around her pale full lips. "Who has children of her own."

"One child. So far. A son," Joan agreed.

"I was about to say as much. Oh, it is all written in your palm, lady. All this past sadness and joy—but also the danger I warned you of. Your daughter's name is Mary . . . Susan . . . perhaps Elizabeth?"

"It *is* Elizabeth," said Joan, marveling at the woman's insight. Was her daughter's very name written on the palm? Joan looked at her own hand with a kind of wonder, trying to make her own sense of the maze of wrinkles and crevices near two score in the making. But now Esmera's eyes were no longer focused on Joan's outstretched hand; again she seemed to retreat into some vision not wholly dependent upon physical contact. Esmera swayed a little on her stool and made a low crooning noise. Joan asked if she were well and received no reply. The crooning and swaying continued and Joan felt afraid again. Was some new warning at hand? She waited.

"I see grave danger for you, Mrs. Stock," Esmera said, her eyelids beginning to flutter a little while she continued to sway on the stool. "And your husband. Here in Smithfield . . . danger close at hand."

"What *manner* of danger?" Joan cried, excitedly.

"I see a beast."

"A *beast?*"

"Teeth dripping with blood, cruel fangs. Claws. Raw, bloody flesh. The odor of death." Esmera began to ramble incoherently; her eyes now opened wide and rolled up into her head. Joan dared not speak and was horrified both at Esmera's vision and her present appearance, which had twisted her countenance into that of a mad woman's. Yet she had no choice but to wait until Esmera's fit passed, which it presently did, the cunning-woman's shoulders slumping and her head falling so that her chin rested heavily on her chest and Joan could no longer see the moist dark eyes. Esmera seemed totally exhausted by her vision. But, looking up, she appeared normal now, and Joan was not frightened as before.

"Are you well, Esmera?" Joan ventured again.

"I am well," Esmera replied in a voice both deeper and weaker than before. "Don't be alarmed, Mrs. Stock. You will come close to death but it shall miss you—with good fortune and . . . the proper precautions. I cannot say the same for your husband, however."

"My husband! You mean he faces the same danger—from the beast you have seen in your vision?"

Esmera nodded her head as if to say yes, it was all to be, fated, as certain as the tracery of Joan's palm.

"And these precautions you mention—what are they?" Joan thought to ask.

Esmera frowned and shook her head. She released Joan's hand and laid it on the round tabletop as if to signal that their interview was over. "I can see no more. Not at this time. You must come again to see Esmera."

Joan rose; the wooziness that she had experienced earlier now returned to intensify the anxiety the cunning-woman's warning had inspired. She looked down at Esmera. "I don't know if I can," Joan said. "My husband and I are in London only for the fair. In three days' time we will return to Chelmsford."

"But you *must* come again," Esmera insisted, looking up at Joan with her large dark eyes.

Joan undid her purse from the broad piece of velvet that girdled her waist and searched for something to pay Esmera, but the woman made a gesture of her hand suggesting that she wanted nothing for advice. "I charge you nothing, Mrs. Stock. I will take nothing from you. Please, believe me, you and your husband are in grave danger. About such matters Esmera is never wrong. Come again, and soon. I may learn more. Remember, you may enjoy long life. I have seen the same in your palm. But the danger is unmistakable. Death is close at hand for you and your husband . . ."

Esmera's voice trailed off. She shook her head with the tragic air of one who knows that there is no controlling what the stars have ordained or fate had inscribed in the smooth palm. Joan felt a chilling sensation in her backbone, compounding her anxiety. She mumbled her thanks to the strange woman and stepped out into the stark sunlight.

Joan's head reeled and throbbed; she was half-blinded by the glare. For a moment she stood staring at Esmera's sign with its grotesque hand and jumble of symbols and felt the very image pressing down on her like the threatening hand of an angry parent ready to strike an unruly child. She tried to shake off the aftereffect of Esmera's prophesy through the force of will, but the unfamiliarity of her surroundings aggravated her confusion. She looked around and decided to go at once to the Close. She wanted desperately to find Matthew and tell him all that had transpired since she had left him.

As she hurried, her brain told her that Esmera's knowledge might have been nothing more than a clever imagination, but in her heart she felt otherwise. Esmera's words had thrust deep into her soul and planted there seeds of uncertainty and fear, and even as she fled Esmera's tent Joan could sense the seeds beginning to grow.

As she approached the Close, Joan saw Matthew emerging from the gate, Babcock with him. The two men were deep in conversation, laughing and gesturing, and for a moment Joan suppressed a twinge of irritation that Matthew could be so indifferent to the danger about him. Had Esmera not *seen* the beast? And what beast could she have seen, save Samson, Babcock's own fighting bear, the terror of Smithfield and bane of foolhardy dogs?

In the twenty paces she traveled between the realization and her arrival at where Matthew stood, her excited brain pictured the creature in startling clarity. The teeth and enormous claws were clean of flesh and blood now. But what of later? How Joan wished she could escape from this horrible place with its vicious animal stench and the blood of the poor, suffering hounds. Men's sport! she thought with disgust.

She interrupted Matthew without as much as a by-your-leave and told him she was sick unto death and wanted to return straightway to the inn, an assertion the great bulk of which was true.

Matthew received this word with alarm. "Sick! Pray God it is no contagion. Did you eat anything since last we met? Bartholomew pig is wondrous rich and can quite undo a delicate stomach."

"I ate no pig, nor sausage either," Joan returned sharply.

"Why, you're as pale as a ghost," Matthew said.

"Paler," observed Babcock, making a sympathetic but helpless face.

"We will go back to the inn," Matthew said. "Are you able to walk or should I find some conveyance?"

"I can walk," Joan replied stiffly, and the truth was she was less sick now, although very hot and weary.

"I'm so sorry, Mrs. Stock," said Babcock. "Pray this indisposition is only temporary. Come, join me for supper this very evening. We'll have a room to ourselves in the Hand and Shears. I'm eager for the both of you to meet my investors. My daughter, Juliet Beauchamp, will also be there."

Joan accepted the invitation as gracefully as her excited state of mind would allow, and looked appealingly at her husband. The two men shook hands, bid each other farewell, and then Matthew took Joan's arm and steered her toward the inn. "It's one of the unhappy consequences of sojourning in a strange place," he said worriedly as they walked. "These sudden revolts and stirrings of the belly."

"Well, it was no pig," Joan maintained steadfastly. "I'll say more anon. For now, I need nothing but to wash off this dust and lie down for a while."

# · 7 ·

"A fortune-teller!" Matthew exclaimed in a tone to suggest that Joan was quite out of her mind. "What, did she cast your nativity water or wound your ears with blather about horoscopes and the conjunction of planets?"

"Don't mock me, husband," Joan warned—grateful, however, that he had saved this outburst of cynicism for the privacy of their chamber at the inn. In the street she had been of no stomach to conduct the quarrel that now threatened. "The woman did nothing more than plow my palm with her thumb and forefinger, from which plowing she reaped a rich harvest of truth."

"Truth, say you?" he scoffed.

"About me. And you. And yes, about Elizabeth our daughter as well—and her child. She said you were constable of the town and in the way of wealth. She said we had a single daughter who in turn had but one child. Why, she even told me our daughter's name. Now, tell me, Matthew, how was this fortune-teller able to do that save she was possessed of some art?"

"Oh, I grant she has art," her husband returned. "Joan, you amaze me—you, a woman whose mind I have always revered for its common sense, its—"

"No more flattery! You have bent your bow, now make from the shaft."

"So, then," commenced Matthew, with a determined sigh and what she thought was a rather fierce expression for him. "Let us begin with my constableship, of which you say this woman informed you. It's no great skill to guess such stuff or my wealth. Look at that gown that covers your nakedness or that French hood that crowns you. A grocer or ironmonger of my income could not have clothed his wife withal, but since cloth is my trade that garment that a gentleman's wife would not have scorned was well within my means. Is my wealth not a likely inference, then? And since your speech betrays you as an outlander, was it not equally probable that your well-to-do husband held some office in his town?"

"She did first suppose you were an alderman," Joan conceded.

"Indeed! And I would wager it was you, not she, who announced that I was a constable."

"It was so," Joan said.

"It takes no great wit to suppose a wealthy townsman holds either office."

"But what of Elizabeth—her name and the fact she had but one child?"

"I cannot say," Matthew replied dismissively. "But on my faith, the knowledge was derived not from your palm but from the cunning brain of the woman. It was a trick, I tell you. From a few stones of accurate information, this kind can erect a great house that seems as real and plausible as God's word. But it is all illusion at last."

"She felt the palm," Joan persisted. "She had a vision of danger, as I have said."

Her husband sighed with exasperation. He stood looking at her as though her case was beyond help, as though he was a physician at a loss for a diagnosis, much less a cure. "I am much surprised that she did not prophesy some curious encounter with an attractive stranger, a long voyage at sea, or the discovery of some valuable roundabout the house. Such stale stuff is the common content of their discourse. Go you to Cow-lane where the cunning-men keep company and watch those goshawks pick the brains and pockets of the innocent and gullible."

"It was a vision of *danger*," Joan insisted.

"A mere variation on the theme," Matthew returned with hardly a pause. "I do not suppose this woman said *what* danger, from *what* quarter it was to come and with *what* exact consequences. Was not the prophecy in fact vague and murky like vegetables floating in a thick soup, nine-tenths of them submerged and the rest barely discernible in the pot? Whoever heard a cunning-woman foretell a stranger's visit but she claimed ignorance of the stranger's name and hour of arrival. It is all gross imposture, the lot of it!"

"Esmera seemed most sincere," Joan said feebly.

"I warrant you, she did. You shall not find in London a more sincere-sounding person. That is her stock in trade. None of them but they ooze sincerity, and it's a cool head indeed that sees through it to the truth."

"I just don't know. I'm confused," Joan admitted.

"Well, given we are in London and in Smithfield, which is the worse, a vision of danger is not out of the way. Of course there is danger—on every hand. Cutpurses abound, as I have warned you. Tricksters on every hand. Sword-and-buckler bullies and saucy bawds. This cunning-woman might have delivered the same prophecy to a Cow-lane alewife and with equal justice."

"She didn't charge a penny," Joan said, as though this were the ultimate verification.

"Now there's the marvel," her husband replied cynically. "A cunning-woman she may be but she's no businessman who sells her wares at such a price. I wonder what she meant by that? No doubt she wants you to return and become a regular seeker of her arcane wisdom, for which, growing dependent on such murky counsel, you will in time become her mainstay. The first visit is but bait for the unwary fish. Beware her lure, Joan. It's all vile deception, every whit."

"And my fears groundless?" she said.

Matthew walked over to where Joan sat on the bed, feeling very dejected and, yes, foolish too. Taking her hands, he opened her palms and studied them, tracing the lines in her left palm with the forefinger of his right, much as Esmera had done not an hour before.

"Upon your palms I see happiness writ and I am but a

clothier, no prophet. I see a fruitful life, a loving and devoted husband, a grateful and dutiful daughter, and a host of admiring friends. Isn't that enough? What, must you seek out the dangers that in truth lie all around and from which God has half-protected us by keeping us ignorant of them?"

It was not an unreasonable question and Joan gave it some consideration. Matthew stooped to kiss her cheek tenderly. "Come, now," he said in a suasive voice. "Don't let's quarrel about this. It's much ado over very little. This Esmera is a kind of entertainer—like the jugglers and acrobats. Her trade is *words*, rather. And hers have given you unrest. So, then, they are but words at last, nothing more."

But Joan was not sure that was all there was to it. In Joan's mind, Esmera continued to cast a spell: she could still hear the strange woman's deep throaty voice, see the dark moist eyes. Yet Joan was weary of arguing. She appeared to concede the point to Matthew but only in exchange for the quiet it would bring, the chance to stretch out on the bed and sleep.

"Perhaps I was gulled after all," she said, forcing a smile to conceal her lingering uncertainty.

"Don't say *gulled*," Matthew said. "You've lost nothing from the experience but a brief hour of happiness that might otherwise have been yours. Say, rather, that you were undone by the heat of the day, the strangeness of the place, and the charm of this Esmera. What is passed is done with. God be thanked that you are my own dear Joan again. For me, that is quite enough."

She let him help her, put her to bed. Like a child again, but now she lacked even the energy for shame, much less protest. He pulled the coverlet up over her and gently tucked it around her neck.

"I have some business at the Guildhall that will occupy me for the next two hours," he whispered. "Come suppertime we'll go upstairs to Ned Babcock's feast and forget our troubles in good fellowship and song. Ned is no mean host, I warrant you. And the cost of the meal is his alone. He won that honor for himself in losing a wager to me."

She thought to ask what manner of wager but the words never came. She listened to her husband's farewell drowsily, as though she had taken a sleeping potion and was fast on the way to oblivion. She had not realized how weary she was until now—from the long journey, she supposed; from the heat and strangeness of the place, as Matthew had argued. With half-closed eyes, she stared up at the netherside of the canopy stretching above her bed like a little ceiling. The dark cloth lacked ornament or design, but in the instant before she crossed the threshold betwixt sleep and awake she thought she saw again the mystical symbols that had adorned Esmera's tent and heard blended with the soft tread of her husband's retreat the low incantation of the cunning-woman's prophecy.

At dusk of that day, Rose again was sent to the muckhill with another bucketload of garbage from Ursula's makeshift kitchen. Her earlier trip had yielded no view of the bearward's helper, but she was undaunted and approached her destination with joyful anticipation. Gabriel was not there. No one was there. The pit had been dug several days earlier to accommodate the refuse the fair was sure to generate and in the waning light it presented to Rose a spectacle of utter desolation. A great moldering heap of filth, a stinking pile that would have been quite nauseating had she not been accustomed to it by now. Standing there, her buckets at her feet as yet unemptied, she stared out over the pit. How she wished Gabriel was at her side to speak of sacred things, to lift her spirits from her sadness. She said the prayer he had taught her and crossed herself (he had not taught her *that* gesture—a vestige of Roman idolatry, he would have said). She began to empty the buckets. As she emptied the last and was preparing to return to the pig-woman's booth, her view fell upon an object sticking out from a pile of refuse. It was a shoe, a shoe that she supposed by some mischance had been cast away. Being of an economical turn of mind, Rose reached down and grasped the toe, thinking that someone's negligence might be her good fortune.

But that there was more there than the shoe she soon realized, as she yanked it forth from the refuse. There was an ankle too, in patched worsted hose, and a lower limb ending in mid-calf in bloody, ragged flesh and bone.

She stared at her discovery with disbelief while a scream of horror welled up inside her. She let the thing drop back into the muck and gave voice to her feelings, a shrill cry of terror and disgust.

She screamed and screamed until someone came. More than one, a whole crowd, gathering around her and the muckhill, wanting to know what was the matter.

"It's Ursula's girl," someone said. "What's her difficulty? A rat bit her, I reckon."

Another voice—Rose recognized it as Jack Talbot's—was more sympathetic. She pointed to the offending object and someone, not the wine seller but someone else, bent over to examine it and uttered an expression of disgust and then ran away.

"It's bloody murder, that's what it is," declared the authoritative voice of another. "Someone fetch the sergeant and the watch."

"Yes," said someone else, "go find Grotwell. He'll want to have a look at this."

"Someone search for the rest of him," said another. "Bring torches."

"Search yourself, if you're so keen."

"Are you sure the limb is a man's?"

"'Tis for a fact, unless beasts are shod and hosed in worsted. Quick, someone go fetch Grotwell."

# · 8 ·

Later the same evening, Joan, physically refreshed from her
two-hours' nap and in a better mind for company, went with
Matthew to the Dolphin, a handsomely appointed chamber
where the inn's guests and their friends could take supper in
private. They were greeted at the door by a smiling Ned Babcock, who was already mildly drunk. Within the chamber, a
round table had been laid. About a half-dozen somber people
stood at a sideboard, where various dainties and a large bowl of
punch had been served. Whatever conversation had been in
progress now ceased with the arrival of the newcomers.

Babcock ushered them in and began a round of introductions. "Now, Francis Crisp you already know," he said with a
forced joviality oddly in contrast to the glum expressions of the
rest of the company. "And this young woman is my daughter,
Juliet Beauchamp."

Joan smiled and nodded at the rather plain-faced girl of
twenty-one or twenty-two. Juliet was small and of compact figure. Dressed in black, she wore the resentful expression of one
not present by her own will. She curtsied at the introduction
and seemed uncomfortable.

With a pained expression, Babcock reminded them that his
daughter had been recently widowed, hence her mourning garments. "A terrible accident," he said, without explaining just
what sort of accident it had been.

Joan expressed her sympathy; Juliet nodded. Joan felt a
coolness between the girl and her father, and her curiosity was
aroused, but before she could speculate further on the cause of
their dispute, Joan's attention was directed to her host's next
guest, a thin, tallow-faced man of about thirty-five, in a hand-

some worsted suit of elegant cut. This, Babcock said, was Mr. John Pullyver. Pullyver was a greengrocer with a shop in Cheapside and a house in Blackfriars. Since Joan knew that many greengrocers supplemented their incomes by lending money, often at usurious rates, she was not surprised to find one among Babcock's investors. Indeed, as Babcock explained, this singularly unprepossessing man was the principal investor in the Smithfield Bear Gardens.

While Babcock's long introduction of the greengrocer was in progress, Joan noticed that Pullyver was casting intermittent glances at Juliet. And when Babcock presently said that the greengrocer's wife had died only recently, leaving him with three small children at home, Joan guessed that Pullyver was a widower in want of a wife—and the wife he wanted was Juliet Beauchamp.

But did Juliet want him? Joan didn't think so. Babcock conducted her and Matthew to his remaining guests.

These included a scrivener named Ralph Chapman and his wife, Margaret. Chapman was tall and loose-jointed and not quite as prosperous-looking as the greengrocer. He was also one of Babcock's investors, but because Babcock treated Chapman with less obsequiousness than he had the greengrocer, Joan suspected the scrivener's investment was also less substantial. Chapman's wife was a round, red-faced woman who in other circumstances might have responded to Joan's greeting with greater cordiality. She seemed a friendly sort, but oppressed by what appeared to Joan more a business meeting than a social gathering, despite the supper in the offing and the dainties already on the sideboard. When Babcock told the Chapmans, man and wife, that the Stocks were from Chelmsford, neither seemed to have heard of the town. "Mr. Stock is constable there," said Babcock.

The greengrocer Pullyver evinced mild interest; he took his eyes off the young widow he wanted and said that he had recently seen at the Globe one of Mr. Shakespeare's plays, which featured a constable named Dogberry. "A very droll, comical fellow, though somewhat deficient in intellect," said Pullyver.

Matthew said he had not heard of such a character or seen the play.

"You *have* heard of Mr. Shakespeare?" asked Pullyver, with an incredulous expression that anticipated a negative answer.

Matthew said that he had; indeed, he had seen at least one of his plays. And at the Globe.

Pullyver, evidently a great frequenter of the Southwark theaters, now began rattling off the names of a dozen plays he had attended during the last quarter. To Joan it was all boasting, probably for Juliet's benefit, although she thought the young woman in mourning looked distinctly unimpressed by it all.

Two other strangers were in the room and Babcock now led Matthew and Joan on to them. One was the Clerk of the Fair, a Mr. Rathbone. Rathbone was a stout, distinguished-looking man with prematurely graying hair. At his waist he carried a watch, an invention still novel enough to proclaim the social prestige of its wearer. Standing by him was a man of about fifty, with the cadaverous expression of an undertaker. This fellow, named Foote, had also something to do with the fair. Like Rathbone, Foote nodded cordially at the Stocks and welcomed them both to London. But Joan was still aware of a tension in the room, as though her and Matthew's entrance had merely interrupted some unpleasantness that would resume once they left again.

She noticed during the introductions that Francis Crisp had wandered off into the corner, away from the other guests. He was dressed very shabbily for the occasion in a garb hardly more decent than that she had seen him in that morning at the pit, when he was hot and sweaty from labor and still stinking of the bear. Crisp's eyes looked glassy and his expression vacant as though his mind was somewhere else, perhaps back at the pit with his beloved Samson. Like his business partner, Crisp had been partaking of the punch in great quantities, and he seemed unsteady on his feet.

The introductions completed, supper was now served. Several waiters came in bearing the first course—a salad of dry greens and cucumbers. "At last," cried Babcock. "The food! Come, let's sit and eat. Let each give thanks to God in his own heart—and express it by leaving not a morsel uneaten."

"Nor a drop undrunk," added Francis Crisp from his corner, saluting the chamber with a newly emptied glass and smiling keenly at Pullyver, who was leading a stony-faced Juliet Beauchamp to her chair.

Juliet was seated opposite the greengrocer and Joan across from her husband. At her left was the Clerk of the Fair and across from her Babcock and his partner. On around were the scrivener Chapman and his plump wife. At Matthew's side was the cadaverous Mr. Foote, whose mordant expression was no brighter at the prospect of a free meal and who studied his plate of greens with the concerned look of one expecting some disgusting insect to be concealed beneath the lettuce.

They commenced to eat. There was little talk during the first course or the second—several sorts of fowl and lumpy pudding. Joan doubted the tall scrivener or his wife were very communicative in the best of times, nor the tallow-faced greengrocer, but she could not remember what funeral or bankruptcy she had experienced that had been quite so solemn. There was something sour in the room, the savory food notwithstanding, and that sourness was something more than Francis Crisp's unwashed linen.

Meanwhile she observed that Babcock seemed indifferent to the awkwardness of the gathering and ate hardily. Matthew did likewise. But Joan had no appetite. The tension in the room had taken it away and the want of pleasant conversation—the spice of any good meal—had left her to her own thoughts, which again turned to Esmera's prophetic warnings. Joan found herself hearing the cunning-woman's deep, thickly accented voice, and her eyes were inevitably attracted to the hands of those at the table. Babcock's were large and ruddy with hairy backs, Crisp's smaller and brown with gnarled fingers, vivid veins, and broken nails. The greengrocer's hands Joan found especially intriguing: Pullyver's fingers were very long, the backs of the hand smooth, white, and hairless, almost puffy, like some exotic vegetable sold in his shop.

Joan was beckoning to the waiter to remove her plate, for she wanted no more to eat, when her thoughts were interrupted by a racket of stomping and knocking at the door of the chamber, and then a loud, commanding voice inquiring of anyone within hearing distance where Mr. Babcock the bearward could be found.

In the next instant, the door burst open and in marched a large, square-faced man in sheriff's livery, bearing a cudgel. At his heels were two other officers.

The scrivener's wife shrieked with alarm at this unceremonious entrance and all rose at the table.

"I am the man you seek," Babcock announced in a trembling voice, waving a napkin at the intruder as though he thought to defend himself with it. "What's your business? It better be honest business, for I am not alone and undefended here." He waved an arm around at his guests.

"What is it, sergeant?" asked the Clerk.

"Oh, it's you, Mr. Rathbone—and you too, sir, Mr. Foote," said the leader of the intruders. He apologized for breaking in, then said gruffly, "I've come in search of the bearward."

"Well, I am he," Babcock repeated, apparently satisfied that the intruders were officers rather than brigands.

"A man is dead. Dead at the fair," said the sergeant.

"And what's that to me?" asked Babcock.

"We believe he was killed—by your bear."

At this Juliet moaned, turned white as a sheet, and slumped into her chair.

"Killed by my bear!" exclaimed Babcock, unsure as to whether to speak in defense of his bear or see to the condition of his daughter. "Why, my bear has harmed no one."

"Well, it appears he has, sir," said the sergeant.

"Come, Grotwell, out with it, fellow," demanded the Clerk impatiently. "This is a serious charge. Give us the particulars."

"A body has been found at the muckhill at the end of Taylor's lane," Grotwell said. "I should say a *part* has been found, for there is hardly more than a shoe and hosed foot and ankle. This same member has been examined by myself and others."

"And?" prompted the Clerk.

"And we think the bear has eaten the poor devil that is dead," said Grotwell. "There's teeth marks on the bone. God knows where the rest of him is."

"Teeth marks," said Babcock, giving the sergeant his full attention now, for Juliet had recovered and, although pale from the announcement, was having her brow moistened by Joan.

"Very *large* teeth," said Grotwell, looking at the bearward accusingly.

Other guests of the inn who had been attracted to the Dolphin by the uproar had now collected at the door and were looking in with anxious faces. The host of the inn himself appeared, a big, burly man who demanded to know whether there was not sufficient cause to raise the watch, for he was convinced a rebellion was in progress.

"We *are* the watch," said Grotwell gruffly, turning to the host and ordering him to close the door and mind his own business. Reluctantly and with much complaining that it was after all his own inn, the host complied. Then Grotwell continued his story. The fragment of body had been found at sundown. By one Rose Dibble, a servant of Ursula, the pig-woman. The girl had screamed her head off and drawn thereby a huge crowd to the muckhill to see. That the body had been ravaged by some huge beast was the general opinion of everyone who had examined the grisly remains.

Babcock denied that Samson had done it; a sobered Francis Crisp agreed, if anything, more vehemently.

Joan gave over attending Juliet and began to pay more attention to the discussion. Grotwell described the remnant of flesh in sickening detail, and Joan thought, *Gnawed by a beast, ripped to pieces by a bear. A bear?*

Esmera's prophecy had been fulfilled, after all! She looked at Matthew. Would he believe her now? He was following the sergeant's description intently; but Joan couldn't tell whether he was making the connection or not.

"Samson has killed no one," insisted Babcock. "Save for the hounds brave enough to come at him. A more gentle creature around mankind one could hardly find. Do you really think, sir," Babcock addressed the sergeant, "that a beast of mine could have made a meal of human flesh and I not know of it?"

"Or I!" echoed Crisp with a fierce expression.

"Do you imagine a poor creature such as he who is dead would have suffered his dismemberment in silence?" Babcock continued, "Look you now, my bear garden is at the very center of the fair, elbow to elbow to a dozen stalls and booths. Would someone there not have heard the screams of anguish, the agony—"

"Father!" said Juliet sharply.

Babcock stopped and turned to his daughter. Juliet's eyes were full of tears, her lower lip trembled. "How can you speak so after what happened?" she complained bitterly.

Babcock turned back to the sergeant, but said no more.

Crisp now took over the defense of the bear. "Even if it was a bear that did it, there's no evidence it was Samson. He's not the *only* bear in London."

"That's true," Pullyver said. "It may have been another creature that did this."

"Come now, sergeant, what proof have you that it was Samson and not some other?" Babcock said.

"Don't I know a bear's tooth when I see it?" snapped Grotwell, heated now. "And indeed there are bears in London, but what of Smithfield? There I know of only one and Samson is his name."

An angry exchange followed between Crisp and the sergeant, in which Crisp said that Grotwell didn't know a bear from his own buttocks and the sergeant said that he certainly did and told Crisp where he might put the bear and his filthy mouth too. The two men were about to come to blows, which would have been indeed unfortunate for Crisp, since he was unarmed, when the Clerk stepped between them and ordered both to be silent. Rathbone said that Mr. Justice Baynard, Chief Magistrate of the Court of Pie-powders, should be notified of the incident at once, but his companion, Mr. Foote, questioned whether this famous court, held during the three days of the fair, would have jurisdiction.

A debate followed between the two men, which was finally resolved in the Clerk's favor. Grotwell sent one of his men to notify the Justice.

Now Matthew came forward and said, "Could it not have been wild dogs who ate the poor fellow, perhaps finding him somewhere dead first, then dragging the body off to the muckhill? It wouldn't be the first time such a thing has happened."

Babcock and Crisp thought this a very fine suggestion, and Babcock said that the very thing had occurred within living memory, to an unfortunate and aged ragpicker who had frozen to death one winter in Holborn and whose body parts were found thereafter scattered over an area of several miles.

"I would have supposed dogs had done it myself, sir," said Grotwell, eyeing Matthew with cautious respect, pending his discovery of just who this well-spoken citizen might be. "The truth appears otherwise. If Mr. Babcock and the rest of you masters will accompany me to where the body was found, each may examine the remains to his heart's content. I assure you that no dog or pack of them killed the man. It was a large animal, and I doubt that it was any other than Mr. Babcock's bear."

"If what the sergeant says proves true," said the Clerk, turning to Babcock and regarding him with a serious expression, "your Samson *must* die by order of law. There's no help for it, not after what happened to your son-in-law, William Beauchamp."

"That was not Samson's fault," Babcock protested.

But it was, Joan thought, a half-hearted protest, uttered with more bluster than conviction. She noticed that Babcock cast a sidelong glance at his daughter. Juliet's face was turned away from her father. The girl was still distraught by the news. And by something else too. Joan resolved to find out more about William Beauchamp's death. It was clear from what the Clerk had said, and Babcock conceded, that Samson had killed him. But what had been the circumstances?

"Grotwell, lead the way," said the Clerk. "Those who wish may follow."

Matthew told Joan he would accompany the others to the scene of the crime, but Joan had little interest herself in viewing the grisly remains or in traipsing about Smithfield after dark. She said that she would go up to their room and wait his return.

There was now a brief leave-taking on all sides. Pullyver said he would see that Juliet Beauchamp was safely delivered to her own home. The Chapmans thanked their host for their supper and begged to be excused from the expedition to the muckhill. Both husband and wife looked pale and distraught. It had been an evening few of them would forget soon.

In her chamber, the door barred behind her and the tall candles flickering uncertainly, Joan sat on the bed, still dressed. Her mind raced with the events of the day: the tour through Smithfield, the visit to the bear garden, her consultation with the fortune-teller, and, most recently, this unpleasant supper and most horrid discovery of murder—if that was indeed what it was. But whatever it was, deliberate savaging by bear or the carrion work of less threatening beasts, it presented to her mind a grim omen. Certainly Esmera's prophecy had been fulfilled and with dispatch. Joan wondered now what greater horrors awaited.

She uttered a prayer for Matthew's safe return and began to prepare for bed. As she did, she wondered who the unfortunate victim of the muckhill murder had been. An itinerant peddler perhaps? Worse, some innocent child astray in that region of stinking devastation? But would a bear have wandered there, unrestrained and unobserved, to do the deed?

That did seem most unlikely.

Then she had a terrible thought; her heart sank with it. What if it was the bearward's helper who was slain—this very evening, while his masters were carousing in the Dolphin—and the monster that had done it was now loose in Smithfield, foraging for more human meat?

She had a vision of the handsome young man she had observed that morning and the girl he loved, and wept softly for the very pity of it.

# · 9 ·

Spectral shapes of men, women, and children, illuminated by torchlight, had gathered around the muckhill. They talked in whispers and moved aside obediently when the officers came. Matthew followed behind the Clerk, the sergeant, and the two bearwards to where several of the sergeant's men had earlier formed a protective ring around Rose Dibble's gruesome discovery.

The truncated limb rested upon a piece of dirty rag someone had found amid the refuse and retrieved to afford a modicum of dignity to the dead man's remains. The foot and calf lay there, the focus of every eye that could see it, like a religious relic, but the response they provoked was not reverence but fear.

Matthew knelt down to examine the remains. The foot was poorly shod and the remnant of worsted hose was of inferior quality and much patched. A fragment of sharp, white bone protruded from the hose and bore the marks of the powerful teeth that had snapped it from the rest of the body, like a twig broken from a dead branch.

It was obvious to Matthew the dead man had not been mauled by a dog. Obvious too that the onlookers were of the same mind. Something had made a meal of some human soul, something large and vicious—much to the disgrace of the fair and the peril of them all.

The whispering Matthew overheard suggested that *something* had been Ned Babcock's bear.

"The creature should be killed forthwith," muttered someone standing behind Matthew.

"Tortured first—drawn and quartered," said a second voice, hard with malice.

"Boiled in oil, blinded, and declawed," said yet another.

"God only knows what other poor devil he's eaten," said the first voice. "Where's the rest of him? That's what I want to know. Scattered hither and yon in this filth, I'll warrant."

Matthew heard these comments at his back and didn't like the sound of them. The crowd at the muckhill was more than frightened; it was looking for someone to blame for the outrage. Ned Babcock's bear seemed the inevitable choice. He noticed that the two bearwards had been strangely silent since arriving at the muckhill, especially in contrast to their vigorous defense of Samson at the inn. Neither man had pushed forward for a closer view of the corpse. Was this because they knew already that Samson *was* to blame—that the great bear was a destroyer of mankind as well as dog? Or was it because they feared to be identified as the owners of this alleged monster?

In either case, the silence of the two men had made them inconspicuous and that was well for both. Matthew knew from bitter experience how quickly a nervous multitude could turn into a raging, howling mob.

Perhaps Rathbone, the Clerk of the Fair, knew this too. He announced that there was little to be done until morning, when the muckhill would be searched for more evidence, announced it loudly so that his voice carried over the whispers of the crowd and the occasional whimpering of children dragged from their beds to see this new wonder. At this, some of the gawkers began to disperse, either because their curiosity was satisfied or because they feared to be compelled to search the refuse for the rest of the body—a task well within the sergeant's right to order. The Clerk directed Grotwell to send the rest of them home.

Then they were alone—the Clerk and the officers and the bearwards and Matthew—in that expanse of awful darkness. The single torch that remained and was held by one of Grotwell's men did very little good in dispelling the eeriness of the place.

"What do you say now, Mr. Babcock?" Grotwell asked, turning to where the bearward stood. "Have you seen what Samson has done? Come have a good look then, and persuade me if you can this isn't the bear's mischief."

For a moment Babcock made no answer to this challenge. Then he said, "I've seen enough. I grant it was no dog." He sighed heavily. "But can you prove it was a bear and not some other animal?"

"Perhaps the lion that is kept and shown in the Tower has escaped and feeds in Smithfield," suggested one of the sergeant's men in a sarcastic voice. Grotwell turned angrily on the man and told him to shut up.

"No lion," Babcock said. "Maybe it was a bear, God knows. But can you prove it was my particular bear?"

The Clerk and the sergeant discussed this. The Clerk thought the evidence was insufficient against the bear or its owner, but Grotwell said the condition of the remains was proof enough for any reasonable man. The two began to argue, with no little help from the two bearwards, who sided naturally with the Clerk. Finally the Clerk remembered that Justice Baynard was the person to decide such a question in the first place and that the same gentleman now waited at home for further report. Grotwell agreed. "Yes, by all means, sir, let Justice Baynard decide. But I swear that if he does not issue a warrant for both bear and bearward within the hour, I don't know the Justice's mind in these matters."

"We will do what Mr. Baynard directs," replied the Clerk coldly. "He is both honest and thorough."

"Let's proceed to Mr. Baynard's house, then," said the sergeant, for it was very late, the air at the muckhill pestilent, and the presence of the corpse unnerving to them all.

One of the officers asked the sergeant what was to be done with the dead man—or what remained of him—and before the sergeant could reply Rathbone interrupted to say that it could not very well be left where it was and that it must be removed. Grotwell said that he had no intention of leaving the evidence where it was for some dog to carry off, and would bear it to the

Justice's house and let him have a look at it. He directed one of his men to wrap up the foot and calf and carry it after him. The officer designated, however, was very hesitant to touch the dead man's remains and begged to be excused from the task. Grotwell cursed him roundly and told him that if he disobeyed a simple order as he had been given, he wasn't worth a damn in the watch and he might lose his office and, yes, rot in the stocks too.

After that, the officer did as he had been ordered.

"Let's proceed to Mr. Baynard's house," said Rathbone impatiently. He was anxious to have the matter settled.

Although Matthew was very weary, he agreed to Babcock's appeal that he go along too. But Grotwell questioned whether Matthew had any proper business accompanying them.

"My friend is constable of Chelmsford," said Babcock.

"Is he so?" answered Grotwell, with a snort of contempt. "A country constable in London? Well, I think he should leave his constableship at home and not meddle in matters hereabouts where he has no authority and less knowledge."

"Do you positively forbid him to come, then?" asked Babcock of the sergeant.

"Oh, let him come, if he wills," said Grotwell, as though he was weary of the subject. "Yet let him keep silent. He may be a constable in Chelmsford, but he is nothing here."

The men moved off and Matthew followed, not because he wanted to but because he could not deny the helplessness in his friend's face.

When Matthew returned, he found Joan in an anxious state. Unable to sleep for worry, she had kept a candle burning, now a mere stub. She greeted her husband with relief and asked him to tell her all that had happened. She wanted to know *who* had been killed and by *what.* She said he had been gone so long she was half-afraid he had met the same fate.

"I looked at the body—what's left of it," Matthew said, sparing her the more gruesome details. He sat down on the bed and began undoing his shoes. "Something more than dog ate him, my oath upon it. Afterward I went with Ned and the officers to see a magistrate who will inquire into the case."

"The Justice Baynard that was spoken of?"

"The very man."

His shoes were filthy from the muckhill. In his stocking feet he walked across the rush-strewn floor to the hearth and with his knife scraped the soles clean.

"They all think Ned Babcock's bear did it, but this Justice is wise enough to want more proof."

"What sort of proof?"

"The rest of the body, which may well show more bear marks as well as who the poor fellow was. Ned has asked me to help him."

"Help him? How?"

"By clearing the bear of blame. By finding the true explanation for the death—for the murder, if murder it was. Justice Baynard wants a physician friend of his to examine the remains."

"I shouldn't think the remains would want a physician at this point," she said.

"This physician is—or fancies himself—capable of drawing a wealth of knowledge from a very few facts," Matthew said, while he undressed. "They all come to the bear pit in the morning—the Justice, the officers. Remains of the dead man come with them. Baynard swears he will get to the bottom of the incident. If the bear's guilt is confirmed, that's the end of Samson—the law will do what dogs couldn't. Also the end of Ned's business venture."

"A pity if the bear is innocent. What do you think?" she asked.

"I don't know what to think," he said.

"What I wonder," she said, "is how the poor man's part got to the muckhill in the first place. Surely he wasn't eaten there—not if the bear had done it."

"I put the same question to the Justice," Matthew said, yawning sleepily. "He wasn't pleased with my sticking my nose in and told me so—more elegantly, however, than Grotwell had earlier when Ned urged me to accompany them. A Chelmsford constable is not worth much in Smithfield."

"Well, it's their loss if they think so," she said with a snort of defiance.

"It isn't really my business," he conceded.

"But he *is* your friend," she said, forgetting her plan to ask him to take her away from Smithfield in the morning. Friendship did count for something in this world of woe and faithlessness.

"I hope Ned didn't find the dead man at the bear gardens and try to dispose of the body himself to protect the bear," Matthew said. "If he was so foolish—"

"It would go poorly with him," she supplied.

Joan made no further comment on the possibility of Ned Babcock's involvement. His complicity had crossed her mind earlier but she had said nothing about it, and she was happy that although her husband had been moved by friendship to provide moral support he had not been completely blinded by old loyalty.

"Whatever happened to Mr. Beauchamp, Juliet's husband?" Joan thought to ask.

"A very sad case," Matthew murmured. "Evidently he was an ill-tempered son-in-law to Ned and provoked the bear once too often. He took a whip to the beast and Samson repaid him with a blow across the head that near knocked his head off. Juliet blames her father for it. Ned says she is ever after him to give over bearbaiting."

"What a horrible way to die," Joan murmured.

"The mark of the beast," Matthew said.

"What was that?"

"What?"

"What you said. Just now. About the mark of the beast."

"Are you thinking of that fortune-teller again?" Matthew asked suspiciously.

"Not she. I was thinking of the other dead man too—the one you and Samuel Hopkins found by the Chelmsford road with the cruel slashes in his forehead."

"A coincidence, surely," Matthew said. "Besides, the puppeteer was found all in a piece."

He climbed into bed as though his last words were the end of the subject and blew out the candle. The room became pitch black, a dazzling darkness. He threw an arm over her and snuggled up close, but she took small comfort from his familiar embrace and gentle words. Soon she heard him snoring softly. Joan was still feeling the pressure of her anxiety, a heavy weight upon her heart. In the darkness of the strange room, her fears multiplied and played havoc with her effort to sleep. Later, she gave voice to her fears even though her husband was too deep in sleep to hear.

"The beast's mark. The three of them. He on the road, he in the muckhill, and Juliet's young husband. It's all passing strange, Matthew, and I think no coincidence, as you suppose."

Rose has stopped screaming. Not that she has lost the will but the ability: her throat is as dry as parched grass and her head resounds painfully with the echo of her own cries. Her alarm has brought more than a few witnesses to her distress, who crowd around her asking first what's wrong with her and then, seeing what she has seen, become quiet and stand or squat there gaping, not sure what is to be done. Jack Talbot has come too. He stands embracing her, like a father. She has buried her face in the curly brown hairs of his chest, inhaling the familiar wine smell of the man and taking a kind of comfort in it. She is shaking uncontrollably, as though seized by a fever.

"Come, girl, come. It's no sin to find such a thing, but a bit of bad luck 'twas you and not some other," says Jack Talbot consolingly.

But she thinks it is a sin. It must be a sin—to find it even, the horrid, ghastly thing.

Smithfield is covered by a thick, smoky darkness. More people, bearing torches, shouting. The word has spread, as such words will, with uncanny speed. But now Rose has told her tale many times over to anyone who will listen, how she found the limb, the savaged flesh. And having told her tale for others to repeat with whatever embellishments they wish, she is led away by the wine seller, his arm around her in a fatherly way. And she has not a tear left for her grief, and the pain in her head is almost more than she can bear.

Ursula is not at her booth. Like the others, she has been drawn to the spectacle, for blood and bone are not things shunned by this generation—and even women and children turn cold eyes upon dismemberment.

"Shall I stay with you?" the wine seller asks.

"Nay, I'll be all right," she says, wondering if she will. For she also wonders who it is she has found in the muckhill and is filled thereby with a terrible dread.

He tells her he must go to see a certain woman living in Cow-lane. On some business, he says. To take her mind off the horror, he asks if she will look in from time to time in his own booth, which is well-stocked in preparation for the next day and unguarded in his absence. She nods her head in agreement. Who knows when Ursula will return? She may spend an hour at the muckhill or maybe two or three, chattering with her gossips, some of whom she has not set eyes upon since last August. There will be much news to share and considerable speculation. Who is the dead man? How did he die? And if murdered, by whom or what?

Jack leaves; she watches him go until his shadow fuses with other shadows in the dark lane. Paul's bell sounds nine plaintive times over the city, echoing to her alert ears as far as Smithfield. And in her loneliness the thought she fears to think insinuates itself into her poor brain. It is her beloved who is dead—sweet Gabriel of the golden voice. Dead and reduced to a tithe of himself.

Her fear makes her smaller; the darkness itself is oppressive, suffocating. Satan rules the night, and she wants to scream again to drive the fear that gnaws at her but her throat is raw and she has no breath.

Suddenly, she feels a hand upon her shoulder, hears a whisper behind her.

She turns and nearly faints from pure relief.

"You're trembling, Rose. Why?" Gabriel asks, alive.

She moans, "I thought you . . . I was afraid that . . ."

The tears come again, a torrent, just when she thought her eyes were as dry as her throat.

"You thought I was *what?*" he asks incredulously, grinning in the darkness.

"Dead."

"*Dead?*"

He laughs an easy, pleasant laugh that quite disarms her anxiety. She wipes away the hot tears.

Then as best she can, she explains what has happened. She cannot read the expression in his eyes but his change of tone suggests that he too is affected by the horror.

"*Who* do they say it was?" he asks.

"No one knows. Only the . . . foot and ankle were there."

He says, "Then they may never know. It's all one. The dead man's soul has gone to heaven—or hell."

He quotes Scripture to comfort her, and within minutes her mood is lightened. She remembers that it is wrong to mourn the dead excessively—and it is easier to follow this admonition if he that is dead is nothing to you, not even a name.

Now she remembers that Ursula is gone. The smoky darkness now seems more friendly than oppressive, for it provides a measure of privacy. The voices at the muckhill—surely all Smithfield must be gathered there by now—are distant. Impetuously she embraces Gabriel. She is unmindful of the acrid bear smell about him, the sudden tensing of his muscles at the embrace. He stands stiff and silent. She is so happy to have him alive and to herself that she pays no heed to his lack of responsiveness. And yet neither does he unloosen himself from her embrace. They stand still, alone, and soon she feels a pleasant heat in her loins, an ache in her breast. Briefly but painfully she recollects her other encounters with men. But this time and for the first time it is different. Gabriel is different. They were wicked, but he is good and his goodness radiates from him like a warm fire.

She lifts her face to his and kisses him. His lips are warm, and her body trembles again; it is not fear that quickens her pulse, elevates her temperature. She begins to experience an exhilarating sense of power now that she can feel, all along her own body, the growing responsiveness of his. She is very pleased. But then she remembers the dreadful Ursula and imagines her thundering down upon them.

"It isn't safe here," she whispers.

"If not here, where?" he asks.

She thinks cunningly, remembers the wine seller and his plea.

"Jack's booth. The wine seller's," she whispers. "He'll be gone these two hours. He said so. He asked me to look in on his goods. I said I would."

She disentangles herself from his arms and, taking him by the hand, leads him down the dark lane, he following childlike and silent, both stepping softly like thieves. For Rose the journey of a dozen or so yards is too long. Her heart is racing; the horror at the muckhill is forgotten. The terrible wrath of Ursula is forgotten. All Rose knows is that her present happiness seems to redeem all the miseries of her young life, all the abuse and brutality of act and word, the grinding poverty and cruel neglect.

She leads him into the booth, pushing aside the canvas that conceals the back parts from the front, where the wine seller's custom will drink from bottle and cup the next day. Inside it is even darker than the night, and closer. She smells the faint sweetness of the wine, oozing mysteriously through the slats in the barrels and casks. She turns to him.

But his mood has changed. She embraces him but now finds no warm responsiveness but rather a shudder of distaste. The journey from Ursula's booth, intensifying her ardor, has diminished his.

"*No,*" he says in a tone that brooks no denial. "It is forbidden."

Forbidden? How can what she feels be forbidden? It is beyond her imagining. She can only stare with her mouth agape at the tall, shadowy figure that is Gabriel, this angel of a man, endowed with God-like power and voice.

She hears his preacher's voice, not unfriendly, but distant: "What we feel in our present condition, unsanctified by the bonds of matrimony, *must* not be. It is Satan, Satan who provokes us, not our better selves, which must not burn with lust but with a sanctified flame of chastity, pure and undefiled. The body is of Satan." He continues even more passionately. "And it is our bodies that long to couple, like goats or flies. The soul belongs to God, but can only remain pure if the body is in subjection to it."

These are hard words for her to understand, so full of love is she. But then Gabriel quotes again the measured cadences of the Holy Book, the language she adores, and understanding comes. She feels the power not of his rejection now but of his love, feels it burning and near-consuming her flesh. Her will is not her own, her resistance is ashes in his fire. A calmness comes over her, a surrender.

"Let's pray," he says, kneeling in the booth, kneeling before a great shadowy malmsey butt as though it were a holy altar.

She kneels down with him, and Gabriel begins to pray.

# · 10 ·

Well before dawn, the clatter of cartwheels and the raucous shouts of hostlers roused Matthew and Joan from sleep. They dressed by candlelight, then went downstairs to breakfast, where all the talk in the great room of the inn was of the man-eating bear, Samson, "the terror of Smithfield," as Joan heard the beast named by more than one, dependent for his information on nothing more than second- and third-hand accounts of those fortunate enough actually to have seen the bear's leavings.

"Come midday, a dozen ballads will have been composed on the subject," remarked Matthew dryly.

"And each with a different story to tell—by an eyewitness," said Joan.

In the gray light of early morning they were on their way to the bear garden, husband and wife speculating on the crime as they walked. Matthew felt sorry for his friend Ned. He said that even if Samson had killed the man, no blame necessarily attached to Ned, yet he would lose his livelihood. Joan agreed things did not look well for either the bear or its owners.

They rounded a corner and entered the fair through Gilt-spur Street. When they came to the bear pit they saw a group of men standing at the entrance. Joan recognized Babcock and his partner, the Clerk, and the barrel-chested, gruff-voiced sergeant who had brought word of the murder the night before. With them were two other men. One was stout and of very grave expression, the other tall and thin and scholarly, dressed in a drab doublet with silver buttons and hose encasing scrawny legs. The man carried a satchel. Babcock saw the Stocks approach and called out a greeting.

"Good day, Matthew! And Joan, God save you."

"God save your honors," replied Matthew, bowing to the stout man and his drab-suited companion. These Joan surmised, since no introductions followed, were Justice Baynard, of the famous Court of Pie-powders, and his friend Thomas Millcock, the celebrated physician of whom Rathbone had spoken to Matthew. Both men regarded the clothier and his wife with a condescending air. Justice Baynard said, "You *again*, Mr. Stock?"

"*Again*, Mr. Justice," answered Matthew politely but firmly. Joan took an instant dislike to the haughty magistrate. "I'm come on Ned's invitation," Matthew continued with easy assurance. "If it pleases you."

"I cannot say it does, sir," said Baynard stiffly. "Yet if it be Mr. Babcock's pleasure, I will not deny you a place here. Pray keep quiet, however. This is the Queen's business we're embarked on."

Matthew made another low bow but said nothing more. The conversation that had been in progress at their arrival now resumed. Millcock, the physician, did the talking. He explained that the satchel he carried was full of instruments of his profession, instruments that he had earlier used that morning to examine the remains of the victim. From his examination, he declared the foot and ankle to have been that of a man in his prime, say twenty-five to thirty, with reddish hair and a height somewhat between five and a half and six feet. A poor man, he said, continuing his observations, as the quality of his shoe and stocking indicated. About the identity of the victim, Millcock could say no more, except that certain incriminating evidence had been found on the sole of the shoe.

"And what evidence might that be?" asked Babcock in a concerned voice.

"*Excrementum ursuii*," entoned the learned man. "In plain English, bear shit."

"All that proves is that the dead man was careless in his footing," remarked Crisp.

"More, sir," said the sergeant, addressing the bearward who had just spoken. "It means that your precious Samson ate him, for how else would he have trod upon the animal's voidings?"

"As easy as yourself," said Babcock, "for there are traces of it on all this ground. Besides," he continued, addressing the physician, "how can you say it is the excrement of a bear and not of some other beast?"

The illustrious physician cast Babcock a disdainful look and said, "I examined it most carefully, I assure you. The residue is from the bear; the properties of the excrement match. The facts admit no other explanation. The dead man was only recently in the company of a bear."

"A bear, not *that* bear," reasoned Babcock. "We have come full circle again. To say a bear killed the man is not to say Samson did it."

Both the physician and the Clerk of the Fair conceded that that was true by order of logic.

Grotwell said he was confident further evidence could be had if only the bear pit were inspected.

"And for that reason we are met here," said Justice Baynard. "Mr. Babcock, lead the way. We shall want to see everything— the accused bear, his quarters, everything."

Babcock bowed respectfully to the magistrate and led the way into the pit. Matthew and Joan followed.

While the Stocks waited with the two bearwards, the Justice, the physician, the Clerk, and the sheriff spread out and searched the compound. This inspection was thorough, but nothing was found. Then they all went into the tent, where they encountered the bearward's helper feeding the bear. Joan, who had thought in the worst of her fears that the young man might have been the victim, was pleased to see him hale and hearty. She smiled and nodded to him as she entered and he smiled back and continued to toss to the bear great globs of bloody flesh that the bear was making quick work of, much to the disgust of the great physician and the Justice. Both men commented on the bear's appetite.

"It's his regular breakfast," explained Babcock defensively. "He eats twice a day, three times if he is to fight."

"He could kill a man and eat him too in less time than it takes to wring a chicken's neck and pluck it naked," said Justice Baynard.

"He's no killer of men," Crisp protested.

They watched the bear devour the last morsels of his breakfast, then beg for more. Blood dripped from his savage jaws. His appetite seemed insatiable. The bottom of his cage was littered with bloody bones.

When he saw that he would get no more, Samson rocked back on his shaggy bottom and regarded the men and the woman with his tiny black eyes.

The physician said he had seen enough. He said that the guilt of the bear was certainly within the realm of possibility.

*"Realm of possibility!"* exclaimed the Justice. "Can you not say with greater certainty?"

"I cannot," said Millcock. "Obviously the animal has the capacity—the strength and appetite—perhaps even the disposition. That's plain enough. On the other hand, both the bearwards swear the bear was not permitted to wander from the pit and no witnesses have come forth to testify to having seen him loose. Had he been, surely he would have been seen and an alarm given. And as Mr. Babcock has stated, to prove the dead man was killed and eaten by a bear is not to prove it was his particular bear. That, sir, is the long and short of it. My work is done."

With that, Millcock directed his gaze to each person in the tent as though to ask if there were any more questions. Then, pleading an urgent appointment elsewhere, he took his leave.

The two bearwards now accompanied Justice Baynard, the Clerk, and the sergeant out of the tent to discuss the matter further. Matthew and Joan remained inside to converse with Gabriel, whom they found a very agreeable, well-spoken young man. Gabriel confirmed that the bear had not been once outside the bear pit and said that he surely would have been aware of it had the truth been otherwise. Their conversation with the helper was foreshortened by Babcock's return. He was all smiles now, and Joan supposed the news was good.

It was. Babcock, almost beside himself with glee, gave a rapturous account of it all. Samson had not been exonerated, but the charges against him had been suspended and the bear was now free on good behavior, a condition that evidently required constant surveillance of the animal and, above all, no more mysterious deaths in Smithfield. But from what Joan could make of the bearward's excited report, the decision in Samson's favor had depended on more than a lack of concrete evidence. Questions of property rights, profits and losses, the reputation of the fair, and the prospect of a larger crowd drawn to Smithfield because of Samson's notoriety had also been considered along with lesser matters such as public safety and the right of the dead man, whoever he was, to be avenged by the law.

"My fortune is now made!" Babcock exclaimed in a transport of happiness.

"How so?" asked Joan, somehow missing the cause of this celebratory mood.

"Very simple," he said. "The Clerk has said it and the Justice agrees. Samson is now the most famous bear in London. A famous man-killer."

"*Notorious*, you mean," Joan remarked, skeptically.

Out of politeness she joined her husband in congratulating the bearward for his narrow escape from public disgrace and financial ruin, but she was not without misgivings. Privately, she thought the bear was guilty as charged and she believed Babcock knew that too and was denying it for perfectly understandable reasons. Babcock had been very lucky, he and his bear. The evidence against Samson, if not conclusive, had at least been more than circumstantial. The body at the muckhill had been ravaged by a large, ferocious animal. That was a fact. The same body, the evidence showed, had been in the vicinity of a bear. The bearwards and their helper swore themselves hoarse the creature had not been out of their sight since their arrival in Smithfield, a claim no witness had come forth to refute. All that was lacking in evidence was something to tie the dead man to the particular bear under suspicion. What Joan could not understand was this: if Samson killed the man, then the deed was done in the bear compound, perhaps in the very tent she now stood! And if so, then how did the man's parts get to the muckhill, more than a quarter mile away?

Samson could have dragged the body there, but evidently didn't since it was unthinkable that such a creature could roam the neighborhood without being seen by someone. That left a human accomplice to consider.

Babcock himself came first to her mind, or Francis Crisp. Or the both of them. But then, suddenly, she remembered how Gabriel made his journey from the pit to the muckhill twice or thrice a day, with the bear's waste. That rickety wheelbarrow with its noxious load. She began to suspect him too.

Yet he was such an amiable, well-spoken young man.

Before it was light enough for Gabriel to see his hand before his face, Babcock had him up and policing the pit and tent. Babcock did not say why, but Gabriel knew. Someone was coming to have a look round, someone important.

But Gabriel had already seen to it that no evidence of human remains could be found there.

It had not been murder, what he had done. Murder was a sin against God, expressly forbidden. He had carried out a command of that still, small voice in his head—the same voice that had told him to kill the puppet master on the London road, the same voice that told him now how nearly he had come to sinning with Rose Dibble the night before in his dream, if dream could inspire such passion in blood and groin. The flames of desire had engulfed him and had painfully singed his conscience, and although he had since sought the means of his repentance, the reclaiming of the special privilege as an ex-

· 103 ·

ecutor of God's judgments on the wicked, the memory lingered and stung.

It had been the Devil's work, his near fall from grace, and he cursed the flesh that so regularly played host to the enemies of his soul. Since his first view of Rose, he had felt a stirring in his bosom. Her dreamy quality he saw not as defect but as sign of God's providential hand upon her. He recognized her as a sanctified sister among the Smithfield harlots. And yet she was also woman, a daughter of Eve, clear-eyed and well formed, supple as a young willow, her mouth small and ripe.

But even these thoughts flirted with evil and the destruction of his personal righteousness.

That morning he had watched while the officers had come to the pit, watched while they poked into corners and stared stupidly at Samson as though the bear would presently confess his own guilt. He recognized the sergeant in his leather jerkin and the clothier of Chelmsford and his little wife in her finery and hated them with a quiet, intense hatred he reserved for those who thought themselves righteous but inside were rotten with concupiscence and worldliness, dressing their bodies for show, bearing themselves with worldly pride and vanity, regarding with haughty stares those for whom honest poverty was a badge of sanctity. The smug, self-satisfied clothier and his wife, the learned man of science, the minions of the law with their insipid faith in the arm of flesh. A book of sermons could not have preached sounder doctrine of their imminent destruction than this parade of fools.

They had discovered nothing. As he intended they should not. All were mired in their own ignorance, as blind as bats.

God's work could not be easily brought to naught. Not by the law of a corrupt state, not by the temptations of his own flesh. Nearly undone by a stirring in his groin—the very seat of concupiscence—Gabriel Stubbs had put the old man from him and had been since his devout prayer of the night before a new man. Now he saw himself in a distinguished company of penitents, beginning with Father Adam. He thought of David and his Bathsheba, Solomon with great Sheba's Queen. There was Samson too, undone, unmanned, unsighted by a woman's wiles. These were men of renown, and Gabriel's weakness had placed him among them.

But not his sin alone. He realized that his present remorse of conscience was proof of his election. *Whom the Lord loves, he chastens.* Sound doctrine. He would be forgiven and strengthened.

The deaths meant nothing, then. His conscience was devoid of offense. The voices in his head, which each day grew more insistent, would be obeyed; and God's vengeance on the wicked exacted.

By two o'clock Matthew and Joan were part of a mighty throng of holidaymakers lining Gilt-spur Street to hear the Lord Mayor of London proclaim Bartholomew Fair officially begun.

Moments before, Joan had stood breathless with excitement and patriotic fervor and nearly deafened too by the explosion of cannon and the clamor of church bells as the Lord Mayor had come riding by, making his way with great difficulty, so large was the press of bodies packing the narrow street, all waving and cheering. Resplendent in his scarlet gown and gold chain of office, the Lord Mayor was preceded by a liveried servant bearing scepter, sword, and cap upon a velvet pillow and was followed by twelve Principal Aldermen of the City, also adorned in scarlet and chains of office and as proudly mounted. The crowd much appreciated this spectacle. They howled with delight, elbowed for positions of better vantage, gaped at the gowns and jewels that were worth a king's ransom.

The Mayor and his retinue stopped before the Great Gate, remaining mounted the better to be heard and seen. As the crowd grew quiet, the Lord Mayor unrolled a large scroll handed to him by an Alderman and began to read the proclamation.

He first commanded that all those present keep the peace during the fair. Then he directed merchants of wine, ale, beer, and bread to sell by honest weights and measures. This was a popular injunction, and there was a great roar of approval from the crowd. When the clamor had ceased, the Mayor went on to enjoin all those who might have complaint not to take the law into their own hands but present their grievances to the Stewards of the Fair, by whom he meant the Justices of the Pie-Powders. In concluding, he called out "God Save the Queen," and the cry was immediately taken up by the multitude, who screamed themselves hoarse with it, at the same time moving toward the gate, so that the Mayor and the Aldermen of the City were at pains to avoid being swept away by the human tide.

Matthew and Joan moved forward with the rest, but the gate was too narrow to admit the multitude efficiently and soon they seemed to be standing dead still with hardly room to breathe. It was then Joan felt a tug at her sleeve and, turning around, saw that it was Esmera.

How long the woman had been just at her back Joan could not tell and was half-afraid to wonder. Cannons began thundering again. Baroom! Baroom! Matthew was facing, doggedly, forward, his eyes fixed on the gate. Joan decided not to call his attention to Esmera's presence, and to try to ignore the woman herself. But Esmera was insistent; she tugged again on Joan's loose, flowing sleeve. Finally, seeing that ignoring the plea for attention was useless, Joan turned around. Esmera mouthed some words, lost in a tumult of explosion and cheering. Her dark eyes implied some new warning. But the crowd suddenly surged ahead, taking Joan with it. A contingent of rowdy apprentices released from their labors for the holiday intervened with laughing, bobbing heads and loud shouts.

Matthew steered Joan through the Great Gate, his face still forward while she looked back helplessly at the vanishing figure, a lone dark face amid a host of faces.

# · 11 ·

At the first pig booth Matthew and Joan came to—not the beastly Ursula's but one with pretty tablecloths and a decent clientele of merchants and their wives—Matthew, having missed his dinner and slighted breakfast, stuffed himself like a gamecock while Joan tried her best to explain about the fortune-teller, whom her husband had caught no glimpse of minutes before and was not pleased to hear mentioned again. Matthew washed down his meat with tepid ale, wiped his mouth upon a napkin, and lectured her on her gullibility. "What did the woman have to say—more dire warnings?"

"She tried to speak," she replied. "I couldn't hear for the roar. Soon we were carried away." Her husband's tone nettled her.

"I warrant you it was the price for her services she was trying so hard to communicate," he said.

"I think it was something more serious," she answered.

"She's at it again then," Matthew said, motioning to the tapster for a refill. "A most persistent creature, this Esmera. Drumming up business with dreadful omens. Well, if you missed speaking for the multitude, I'd call it good luck. I supposed you had given up this silliness. The woman is a fraud. It's as plain as the nose on your face."

Joan began to protest that it was not so plain. She did not like this cynical vein in her husband and was not accustomed to it, for she had always found him an open-minded man, ready to give the strange and not readily explained the benefit of doubt. Had he not always lent a sympathetic ear to her own prophesies—her glimmerings, as she called them—the unbeckoned visions that from time to time in her life had betokened both the evil and the good? Or had his respect for her own gifts been only seeming tolerance for an addled female he must not censure, for she was his wife? Men! For a moment she contemplated a world without them, then came back to reality again.

Matthew was continuing his diatribe against Esmera, so strongly worded as though the woman had already her hands in his own pocket. He had never seen her, but he knew her kind—given to a devilish eloquence, cunning and subtle insinuations. Joan realized that it would do no good to argue further. It wasn't, after all, that she really needed her husband's approval. She was a free-born woman, was she not? No puling wife harnessed to her husband's wagon. She had visited Esmera by herself when she was neglected because Matthew would go on another hour with his friend. She decided to visit Esmera again. She had the remainder of the afternoon before her and no household to manage. Why shouldn't she, if it was her will?

Matthew, seeing no further opposition to his counsel, went on to another topic. Husband and wife finished their meal. Then Matthew said, "Peter will be all in a stew with me gone from the Close. He's such an earnest, conscientious fellow, God save him, and as straight as a candle in a socket. I must return to the Close. Will you come with me? Here, you're finished. What time of the day must it be?"

She said she would not return to the Close; rather icily she said it.

"Will you go back to the Hand and Shears? I should accompany you—"

"I can look out for myself," she said. "Go to the Close. You said yourself just now that Peter will be at sixes and sevens without you. Go to the Close; look to your cloth."

"You will go back to the inn, then?" he repeated, lifting an eyebrow of suspicion. "But not to this Esmera, this mountebank?"

Now, she thought, he *was* being too overbearing with her. "If I will, husband, I shall," she replied shortly, her hackles up.

"What, am I a dewy-eyed calf that must be tethered to a post or ever in sight of its mother?"

"Surely not, I only meant—"

"Your meaning was plain, Matthew, and I like it not."

She held her peace with that determined look that brooked no impediments, while he explained with a worried expression that he had no wish to restrain her liberty. She was free to go and come as she pleased. If it was her pleasure to reject his counsel, which he had provided only for her good, then he would rest content. He forced a smile of conciliation and reached over to kiss her cheek, trying to mitigate her rising indignation with a merry countenance. She permitted the kiss, accepted his submission, but now she was resolved she would not be tethered or restrained, parented in her grandmotherly years, nor have her own good reasons belittled by a man's counsel—even if the man was her husband.

"Godspeed, then," he said.

"Godspeed to you, Matthew."

"When will I see you again?"

"Later. I'll come to the Close. Watch for me."

He said he would, and she moved away—like a river lighter pushing off from the pier to join the larger traffic in the stream—and was presently lost in the crowd.

With rising excitement, she maneuvered among man, beast, and gear, trying to recall exactly where the fortune-teller's tent was situated among the lanes of booths and stalls. But everything appeared different now—now that the fair had begun and Smithfield swarmed and roared with beating drums, bugles, and the hoarse cries of sellers in the fierce competition to be heard. "Buy, buy, buy," they screamed, booth seller and itinerant peddler, proclaiming their own goods and decrying their neighbors'.

Realizing she was lost, she stopped in the midst of the current, feeling the pressure of movement at her back and the murmur of complaint when she became an impediment to it, for all seemed to move now in the same general direction—

toward a distant drumbeat signaling, she supposed, an exhibition of dancing dogs, a freak of nature, or a puppet show. She moved out of the way and found herself next to a shabby costermonger with a basket of pears in one arm and his other extended with a sample of the globular fruit in hand, offering it to the crowd. "Pears, pears, fresh and sweet," he cried in a rasping voice. He was an old man, toothless, with a savage scar across his forehead.

"Please, I am looking for the fortune-teller. Esmera."

The costermonger turned at her voice and prepared to give her the ear; she was forced to ask her question again.

"A fortune-teller, you say? I'faith, good woman, there's many a one at Bartholomy Fair," he declared in a cranky old man's voice, blasting her with the fetid breath of rotting gums.

"Her name is Esmera," Joan explained, pronouncing the foreign-sounding name slowly and deliberately. When it was obvious the name meant nothing to the old man, Joan described the tent.

"Stars, you say? An image of the heavens?" The costermonger nodded and scratched his chin thoughtfully. He said he thought he knew of such a woman after all. He had passed such a tent as Joan had described within the hour. Had sold five or six of his pears there to this same woman's patrons, glad to have a sweet, succulent pear of the sort he carried in his basket. The pennies he had received for them were still palm-warm in his purse.

"And *where* was this tent?" Joan asked, impatient with the old man's prattle.

The costermonger shrugged and shuffled his feet, staring down to the little leather bladder at his belt. His purse. Joan got the idea. She bought two of the pears, and the old man took her money and raised his head like a dog sniffing at the wind, looking all about him. He pointed up a lane of stalls Joan had not yet explored. But Joan was doubtful. The two pears she had purchased as a price for her information looked neither sweet nor succulent, and the way he had shown her to Esmera's tent seemed not at all familiar. And yet what was she to do? If Esmera's tent was not where he said, then she would give over her search. She would return to the Close, grant her husband his share of wisdom, and allow God to determine her fate and his.

This lane was occupied by sellers of candies, toys, and cheap souvenirs hawked from rickety booths made of slender poles with ragged canvas tops. Joan saw a great many children in the lane (to one of whom she gave the pears gratis) and an equal number of laborers, idle riffraff, unattached young men—many flirting with the sellers, mostly girls of their own age in muslin caps and aprons like milkmaids.

Joan passed resolutely by the candy and the toys, the pretty wooden figurines and the samplers with pious sayings, the bottles of colored glass and the bewildering assortment of geegaws fetched from as far away as Poland or Moscovy. On another occasion these things might have caught her attention for a moment, but today she had no leisure. She ignored the invitations to buy extended by the sellers, who recognized in this little woman in velvet hood and cape a person of means; she ignored them still when the invitations turned to insults at her indifference. They called her "mistress nose-in-the-air" and "mistress high-and-mighty," and she blushed with shame and embarrassment as she became the object of ridicule of both the sellers and their customers, whose heads turned to look upon every new thing and who were as pleased to stare at Joan as at the bull with the fifth leg or the boy with the man-size pizzle. How she wished again she had never set foot in London, never braved filthy Smithfield. How she wished she was back in Chelmsford, where her reputation and person were secure. She was at the point of retreat when she glimpsed what she sought—the familiar shape and gaudy hue of a tent only a few yards ahead where the lane of stalls came to an end in an expanse of field.

She pushed on, jostled by the crowd, and a sudden opening of the way revealed her journey's end. There it stood. The sign in front boldly declared the owner's name and profession. The mystical symbols on the tent confirmed it. Before the tent, a small company had gathered and had arranged themselves in an orderly file, attracted, Joan supposed, by a curiosity as powerful as her own.

The line began a few paces from Esmera's tent flap and extended twenty feet or more along the bank of a ditch of brackish water. Conducting Esmera's patrons in and out was a scrawny little man in a sweat-stained jerkin that appeared just snatched from some ragpicker's cart. He conducted his business—opening and closing the tent flap, taking pennies, smiling and bowing—with much ostentation and ridiculous ceremony that was the source of some amusement among the crowd. In his duties he was assisted by a wretched boy, so pale and thin he was the very image of ravaged mortality, who scrambled up and down the line exhorting those waiting to be patient, assuring them that the wise woman would converse with them all, and warning them against falling backward into the ditch whose bank, he declared in a high-pitched, whiny voice, was exceedingly treacherous.

Joan found the stench of the ditch almost beyond endurance and wondered that other of Esmera's patrons could brave both it and the heat of the day, but those in line seemed indifferent to both sources of discomfort. A mixture of condition and sex, they stood quietly facing the tent door or with backsides to the ditch, conversing among themselves with the familiarity of old acquaintances. She was not surprised when, joining the line a few moments later, she discovered that the matter of their conversation was the cunning-woman herself, who was evidently more famous in the neighborhood than Joan had ever supposed.

In front of her was a stout, goose-faced housewife wearing a dark purple smock with stains beneath the arms like half-moons. She was girded with a crisp white apron and although her face was red and moist, she seemed more than content to be where she was. The woman turned to regard Joan with an ingratiating smile and began to praise Esmera. "Worth every penny," exulted the housewife, nodding with the self-assurance of one who knows a bargain when she sees it. "She told my cousin all that she did as a child, then prophesied that she would find riches at her door. Within a fortnight all came true!" The woman's voice dropped to a confidential whisper and her gray eyes bulged. "Her own brother, not seen in five years or more, came tripping home from sea, him all full of coin and silver baubles he had from Spaniards with whom he had crossed swords. The family is nigh unto wealth now, and they owe all to Esmera."

Joan thought the woman's reasoning hid a fundamental error; for even if Esmera foresaw the future in a patron's palm, was she due thanks for shaping it? But Joan kept her reservations to herself and the housewife hugged her aproned belly self-protectively and smiled with glee in contemplation of her cousin's wealth.

The woman's neighbor, a plainly dressed girl with a scarf on her head, had overheard this exchange and now joined in the conversation. She confirmed the impression of Esmera that Joan had just received from the housewife. Esmera was indeed a wonder. Her prophecies were the talk of the town. In the reading of palms she was as skillful as Drake or some other great captain in steering the straits and uncharted waters of the future. And all in the human palm! Those lines, wrinkles, bumps, crevices of pink flesh! The girl tugged at her scarf and said she did not mind waiting in the line, although she confessed of once nearly slipping backward into the ditch (and had she not seen a rat the size of a spaniel plop there in the scum!). The line was not half the length she feared it would be. Her confidence in Esmera was unshaken. She hoped the wise woman would help her choose between the two young men vying for her affections.

But the line did advance slowly, Joan thought as the afternoon waned and the chatter of her neighbors in the line grew tedious. She began to have second thoughts about her quarrel with Matthew. Had he been right all along? Was she being manipulated by a clever schemer—a guller of the ignorant who knew subtle ways to arouse curiosity and instill fear? Joan was in a good mind to leave, to return to the Close as she had promised. But she had invested so much time waiting. There was her pride too. No mere thing, that!

She decided to wait.

The sight of a familiar face at the tent door now caught her attention. How could she not have recognized that long, tallow-faced figure in the same suit he had worn the night before? It was John Pullyver, the greengrocer. She wondered she had not seen him there, then decided he had paid someone to hold his place in line. But it was certainly Pullyver. There could not be two in London so alike.

Pullyver was walking in her direction, skirting the edge of the line, and somewhat furtive in expression. When he was about to pass Joan, apparently without seeing her, she called out his name.

"Mr. Pullyver, a very good afternoon to you, sir."

The greengrocer stopped at the sound of his name and looked her up and down quite impertinently. He did not seem to recognize her, and Joan found this nettling. Obnoxious man, was she that common that he did not remember having conversed with her less than twenty-four hours before? She decided to revenge herself for this slight of her person. Meanwhile, Pullyver continued to regard her, taking in the velvet hood and cape, the handsome jewel on her marriage finger, the gown of a woman of some means, though a country woman indisputably. Joan could follow the man's thinking in his face. His expression softened; he assumed an air of politeness and spoke her fair.

"Good day to you, mistress. Taking the air of Smithfield, I see. Delighted to see you . . . again."

Pullyver's expression remained perplexed. His manner was awkward. And for a moment the thought passed through her mind that the greengrocer knew very well who she was and for some obscure reason was pretending forgetfulness.

"I see you have been inquiring of the prophetess," she said.

· 114 ·

"Oh, *she,*" Pullyver said dismissively, casting a glance back at the tent from which he had just emerged. "Yes, just a little matter regarding the disposition of my goods. Where to place this vegetable or that fruit—all to breed the better commerce. A man of business looks out for every opportunity to improve himself."

"Oh, indeed he does," Joan agreed, smiling broadly. "Especially one in the way of a fair wife. And I am here"—she noted the furious blush on Pullyver's face at her remark about the wife—"to satisfy a whim of my husband's."

She savored the irony of this innocent falsehood. Whim of her husband's indeed! But why was Pullyver really here? She held him with her chatter. He seemed eager to be gone. But after a few minutes her inventory of casual topics had been exhausted.

"Well, I really must be off," he said, tipping his hat. "Business elsewhere. So hot here in the sun. And the stench from yonder bank!" The greengrocer made a face of disgust and raised a handkerchief filled with pomander to his nostrils. "Give my regards to your good husband."

"I shall, I shall," said Joan, smiling slyly and replying to his courtesy with a bow of her own.

She watched Pullyver until he reached the end of the line and then turned up the lane of candy sellers, where he was joined by a woman with whom he stopped to converse. Joan recognized the woman too. It was Ned Babcock's somber daughter, her mourning garments sharply contrasting with the gay attire of most of the holidaymakers.

The pair exchanged some words and then went on together. How Joan would like to have been privy to that conversation! She wondered what the both of them were up to, for indeed they seemed up to some intrigue, although she could not imagine what it was.

But now she had moved up closer to the tent and her heart began to beat with anticipation. The girl with the scarf went in and came out again, all within a very short time, and yet whatever Esmera had said to her had obviously pleased her greatly, for she came out grinning from ear to ear and wished Joan good day.

Now Joan's turn had come at last. She paid her penny to the little doorman and he lifted the tent flap. She went in.

Esmera was seated as before. Her hands with their long bejeweled fingers entwined rested upon the round table. Esmera was looking down, her head slightly bent in the pose of an anchorite. She was wearing her hooded robe and Joan wondered how she could endure it. The heat in the tent was stifling.

Esmera looked up and recognized Joan.

"I wanted to speak to you at the gate," Joan said, "but I couldn't hear you for all the noise. What's the message you have for me? It's something terrible, is it? Something more about my husband and me?"

Esmera's expression, a mixture of pity and fear, confirmed Joan's worst suspicions. It *was* something dreadful, and it *did* have something to do with Matthew and her.

"Please sit down, Mrs. Stock."

Joan was more than ready to sit down. The heat had made her faint and the growing anxiety in her bosom was also working to undo her. She sat down on the stool opposite Esmera and fixed her eyes on the woman. The expression on that strangely exotic face softened and became sympathetic.

"I have seen a vision," Esmera said.

"A vision?"

"Of death."

Joan's heart sank. She beat down an urge to flee. But she knew she must remain.

*"Whose?"* Joan asked, afraid to learn but knowing the question must be asked, yes and answered too.

Esmera leaned forward and stared at Joan intently. "You are in graver danger than I supposed before, Mrs. Stock," she whispered conspiratorially, her long face made somewhat pale by the intensity of her concentration.

"So you said when last we met," Joan said. "I came because I thought you might explain from what quarter the threat of death would come. Your expression in the crowd convinced me you had perceived some more certain danger than before."

"Ah, and so I have."

"And that danger is . . ."

Esmera closed her eyes; her head began to sway from side to side; she was lost in some trance, all the while making a soft crooning noise and clutching Joan's hand as though she were able to decipher the lines in the flesh by touch alone.

Then the crooning and swaying stopped and Esmera opened her eyes and seemed to stare at something in the middle distance. Joan sat transfixed, her heart beating at an accelerated rhythm. She was half-sick; her clothing clung to her; and yet she knew nothing could make her leave now. She must find out what Esmera knew.

"Who was it you saw in your vision?" she repeated urgently, unable to endure longer the suspense.

"I see a body of a dead man," Esmera said in a faraway voice. "I cannot see his face, only his shape. I see his murderer too. And the weapon with which the deed was done."

"Weapon? It was no beast then?"

"Oh, it is a beast indeed. The worst of beasts. The most malign of God's creatures. The only beast that will kill its own kind when its belly's full and its other lusts are satisfied. I can see him triumph in his crime. He laughs at his victim. He thinks himself very clever, and the worst of it is that he *is* clever indeed. The body of his victim is discovered but no one suspects the cause of death—no one save one."

"Who?"

"Your husband."

"But you said there was a weapon?" Joan blurted. "Surely the cause of death would be evident to all."

"I see the weapon," Esmera repeated solemnly. "A blade, long and very sharp. The murderer is clever. He has killed but the crime goes undetected. How, you ask? How is this done?

An excellent subterfuge. The murder seems to be the work of another. The death lies at another's door. The murderer lives to kill again."

"What of the dead man? *Who* is he?"

Esmera shook her head. "I cannot tell."

"Why not?"

"I cannot tell," she repeated. "His face is concealed."

"And the murderer?"

Esmera shut her eyes again; a slow grim smile traveled across her face. "I see the murderer walk behind his victim. I see him reach for the long, pointed blade. Out it is drawn from its place of concealment, like an eel slithering from a clump of marsh grass. It is thrust in and again." Esmera made a grimace of anguish as she repeated the phrase. Her body convulsed in dumb show of the vision; her eyes rolled up into her head, flashing their whites while the pupils grew small. Aghast at this manifestation, Joan could make no reply. Shortly, the fortuneteller's fit ended, and Joan was able to catch her breath.

"Surely this is murder plain and simple," she said in a trembling voice. "It's impossible to think it would not be recognized as murder."

"The murderer is a devil, as I have said. I see these jabs so violent and fatal, but in my vision of the corpse I see no wound made of man. Only raw, exposed flesh and bone where the dead man has been devoured."

"*Devoured!* First slain, then eaten. Awful to think of!"

Joan quickly worked through the bloody scene in her imagination while Esmera, tranquil now, seemed to slide into another trance. Surely, this was a beast, this murderer of which the fortune-teller spoke. Foisting off on some dumb brute beast the blame for his own crime! But the victim! Who was the victim? Was it the poor wretch of the muckhill or some other yet to be? She hurled the question at Esmera, but so deep and imperturbable was her trance that Joan was forced to wait until the fortune-teller emerged from it. Minutes passed; Joan's imagination conjured up horrible scene after horrible scene—all of which involved her husband. Now she was beset by grief and guilt as well as horror. Oh, Matthew! How sorry she was now that she had rankled at his counsel. Were his admonishments so insufferable then, aimed as they were at her good? Was he the one whom the murderer would strike next? Or was it Joan herself?

"If it is my husband whose body you see, tell me, for Jesus' sake. Who is it that lies dead and bloody?"

As if in response to Joan's appeal, Esmera opened her eyes at last. Her dark pupils enlarged, glistening with a cold, dispassionate acceptance of fate, and Joan felt that acquiescence to what could not be changed was being forced on her. Then Esmera answered the question slowly and deliberately. "I can see no face, only the terrible wound. At least I cannot see *now.* Perhaps on another time the vision will be clearer, fuller. But this I can truly say, Mrs. Stock—you and your husband are in grave danger here. Take my advice and go home. Go home to Chelmsford. Go home before it is too late."

"Was there not more in your vision?" Joan asked quietly.

Esmera shook her head. "Only this—death stands in the way of you both."

"Dear God!" Joan exclaimed, deciding she could stand no more. She stood, jarring the table while Esmera looked on calmly. "Blessed Christ, make it not so."

She turned and without another word to the cunning-woman pushed aside the tent flap and emerged into the open air. She nearly collided with the penny-gatherer and trod upon the feet of Esmera's next customer; she mumbled an apology to them both and hurried on. By the time she reached the bottom of the toy sellers' lane, her stride had become a steady jog that provoked more than one surly complaint from those she elbowed and jostled in her panic and once, at least, the cry of "Stop, thief," from one sure that no honest motive could so propel the little woman through such a throng.

# · 12 ·

Arriving breathless at the Close, Joan found Matthew gone from the booth, which was attended only by Peter Bench, still reading his book of poems. "Oh, Peter," she gasped. He saw how distressed she was and put the book aside.

She did not endeavor to explain; it was all too complicated. She asked where her husband had gone and Peter told her he had gone to the bear garden some few minutes before. She felt another lump of anguish rise in her throat.

Without thanking Peter for this information or indeed saying another syllable, she was off again, caring nothing for the spectacle she was making of herself, darting around like a startled hare.

At the bear garden, at which she arrived within ten minutes of leaving the Close and not without considerable difficulty for the crowds, she was dismayed to see another long line waiting to pay and get in, as though nothing could be seen or done at the fair but one must form a line to do it. She scanned every face and did not see Matthew. She concluded he must be inside already.

Francis Crisp was taking admission at the gate. She ran up to him to ask where Matthew was and he told her that he had gone inside. "Pass ahead yourself, Mrs. Stock. Don't bother about paying. Compliments of the house."

Inside the noisy bear garden she found the tiers of seats already full and standing room only below, where the view of the proceedings was the poorest, blocked by hats and shoulders moving about in a constant stir. She insinuated herself amid the bodies until she arrived at the paling separating the spectators from the pit itself, ignoring the slurs upon her character from every side for her boldness.

She looked all around, above, and below, in the tiers. Her vision blurred. A dozen faces she spotted might have been Matthew's but hats concealed faces and some faces were turned from her in the direction of the bear's tent. The crowd was clamoring for the bearbaiting to begin. Braces of hounds, soon to be in combat with Samson, joined the uproar. She realized it was hopeless. She prayed Matthew was *here* and safe, but how could she be sure until she saw him with her own eyes? And even then he was surely vulnerable to the murderer of whom Esmera had spoken and in whose existence Joan now believed beyond doubt.

A trumpet blared somewhere behind her—a long, elegant flourish that, concluding, provoked a mighty cheer of approval from the throng who understood this was the signal for the contest to begin. In the center of the pit Ned Babcock now appeared, smiling proudly and holding his arms aloft as a gesture of silence to the noisy crowd. When the clamor lessened— silence was too much to ask of such a rout—Babcock spoke. He welcomed the spectators to his pit, which he called the Smithfield Bear Gardens, its more elegant title, and referred to those present as "good gentles" and "honored and distinguished guests everyone" as though he was speaking to the cream of society and not to as great a hodgepodge of every condition of man and woman as Joan had ever seen. Most were already drunken and had been so since midday, for the great heat had caused enormous consumption of every kind of liquor. And the sobriety of the rest was imperiled by the general atmosphere of holiday misrule. Nonetheless Babcock paid them more than their due. He made a very low bow to the tiers and another to those standing and then said they should all presently witness a spectacle of ursine puissance not to be matched at the bear gardens of Southwark or by other famous bears of the town he then proceeded to name.

This boast provoked many a cynical guffaw and denial from the impatient crowd. Meanwhile the dogs, who had been confined in a small enclosure in front of Joan, began to bark and whine so that Babcock's final remarks before disappearing into Samson's tent were completely lost on the crowd. These same dogs had been raised to such a pitch of excitement by the human noise and the smell of the bear that they now were practically beyond the control of their keepers. They began to fight with each other, and their keepers were at great trouble to separate the most belligerent of them; at last one of the animals, a particularly scrappy little spaniel, was so bloodied in an encounter with a larger dog that he was quite unfit to fight the bear and had to be removed.

Meanwhile Joan, only vaguely aware of these happenings and caring less, continued to search for her husband in the crowd. Her searching was by eye alone, for she was unable to move from where she stood. It was not therefore that she could have done anything had she seen him. But just seeing him, and seeing him whole, would have been sufficient at this moment, for she had a terrible fear that somehow he had been swallowed up in the multitude and she should have to go back to Chelmsford alone with not even his dead body for company.

The quarreling dogs had caused a delay in the proceedings. But their owners had now regained control and still the bear did not appear. The crowd began to boo and hiss and presently Francis Crisp came out of the tent and made motions for them to be quieter. His efforts were futile; the uproar increased. Crisp went back inside the tent.

A moment later he appeared again, pulling a chain at the end of which was Samson, who was wagging his shaggy head and thrusting his nose forward in the air to sniff out the scent of the dogs.

At the appearance of Samson the crowd's boos turned into cheers. Crisp chained the bear to the tethering stake and as if on cue Samson rose to his hind-legs and stood manlike, pawing the air as though saluting the assembly—like an old Roman gladiator about to give mortal battle. "It's no wonder he could kill a man," someone said near to Joan, by which she understood the word had spread about the dead man. Joan felt yet another chill of apprehension. She futilely stared about her in a renewed effort to find Matthew.

A short, thickset man in a loose-fitting shirt led his dogs forward and unleashed them one by one, so that each animal sprang forward into a position just beyond the extent of the bear's swing. The crowd roared. Samson glared at the dogs with his small eyes and then took a mighty swing at the closest, catching a small, scrappy hound on the side of its head and sending it flying to within a few feet of the paling. While the dog lay stunned by the blow, his confederates now joined the attack, and in the fray that followed Joan could not hear the sound of dog or bear for the boisterous enthusiasm of the crowd for this bloody spectacle. Samson was now on his hind feet, pawing the air threateningly, bellowing and flailing at the attacking dogs. One spaniel, more courageous than the rest, attacked the bear directly and for a moment hung upon his chest, his teeth fastened into the thick fur, until Samson caught the creature in a hug that crushed the dog's spine, then let him drop at his feet. In the meantime the other dogs were circling, snarling, and lunging, alert for any part of the bear's anatomy that they might attack with impunity. Their fangs were bare and dripping with saliva, their eyes intense. The bear swung round and round, letting fly with his arms, crouching to protect his midsection, and then growing erect again with a threatening suddenness. Samson caught one dog on the side of the head and sent him sprawling into the dust, his head a bloody pulp. The bear shredded the fur from another's back and broke the forelegs of a third, before the remaining attackers, recognizing the superiority of bear to dog despite their numbers, began to lose enthusiasm for the fight. Scampering over the bodies of their fallen kennel mates, they went whimpering back to their crestfallen master, who gave the bloodied survivors a few good kicks for their pains.

The conclusion of the fight brought frenzied applause from all sides as onlookers scrambled to collect their winnings, which evidently were based on both the winner of the combat—bear or dog—and on the extent of the destruction—three dogs fallen out of the brace of half dozen who had commenced the attack. But Joan thought the whole spectacle the most disgusting she had ever witnessed. The fight confirmed what she had long believed: that here was the most abominable of sports for a Christian. And the worst was that as anxious as she was for Matthew's safety and disgusted at the spectacle before her, she was now forced to stand as witness to this carnage while God only knew what mortal mischief her husband might be subject to, assuming as she did that he was somewhere within the confines of the bear garden. While bear and hound tore at each other with tooth and nail to the delight of the multitude, Joan could think only of the deadly blade so vividly described in Esmera's vision, a vision enacted for her again every time one of the drunken louts she was wedged between jabbed an elbow in her ribs or shoved her from behind in the general excitement.

It was with great relief, then, nearly an hour later, that she heard the trumpet sound the conclusion of the baiting. The crowd began to disperse. Now she was at pains not to be trampled as the unruly lot rushed toward the narrow gate, pushing and shoving, even more quarrelsome after the excitement of the baiting than before and all eager to move on to quench their thirsts at the nearest ale- or wine seller's booth. She had passed through the gate herself and was standing about helplessly, not knowing where to search next for Matthew, when Francis Crisp, coming up from behind her, tapped her on the shoulder and gave her the benefit of his horsey grin. "And how, Mrs. Stock, did you and your good husband enjoy the baiting? Tell me, did not Samson give those curs their due? They're a bloody chastened lot of dogs now, I tell you."

Joan interrupted Crisp's review of Samson's exploits by informing him that she had never found her husband.

"Not found him! Well, and no wonder with such a multitude. But I saw him enter just minutes before your arrival. Perhaps he's gone to speak to Ned."

Joan thanked Crisp for this information and hurried back inside the pit. Here she found a few stragglers arguing about the baitings and a dog owner nursing one of his wounded charges. She walked toward Samson's tent and saw Matthew talking with Ned Babcock in front of the bear's cage. Samson was at work licking his wounds, several savage rents in his thick coat. Matthew and the bearward were in such earnest conversation that neither noticed her approach.

"Thank God you're safe, husband," Joan said.

"Safe enough," Matthew replied, turning to receive her embrace, but appearing very solemn-faced.

Joan was about to blurt out her report of Esmera's latest warnings when her husband interrupted her.

"There's been yet another murder," he said.

Startled at finding her own worse fears realized, she could only stare back at her husband, and then at Ned Babcock. The bearward nodded his head in agreement.

"Murder for a fact. There's no denying it," said the bearward.

# · 13 ·

Samson, in his cage, made slurping noises with his tongue as he licked his wounds. Ned repeated the story he had just told to Matthew while Joan listened, her heart in her throat. "It's Jack . . . Jack Talbot," Ned said with an anguished expression and speaking in short gasps as though winded. "He's a wine seller . . . his booth is nearby. I found what's left of him . . . in a pile of muck. O Lord! Just behind the tent. The baiting was over. I had gone out with a shovelful of bloody straw—couldn't find Gabriel my helper anywhere. A flyblown corpse is Jack now, God pity him. Skewered in a dozen places and with cruel slashes on his forehead. A devil's work to be sure, Mrs. Stock, as I just finished telling your husband." Ned's eyes filled with tears; his face was pale; his large body trembled.

Matthew asked, "Have you sent word to the Justice?"

"Not yet," he replied. "There wasn't time. I just found the body, not a minute before you entered. Good God, what bad luck for us all."

"Especially for the wine seller," Joan observed.

"You don't think this will be blamed on Samson, do you?" Ned asked Matthew.

"I shouldn't think so. But the authorities will have to be told. And the sooner the better. Maybe, in the meantime, I should have a look at the body."

The bearward nodded his agreement, then looked with concern at Joan. "It's an ugly thing, Mrs. Stock, not fit for a woman to see."

Joan was sure it was no pretty sight, but having endured an afternoon of carnage she was positive another glimpse of blood and mutilation could do little damage to her already violated sensibilities. Besides, she didn't want to be left out of an inquiry in which she had come to feel personally involved. The dead man was a stranger to her, but she felt in her heart it might have been her husband whose brutalized corpse she was about to view.

Ned led the way out the back of the tent and round a corner to a narrow alley separating the booths facing one lane from those facing the other. The alley was piled high with litter and garbage from the booths. As soon as she entered it, the fetid odor of decay assaulted her nostrils and made her recoil with disgust. She saw a pile of refuse partly covered with a raggedy tarpaulin. She stood close to her husband as Ned reached down and pulled the tarpaulin back, revealing the dead body of the wine seller. He was sprawled face down on a mound of stale, crusted ordure and trash as though it were a great teat he was sucking on. His filthy bloodstained jerkin showed where a weapon with sharp point had punctured the flesh, time and time again.

A wave of nausea passed over her, made worse by the grip of dread around her heart. It was Esmera's vision come true, the vindication of the fortune-teller's powers. Joan turned her eyes from the scene, struggling against the urge to run.

"That's how I found him, Matthew," Ned said. "I didn't move him at all. I saw at once it was Jack. He was a good soul."

With his hat in his hand in an attitude of respect, Ned Babcock pronounced his words slowly and deliberately, as though composing an epitaph. Joan braced herself for another view of the body and turned slowly. Her husband was kneeling down by the pile. His face was very pale and glistened with sweat. His presence hardly disturbed the legion of flies that crawled upon the corpse and buzzed madly in the air around it.

The three were now joined by Francis Crisp, who had come looking for his partner and had heard voices in the alley. He wore a grin of satisfaction on his long face that vanished as soon as he perceived what it was that had drawn them into the narrow alley.

"God's blood, who's *that?*" he said, his jaw falling slack.

"Jack Talbot," muttered Babcock with a heavy sigh. "He's been murdered."

"Murdered!" Crisp said, stepping backward and crossing himself.

"You'd better go fetch the Clerk of the Fair—and Justice Baynard too," Babcock said to his partner. "Tell him a dead man's been found. Tell him too that our Samson had no part of it."

As Crisp ran off in compliance with this direction, Joan watched as Matthew gently turned the body of the wine seller onto its back. She suppressed a cry of horror as she saw the dead man's forehead.

"Jesus in heaven!" exclaimed her husband. "I've seen *that* mark before."

The dead man's countenance was curiously peaceful despite the filth that covered his face and the painful manner of his dying. But on his forehead were rust-colored streaks of dried blood radiating outward in a fan from a point between his brows, as though some beast had placed his claw upon his forehead, tearing the flesh to the bone with his nails.

Joan remembered Matthew's description of a similar mark on the forehead of the murdered puppet master.

"It is the very same mark, to the life," Matthew said, turning to look at his wife. "Made, doubtless, with the same weapon—stolen from the puppet master's sheath. A poniard. The murderer carried it off, just as I had supposed."

"The murders were committed by the same hand, then," Joan asserted.

"How could it be otherwise? Here's a grisly signature!" Matthew said. "Poor miserable creature. Done after he was already dead—like the puppet master. A mark of vengeance or a crazed mind. Perhaps both."

Matthew left Jack Talbot lying face upward. He tried to brush away the flies, but it was futile. He pulled the tarpaulin back over the body and quietly explained to Ned Babcock about the grisly murder on the London road near Chelmsford less than a week before. Babcock listened with interest. He seemed eager for any facts that might serve to disassociate himself or his bear from the death of the wine seller.

"Your bear won't be blamed for *this*," Matthew said reassuringly. "But the finding of the corpse near your tent won't enhance your reputation with Justice Baynard. That's two dead men in as many days."

Babcock heaved another sigh and rubbed the moisture from his ruddy face. He resembled a chastened schoolboy in his stance.

Joan noticed the wheelbarrow was not about and remarked on it. "It's Gabriel's, isn't it? Was it not his duty to carry off the refuse? Shouldn't he have found the corpse himself?"

Babcock made a perplexed face and then said, "I can't find him. I haven't seen him since before the baiting. It is his duty to keep Samson's quarters clean, as well as feed and water him. He carries the dung to the muckhill twice a day, in the morning and then again after suppertime. I'm in for a heavy fine from the Smithfield beadles if I'm caught allowing this muck to collect here. He should have moved it all in the wheelbarrow. That's his job. Now, you don't suppose *he* did this, do you?"

Matthew and Joan exchanged glances. The face of the handsome, well-built young man flashed through her mind. The image was followed by that of the slim, dark-haired servant of Ursula the pig-woman, and Joan shuddered. If Gabriel were the murderer, never had a murderer's face showed less guile or menace. Was it possible? If it was, Joan worried for Rose Dibble.

But her husband was already considering the possibility.

"He was only recently employed by you?" Matthew asked Babcock.

"Yes. When Simon Plover was kill—" Ned Babcock stopped in midsentence, flushed, then continued hurriedly, "Disappeared, I mean. You see, he vanished in thin air. Then this Gabriel Stubbs showed up and said he was out at elbow and needed employment. He seemed like a sturdy and dependable lad, a deep thinker too and religious, which things Simon never had been—what with his drinking and wenching. So when Simon disappeared, I hired Gabriel."

"Not disappeared," said Matthew in a sudden inspiration triggered by his friend's slip of the tongue. "Was *killed*, as you started to say just now. It was Simon Plover whose leg and foot were found yesterday in the middenheap, wasn't it?"

The bearward made no response to the charge, but his slumped shoulders and fallen expression acknowledged the truth he had tried to conceal. An awkward silence followed, then he said: "The hose Simon wore were once mine. I gave them to him out of simple charity. He patched them himself and wore them always since they were all the simple fellow had. I recognized what was left of them, knew it was Simon who had been eaten. Samson was already in bad repute for my son-in-law's death. I lied to protect the bear."

"And your business," Joan added, rather severely.

The bearward admitted it was true. He was not a rich man, he said defensively, regarding Matthew as though to suggest that some in the present company were and that therefore they should be charitable to those less fortunate. All he had in the world was invested in the bear garden. If this venture failed, it would be the last in a line of failed ventures. His creditors, his investors, Pullyver and Chapman, would take everything. He regarded Matthew with a look of desperation.

"It is very likely Simon was murdered *before* he was eaten," Matthew said. "Possibly murdered by your present helper, Gabriel Stubbs." Matthew suggested they have a look at where Gabriel slept and among his personal possessions.

Ned Babcock led the way back into the tent. He showed them the corner where there was a simple pallet covered by a coarse homespun blanket. A worn leather pack was propped up against a hogshead of water that the bear drank of. Matthew opened the pack and emptied its contents on the pallet. There was an extra shirt, an old pair of hose, and a greasy jerkin. There was also a pen and ink and a tablet of foolscap.

Matthew said, "This Gabriel came to work for you the day your previous helper disappeared. A coincidence, you supposed—a piece of good luck to find a dependable lad in place of a lout. Gabriel is from the north country. His speech betrays that. He must have come down from Norwich or thereabouts, passed through Chelmsford, and then on his way to London. The puppet master, seeing so goodly a young man afoot, offers him a ride, for which mercy Gabriel Stubbs kills him and gives him the beast's mark as a memento. Steals, then, the puppet master's horse and his poniard. With the horse he makes for Smithfield. With the poniard he has killed the wine seller, for what reason God only knows, but we shall discover for ourselves with patience and industry. He probably sold the horse when he arrived at Smithfield—that would be no difficult task, Smithfield being as it is the best of markets for horseflesh. Somewhere he must have met this servant of yours—at a tavern perhaps, or a brothel. Maybe he was interested in the bear. Maybe he had never seen one before. Maybe he just needed employment, or the two of them quarreled over the reckoning or a girl. London is a cold city for strangers."

To Joan these speculations now began to sound too rich in her husband's fancy although she was still marveling at his shrewd guess at the dead man's identity. She understood how the boy might kill the puppet master. A horse was worth something—five pounds if in good condition, at least an easier journey to London. But why kill Simon, lazy lout and scoundrel though he may have been? She could hardly believe anyone would kill just to have a place in a filthy bear pit.

Matthew was picking his way through the straw of the bed, raking it with his fingers, an expression of intense concentration on his face. "What's this—a treasure?"

It wasn't a treasure. It was a penny pamphlet like those sold in the bookstalls, much dog-eared and besmirched from handling. Matthew read the title aloud: "A *Faithful Discoverie of the Sundrie Shapes in Which Satan Hath Appeared from Antiquity to Present Times.* Pleasant summer reading, I warrant."

Matthew flipped through the pages, reading silently.

"*His* book?" Joan inquired.

"It couldn't have been Simon's," Ned remarked. "Not the religious type. Besides, he couldn't read."

"Stern Puritan warnings about the Evil One—an inventory of satanic manifestations," Matthew said, keeping his eyes on the rumpled pages. "This Gabriel is evidently a scholar. All the margins are written upon. See here." He held the page open so that Joan and Ned could read too. "Here, for example. The author mentions the Beast of the Apocalypse. And next in the margin someone—this Gabriel doubtless—has written, '*Verily, I have seen this shape myself and can testify that it is so.*' And here, on this page is a drawing of the very Beast described in the sacred text. He's not much of an artist, I'd say."

Joan took the pamphlet and looked at the page. Before her eyes she saw the crude drawing of a fantastic creature, with immense glaring eyes, wings, horns, and large paws. "I've never seen such a creature under God's heaven."

"The boy affirms that *he* has," Matthew remarked dryly.

Babcock took a look for himself. He said he had never seen such a beast—and hoped not to—although he added that he meant no disrespect for Sacred Writ. Then he said, "The feet resemble Samson's. Look at them. They're bear claws, right enough."

Both Matthew and Joan took another look. Indeed the feet of the beast did resemble the feet of the bear. In this detail, at least, the drawing was quite faithful. Observation of the original had obviously inspired the artist to greater skill.

"Bear's claws. The mark of the beast," Joan said in an almost reverent whisper.

"If this is Gabriel's book, and all evidence suggests that it is, then he is a furious Puritan as well as a murderer," Matthew said.

"A crazed mind, his comely appearance notwithstanding," Joan added, marveling.

Matthew took the book and continued his perusal while the

others waited for the next discovery. It was not long in coming. "Here is proof positive," Matthew declared, looking up with a grin of triumph. He turned the book around so Joan and Ned could see for themselves. On the last page of the pamphlet, only half of which was printed upon, an open space had been covered with a crude drawing. It was not a creature but a symbol—five lines drawn from a single point, splayed outward like the prongs of a rake or the claw of a beast.

"Gabriel is our man!" Matthew said. "Thrice a murderer—and perhaps a murderer again if not prevented."

Joan looked around the interior of the tent nervously. Where was Gabriel? Stalking another victim with his poniard, concealed doubtless in his shirt, its point needle-sharp and bloody? Perhaps he had fled Smithfield, leaving his pack and precious pamphlet behind in his flight. Maybe now he was halfway to Plymouth or Norwich?

And yet that did seem unlikely. Had he intended to escape, he would surely have escaped beforehand. No, certainly the pamphlet suggested he had some maniacal mission in his head that, remaining unfulfilled, would keep Gabriel—oh, the irony of that angelic name—around until his own good time.

# · 14 ·

Francis Crisp returned, bringing the Justice, the Clerk, and the sergeant with him. The three men had been apprised of what they would find in the alley and they regarded Ned Babcock and the Stocks with the disapproving look reserved for convicted felons and other unsavory types. Cool greetings were exchanged, then the newcomers and the others went into the alley to see the dead man for themselves.

"A wine seller, you say?" remarked the Clerk, taking his turn at peering beneath the tarpaulin and damning the flies and smell at the same time. "I partly knew the man."

"He's Jack Talbot," muttered Ned Babcock beneath his breath. The bearward had come up silently behind the Clerk and looked down at the body. He shook his head sadly. "An honest man, Jack. His booth was not a stone's throw from here. He was very big with Ursula the pig-woman."

"Oh, *that* slut. There's disreputable company, to be sure," said the Clerk.

"Mr. Stock here thinks he knows who did it," Babcock said, nodding toward Matthew and speaking with the forced confidence of a man who knows his own guilt is yet to be disproven.

"Does he?" answered Justice Baynard, turning to Matthew and regarding him with new interest. "And just what is it you know, sir?"

Joan listened as her husband began a recital of the facts as he now understood them, including a description of the dead puppet master whose body had been found near Chelmsford. He added that the peculiar way each body had been marked left little doubt that the murders were the work of the same man.

"And that person is—?" prompted the Clerk impatiently.

"Almost surely it is Mr. Babcock's helper we seek—Gabriel Stubbs," Matthew said.

Matthew now showed the Justice and the Clerk the incriminating pamphlet with its strange drawings and commentary. The Justice examined the pamphlet and shook his head, agreeing that it was the Devil's work if ever he saw it. The Clerk also took a look. He said that the curious clawlike figure was the mark of the Beast. He said he would swear to it.

"And this same mark was carved in the forehead of the dead man you found in Chelmsford?" asked the Justice.

"What manner of man was this puppet master?" the Clerk asked Matthew.

Matthew described the puppet master to the best of his recollection. The Clerk said he knew the man. "Why, it's James Fitzhugh! Many a year he and his little folk have come to Bartholomew Fair. And now he's dead!" The Clerk shook his head sadly. "Dead like this one here, murdered in cold blood."

Matthew assured the Clerk that the puppet master indeed was dead. Buried too, in Chelmsford churchyard. "And with the same vicious mark etched in his flesh."

"Lord have mercy upon us all," said the Clerk.

But Grotwell cursed and so did Francis Crisp, who had been silent all the while.

"Well, Mr. Stock," Justice Baynard said, regarding Matthew with more respect than before. "You've done well in discerning all this wickedness and have our thanks for it. As for you, Mr. Babcock, it seems your bear is cleared of blame. At least in this new enormity, for this is clearly human mischief we gaze upon. Now this Puritan Stubbs must occupy our attention."

"But why would Gabriel have killed Jack Talbot?" Babcock asked with an expression of puzzlement on his great round face.

"He must have lain in wait for him in the alley," conjectured Grotwell. "When the wine seller's back was to him, the boy thrust home." Grotwell made a sudden violent motion with an imaginary blade. It was all very dramatic, and the gesture had its effect on the others. Joan shuddered at the very thought and could not bring herself to look again at the dead body of the wine seller.

"I suspect, rather, that the deed was done inside the tent yonder," Matthew remarked casually.

Grotwell, not pleased at having his own theorizing disputed, frowned at Matthew and wanted to know just how the Chelmsford constable had arrived at that conclusion, which seemed to him contradictory to the plain fact that the body lay where it was and the alley, being narrow and private, was as fine a place for murder as any he knew of in Smithfield.

"Go on, Mr. Stock. Tell us," said the Justice, interested.

"Well, sir," said Matthew, addressing his remarks to the Justice. "The dead man's jerkin is soaked with blood from the wound, yet there is hardly any blood here on the ground roundabouts. Now the tent floor is strewn with straw, some of it freshly laid, I have observed. Especially around Samson's cage. The wine seller might well have come into the tent to have a look at the bear and Stubbs stabbed him while his back was turned. Then Stubbs took pains to clean up the bloody straw so as to remove any evidence of the death—perhaps after lugging the body out here, where it would not be seen. Sooner or later he would have disposed of the body the same way he disposed of Simon Plover."

The mention of the former helper brought startled expressions to the faces of nearly all the men present. There was a silence while the Clerk looked at Matthew and then at the Justice.

Matthew said, "There was a third victim. Simon Plover, Mr. Babcock's former helper—the one before this Stubbs. Stubbs killed him too and fed his body to the bear. It was Plover's bloody foot and shank that were found yesternight at the muckhill."

"Jesus!" gasped the Justice. "Do you mean to say—"

Matthew nodded solemnly. Fortunately for Babcock, the officials were too dumbstruck by this revelation to care how and when the identification of the body had been made, or to infer from it that Babcock had known the truth from the beginning. Indeed, Matthew's assertion that Simon Plover had also been a victim of the young Puritan was, as Joan well knew, based entirely upon circumstantial evidence. But the circumstances as now understood pointed all in a single direction: at the guilt of the handsome young man with the soft voice and pleasing eye.

"This fellow is mad indeed," said the Clerk, whose anxious expression suggested he was still obviously working through the grisly scene Matthew's disclosure had evoked.

"If Stubbs thinks his murder has been concealed for the present, he'll surely return," observed Justice Baynard. He asked Babcock for a description of his helper and Babcock provided one, not neglecting to mention the young man's sterling good looks and his limp.

"A limp, has he?" said the Justice. "All Smithfield must be searched. We can't assume he'll return, although he certainly may."

"He won't if he thinks we're waiting for him," Matthew said.

"That's right, Mr. Stock," the Justice said. "Well thought of." The Justice looked around him. He ordered Grotwell to fetch the rest of the watch. Babcock said he thought those present would be a match for the boy should he return. They were all still planning what was to be done and who should do it when their attention was diverted by the sound of a railing voice within the tent.

Ursula appeared. She was fuming and cursing Grotwell, who had her in tow and who explained over her thunderings that he had found her wandering around in the compound looking for Jack Talbot. Someone had told her he had come to this same bear garden earlier that morning and had not been seen since and indeed had not opened his booth for business although there was as great a demand for liquor of every kind as Ursula had seen in twenty years because of the great heat.

"Jack is *here*, beastly woman," the Justice said scornfully, pointing a finger at the tarpaulin that had been pulled over the body again. Grotwell walked over and lifted the tarpaulin.

"What is this?" Ursula asked gruffly, peering at what the tarpaulin concealed. "Jack?" she said, then cried out with anguish.

· 137 ·

"We think it was Gabriel Stubbs who did it," said the Justice. "Mr. Babcock's helper."

Ursula straightened up and looked menacingly at Ned Babcock. "The bearward's helper! Well, damn his rotten soul, then." She clinched her jaw and made both hands into fists. Her bosom heaved. "My prophetic soul, if I didn't suspect the whelp from the first day I laid eyes on him. Did he not come round practicing his lechery on my own servant, Rose Dibble, a lazy, idle creature with no more brains than a cabbage? See now where this all has led—to the death of poor sweet Jack, who was ever as tender with me as with his own blessed mother. I swear 'fore God it's all true."

"If this Rose you speak of had anything to do with Stubbs, we should speak to her as well," said the Justice. He turned to Grotwell. "Go fetch her—this Rose Dibble. And do gather your men as before I commanded." Grotwell went to do what he was told.

Ursula said, "Aye, fetch the slimy grasshopper's thighs, for I will pluck out her eyes and make soup of 'em."

Ignoring this terrible threat, Justice Baynard went on with his instructions. "The hue and cry must be raised," he said.

But the Clerk, a cool head in emergencies, said he wondered about the wisdom of such an action.

"Wisdom?" asked the Justice, amazed that such a practical and seemingly obvious expedience should be questioned. "And why not? The crazed fellow will escape—and he may kill again."

"Because, sir," said the Clerk in a calm, steady voice, "if the hue and cry is raised you will create a panic at the fair. The booths all round will be emptied of custom as the fainthearted burghers flee from the alarm of murder. And the deaths will surely be multiplied, as the more villainous use the opportunity to disguise their own crimes of violence. No, sir, the madman must be found indeed—for the sake of justice and public safety. But let us not resort to the hue and cry but proceed with discretion and policy. A public announcement will do no more than alarm him and the citizenry. Nor would such a ruckus be pleasing to Her Majesty, who all the world knows comes to the fair tomorrow."

Concluding his plea, the Clerk looked to Matthew for support. Matthew, a man of business himself, was not unsympathetic to the Clerk's argument. He agreed that a hue and cry would probably drive Stubbs away rather than result in his capture. During the next few days Smithfield and its annual fair would be the most densely populated square mile in England. Finding a single boy who by girth and height was in no way remarkable and who might disguise his appearance with very little trouble would be like finding a certain ant in an anthill. And if Stubbs did escape, crazed as he obviously was, who knew what mischief he might do elsewhere?

"A carefully organized search of a few men," said Matthew, "may yield better results than a rampage of every drunken roisterer in the fair—who will have many a young man remotely resembling Stubbs hanged to every tree limb for the simple joy of watching them dangle. Besides, Stubbs may not know we know of his mischief, and he may yet return if not frightened away by our assembly."

"Will you lend us a hand in the search, Mr. Stock?" asked the Justice. "You know this Stubbs by sight."

"I'll give what help I can," replied Matthew resolutely. He suggested that the bearward's investors—Pullyver and Chapman—also be recruited for the search. "They're true men and know both Stubbs and Smithfield well," Matthew said, glancing at Babcock for support.

The bearward agreed, and Francis Crisp was sent to fetch the two men. Joan offered her help also, ignoring the fact that her aid had not been solicited. "Perhaps Stubbs is with Rose Dibble," she conjectured aloud. "If we find the girl, then . . ."

"And the sooner the better for her, it would seem," said the Justice darkly.

"I'll find them both, wherever they have concealed themselves," Ursula growled. The pig-woman had been silent during the forgoing conversation; her round, red face was streaked with a few pendulous tears. Now the thought of the fugitives had reawakened her wrath and desire for vengeance. Breathing heavily, she presented a frightening picture of imminent female violence, her nostrils flaring, her fists clinched like iron mallets.

"You'll do nothing of the kind," snapped the Justice. "Go about your business. Say nothing of what has happened here. Not to a soul. If this Rose of yours comes back to the booth or is there when you return, do nothing to her. Say nothing about Talbot or Stubbs or murder or such matters. Do not commit any violence upon her body, but bring me word at once to my house near Pie-Corner."

Somewhat grudgingly, Ursula indicated she would obey these instructions, but her nostrils continued to flare and her heavy breasts rose and fell like blacksmith's bellows. With swollen red eyes full of hatred she glared at the Justice and the Clerk, and then at the Stocks too.

"And should you see Stubbs, you are to do nothing either," the Justice warned as Ursula went off.

"Now," said the Justice to the others with a sigh of resolve, "we must indeed organize ourselves. As for you, Mr. Babcock and Mr. Crisp," he continued, regarding the bearwards sternly, "you are not to be blamed here, nor your bear Samson, who now appears an innocent accomplice of a maniacal Puritan. Yet I would look to your own safety. Stubbs's possessions—including this cursed pamphlet which seems to have inspired his madness—remain here. He may return for them. In the meantime, his weapon is not to be found and it is more than reasonable to assume he has it with him and intends to use it again. I would watch myself very carefully if I were you. When is the next baiting?"

"Tomorrow, sir, in the morning," Babcock said.

"Well, then, pray we have our murderer in hand by then. The baiting is certain to draw another huge crowd to the pit and that can only frustrate our efforts, if Stubbs is still at large. Certain it is he will be wary of capture."

While these things were being said, Joan stood thinking of Esmera. The woman had been right about everything—the beast, the murder, the instrument of death. All she had seen in her vision as quickened by the touch of Joan's hand. And all had come to pass. Except for her own and Matthew's share of the risk. That had not happened. Not yet at least; she prayed God it wouldn't.

Yet despite her anxiety of the day and the awful revelation of the murders, Joan felt some degree of satisfaction. Her own trust in the fortune-teller had been vindicated. Matthew had been proven wrong, and like any strong-minded wife of an equally strong-minded husband, she longed to exult in her victory. But the alley was not the place, and the company was wrong too. To the Justice and the Clerk, content it seemed to exclude her from these dangerous proceedings, she would surely have appeared as unsound of mind as the crazed boy they now sought were she to begin discoursing on the amazing parallels between these dire murders and the cunning-woman's prophecy.

Justice Baynard assigned Matthew to patrol the lanes immediately adjacent to the bear garden. "Look in every booth, scan every visage, Mr. Stock. There's a few hours of daylight left at least. Take advantage of it before darkness. Master Clerk and I will wait here for your return."

Matthew advised Joan to return to the inn. It was late. Surely she wanted a good supper after the day's excitement.

But Joan was not hungry. How could she think of eating after a long day of animal and human carnage, startling revelations, and the threat of further murders in the offing? She said she would keep him company on his patrol. She too knew the fugitive by sight—and Rose Dibble too. Four eyes were better than two, she reasoned.

But Matthew insisted that it was too dangerous. He insisted she return to the Hand and Shears. And so she would, if he had anything to say about it.

# · 15 ·

Gabriel Stubbs is on his way back to the bear garden, pushing the empty wheelbarrow before him and whistling a hymn. He has just turned down the narrow, twisted alley between the booths when he glimpses the assembly of men clustered outside Samson's tent. He stops dead in his tracks. His pulse races. He makes himself flat against the ratty canvas side of a confectioner's booth, watching like a fox whose keen eyes see every movement—every twitch, flutter, and blink—of its victim in a distant field, while from the lane-side of the booth, quite out of sight, comes the frank, ribald laughter of sinners gluttonizing on marchpane and other dainties, such sweet stuff to rot the gums and destroy the soul.

Among the men he recognizes his employers and the Stocks, husband and wife. The Clerk of the Fair is there too, a very proud man. Gabriel Stubbs also sees Grotwell, the sergeant of the watch, emerging from the tent with that obstreperous she-devil Ursula at his tail like a fury, railing and cursing.

Yes, the wine seller has been found, Gabriel Stubbs thinks, worse luck.

The sergeant lifts the tarpaulin and shows what's beneath to Ursula, who cries out as though she herself were just stabbed and slashed and bloody. The men converse. Gabriel Stubbs can hear nothing for the noise of the lane, but because of her gestures and expressions he can discern that Ursula demands to know who has murdered her friend. But if she is being told, Gabriel cannot tell; the words are lost in the air. At the safe distance he must maintain from these proceedings, all is a dumbshow of gesture and grimace.

But his deed has been discovered, that's plain. And he fears they have found out his part too. Then he thinks that perhaps they have not. Did not the death of Simon Plover (foolish knave!) remain a mystery to them, thanks to the good offices of a hungry bear ignorant of the distinction between human flesh and butcher's offal? Might not this new death, so sudden and inexplicable to them, be laid at the door of some nameless malefactor? Are there not a devil's plenty of such sort at the fair, not to mention old enemies of the dead man rubbed raw by some new or imagined grievance?

Gabriel is in a quandary and much in need of a burst of revelation on the matter. Should he go forward, reveal himself, or remain concealed? Quickly and fervently, he offers a prayer that floats upward in the heavy air but to no avail, for no answer descends to illuminate his darkness. At length he concludes the decision must be his own. He decides to remain away from the bear garden until he can determine which way the winds of suspicion blow.

For the killing of Jack Talbot, Gabriel Stubbs feels neither remorse nor strong satisfaction. He feels very little if the truth be told. If he has thought about the incident at all, he has thought about it as a sacrifice—holy violence he has been bidden by his voices to perform and from which, therefore, he feels detached, as though it all were some other man's act. But the necessity of disposing of the body has been in his mind since the death, for the disposing was yet to be done. Or was, until now. Now Gabriel can see it is too late. The body is found. But has Gabriel covered his traces?

This concern provokes a recollection of the circumstance of the death, which in the interim has been suppressed in some obscure corner of his memory. It now comes forth and he remembers the living, breathing, damned soul who had provoked the act in the first place.

It happened this way:

Not long before the commencement of the baiting, Jack Talbot appeared at Samson's tent, not to see the bear as it might have been supposed, but Gabriel himself. Both of Gabriel's employers had been at the time occupied elsewhere: Crisp at the gate, Babcock inside the compound directing spectators to their seats. The wine seller had come in while Gabriel was preparing to open the cage to let Samson out of it, come in griping about how Gabriel and Rose had made use of his booth and bed for their lust, as he termed it. Before Gabriel had had a chance to reply, the wine seller was shaking his fist at the boy's nose and calling him a filthy whoremaster and knave. "Did I not spy you twain come sneaking from the booth yesternight? Do you suppose me a fool to be horned and gulled of my right?"

"She's not your wife," Gabriel had said.

"Nor is she yours so to use her," snarled Talbot.

"I never used her."

"Liar! Lousy lecher! Smooth-faced bearer of bear's turds!"

Pure jealous rage, that's what it had been. Gabriel was wise enough to see that. It was the wine seller who was the lecher, the liar, the infidel and corrupter of innocent womanhood, not *he*.

Talbot finished his tirade with a mighty oath in which the entire trinity—Father, Son, and Holy Ghost—were incorporated and blasphemed. Gabriel could endure it no longer. When Samson, excited by the dispute, snarled suddenly, Talbot turned around to face the cage. In the same instant, Gabriel drew his poniard and shoved it between Talbot's shoulder blades, driving him hard against the iron bars.

He held Talbot there while he stabbed again and again until the wine seller's jerkin was bloodsoaked. Then he allowed the body to slide down the bars into a heap at his feet.

Gabriel knelt down beside the body, his heart thumping with such rapidity and loudness that he thought surely it could be heard above the ever-increasing din of the spectators outside the tent. His anger had driven him into a frenzy but he retained sufficient presence of mind to be aware of his danger. Any moment Crisp or Babcock or the both of them could come walking into the tent to inquire why Samson had not been brought forth. And what should they think, finding him thus, bent over a dead man—and a bloody knife in his hand to proclaim him murderer?

He turned the wine seller face up and saw by the man's flickering eyelids and shallow breathing that by some strange fortune he still lived. Gabriel finished his work quickly. Then he dragged the body out the back of the tent into the alley and covered it with the ragged tarpaulin he found there. He returned to Samson's cage, scooped up an armful of bloody straw, and carried it outside to the wheelbarrow. He returned again to spread fresh straw before the cage, then went out again to the wheelbarrow and pushed it up the alley and around the corner to the butcher's booth, where human blood and animal would be indistinguishable and unnoticed.

He remained away from the bear garden during the baiting, returning as soon as it was done. It was then that he had seen the body had been discovered. Discovered before he had had a chance to get rid of it.

Now there is one last thing that Gabriel recalls in the sequence of events that is fast slipping into oblivion. He remembers that as he stared down at the dying man there appeared a little film of blood upon his lips. Like wine, wine so thin and watery that it is pink. The man's eyes are dark and glassy like stagnant pools overhung with thick willows. Then, for a moment—and for a moment only—Talbot's face is transformed into something strange and terrible. The pasty flesh becomes as black as an Ethiopian's. The dark eyes grow red and glaring. It is a devil's visage, the face of the Adversary, the demon of the worst of Gabriel Stubbs's nightmares.

Gabriel watches them from his place of concealment, the little cluster of men. He watches as they go back into the tent. Now he must find Rose, he thinks. Find Rose before Ursula does, before the sergeant and his men do.

He takes a shortcut to the pig-woman's booth and sees in the midst of the confusion there Rose struggling to serve fifty clamorous customers with only one other tapster to help. It takes a while for him to catch her attention, so great is the multitude all shouting and elbowing each other for service as though what is offered for sale here is the last pig and beer to be had in the world.

He tells Rose she must come with him, straightway.

She flushes with pleasure at the command, but she is confused too. She looks around her as though to ask: How can I leave now with Ursula gone somewhere and only Harry Borden to help with this rout?

"The Lord wills it," says Gabriel, fixing his eyes on her, breathing the words in such a way to suggest they are not his, but some higher power's.

She pales at this dreadful summons but still looks doubtful. A hundred voices now seem to bark in her ears, demanding her immediate attention, but she ignores them all, her attention fully upon Gabriel.

He takes her hand and leads her away, her apron still about her waist and behind her expressions of anger and amazement. "What? Shall we not be served? Is this a time to dally?" How can she be so bold as to desert her plain duty to provide for the hungry and thirsty of the fair?

Gabriel leads her on, searching for a place where he can talk to her privately. He needs a hiding place too—at least until he can determine whether the blame for the wine seller's death has been laid at his door. If he runs too soon, he will only make himself look guilty. If he returns too soon, he may be seized. He needs an ally, and Rose is she.

As they move through the crowded lane, Gabriel thinks of where he can take Rose, a fine private place, not quiet—as no place in Smithfield can be at fair time—but out of the way of prying eyes at least. It is Talbot's own booth. Irony of ironies. As it concealed the two of them the night before, it will do so now, he thinks. Its owner will never return, and it will be shunned by those few who know of the death as an unfit resort for the living and an unlikely hideaway for the dead man's slayer.

Rose expresses no surprise when she sees the booth and understands that it is their destination. She has followed obediently, seems to be in a trance of sorts, like one not fully awake to the light of day. Gabriel pulls her after him into the back parts of the booth. Grasping her firmly by the shoulders—how thin and frail they feel beneath the cheap cloth of her shift!—he tells her that they must be very quiet here, for he is sought by certain officers.

"Officers?"

"Jack Talbot is dead," he says.

Rose stares back wide-eyed, then around the dim interior with its stock of cask and butt.

He tells her as much of the truth as he thinks fit for the both of them. "It is certain the blame will be laid upon me. I was the last person to see him quick."

He tells her then (she being still too stunned by this dreadful news to answer) how Talbot came to the tent. To have a look at the bear, he says, and then began to complain because he had caught sight of them in the booth the night before. He tells her of the wine seller's slanders. She flinches at the names, for she understands their meaning. She can hardly believe that this is all true, that Jack is dead. Like her mother, her father, never to come again. He must explain it all again, Talbot's coming, his slanders. About the death he is deliberately vague.

She stands in the shadowy space that keeps much of the day's light from the enclosure but little of the street noise. She listens to his story intently.

"I fear I'm the one they'll blame, not understanding the man he was. A slanderer, vicious, a tool of the Evil One."

"Are you sure he's dead?" she asks.

"I'm sure."

"But we can't stay here. I must go back. Ursula—"

"You cannot go back. Not yet. I must tell you more."

He is tempted to tell her about the vision—the terrible countenance of the dead man. He explains that he must stay hidden, at least for the time being, and that she can do him and God a great service.

"A service. A service for God?" she asks, wide-eyed, trembling a little.

"Nothing less than that," he says.

"Speak but the word," she says.

He bends down and kisses her on the cheeks, still warm and smoky from the roasting fires. He tastes her tears, feels her supple body molded against his own, feels her heart fluttering like a little bird trapped in a hollow tree.

And Rose can feel against her breast the hardness of steel within Gabriel's bosom.

She looks at him in sudden confused alarm, drawing away, her body as taut as the blade physical closeness has revealed.

Too late he remembers the poniard, strapped in its sheath next to his heart. "Oh, this," he says casually. "It's for my protection." Slowly he removes the weapon and shows it to her. He does not remove the instrument from its long cylindrical case. He handles the weapon gingerly, unfamiliarly, as though he had no skill in its employment. He lays it down in the straw at her feet, a tribute. "Here," he says softly. "I'll put it aside if the thing alarms you."

He stares long and hard at her white face, gauging her response. She seems nervous and uncertain. He begins to explain that God never forbade the defense of oneself and that there is no evil in a weapon but only in its unlawful use.

And what is unlawful?

Why, that which the Lord of Heaven expressly forbids. False witness, adultery, covetousness, disrespect for parents, murder. That which the Lord commands is not unlawful, is not a sin. Hence if a killing were done by divine command, it would be no sin. The conclusion follows as the night the day. Doesn't it?

Rose thinks about this, then admits at length that it must be true. What God commands cannot be sin, since sin is disobedience. But she is more persuaded by Gabriel's voice than his logic.

He puts to her a case of conscience, using the simplest of terms and propositions, as one might explain a difficult circumstance to a child. Suppose, Gabriel says, a man were ordered to kill—by God. The victim being no innocent soul but a damned villain or cruel tyrant or sorcerer or any other of Satan's progeny, wicked to the core. Would it not be a righteous act to obey God and kill the evildoer in such a case?

He must describe these particulars twice before Rose understands, but once she understands, the principle is fast in her mind. She agrees that to kill under such circumstances and with such sanction would be no fault. Indeed, to disobey in such a case would be the sin.

"Even if the damned villain were a seeming friend—as was this wine seller?" he asks, continuing his catechism.

"Nay, no sin surely."

"Or a person of note, a gentleman or a lord?"

"Nay," she says. "Even a great one."

"Or for that matter, a king or a queen?"

She nods.

The lesson continues. Rose listens enraptured, her dark, wide-set eyes large and bright. Only half she understands of what he tells her now, these mysteries of godliness, the privileged information of the Elect. But more than half is enough. She is in love with this young man and is no longer able to distinguish him from the God of whom he speaks with such eloquence and familiarity.

The lesson ends. Now she understands that Jack Talbot's death was God's will. That Gabriel was the instrument of that will she also understands, though Gabriel has only implied it. All this she accepts; she feels no anxiety; she is at peace. And Gabriel too is at peace because he has found an ally in Smithfield, in this Babylon of wickedness, and perhaps too, a disciple.

But suppertime is drawing on and Rose's mind turns inevitably to the world outside their hiding place. Surely Ursula has now returned to her booth. And found Rose gone. Surely the pig-woman's rage is now at the full and stirred into a hurricane by the unaccountable absence of her servant. Rose can already feel the blows, not to mention the words that slash like razors, a thousand abusive epithets from one with a genius for calumnies.

"The beastly creature will be mourning for her friend and seeing to his burial—too full of grief to worry about you," Gabriel says to pacify her anxiety.

But she continues to fret and Gabriel, eager now to know where he stands with the bearwards and the officers, shapes his plan. He will send Rose to the bear garden to pick up any odd scrap of news about the wine seller's death. She will return to report, avoiding Ursula at all cost. If he is suspected, he will flee, taking Rose with him. If unsuspected, he will invent some plausible excuse to account for his absence, resume his menial duties, and await, as before, the appointed hour.

All this he conveys to Rose in urgent whispers, repeating each instruction so that she understands perfectly what she is to do and why. Then he prays over her, long and solemnly, invoking God's blessings on the speediness of her legs, the alertness of her ears, the sharpness of her sight—all essential in this daring enterprise. He kisses her chastely on the cheek after the amen is pronounced, the cheek still warm, still smoky from the cooking fires, and admonishes her one last time to remember whom she serves and in how great a cause, while darkness comes cranking down on Smithfield like an iron portcullis, massive and final.

# · 16 ·

The faces Matthew and Joan sought among so many faces had eluded them during their tedious patrol. Now the gathering darkness made matters worse. A riot of color in the sun, Bartholomew Fair took on a more fantastic and sinister aspect under the mantle of night. Torches and lanterns provided the sole illumination for the shadowy streets, yet the narrow passages were as jammed as ever and the rowdiness of the crowd increased as darkness conferred anonymity on them all. Roisterers and bullies became more threatening, shouting insults and challenges at strangers, all for the pleasure of a casual brawl. Whores became more insolent, the drunks drunker, pickpockets more daring.

But despite these things, Matthew and Joan continued their search. Up and down the streets they went until their cobbles and signs, doorways and windows were as familiar to them as those of Chelmsford's own High Street. It seemed to Joan that the pair of fugitives must surely have disappeared from the face of the earth.

"This is useless, Matthew," Joan said at length, footweary and with a growing sense of the futility of it all. "Surely Stubbs has fled the city—and taken Rose Dibble with him."

"Or he's killed her, like the others," answered Matthew gloomily.

But this unpleasant thought had crossed Joan's mind even as she spoke of their flight. She feared it was true, but her mind recoiled at the image of another brutalized body, especially the girl's. For although Joan had never spoken to Rose Dibble, she had a feeling of protectiveness for her that sprang from Joan's own motherhood and nurturing instincts. Even if Rose were still alive—and God keep the girl if she was—she was in great danger. Stubbs was clearly mad, and madness knew no restraints. Anyone coming in contact with the seemingly pleasant young man might be deceived by his charm, then victimized after. Joan shuddered at the thought.

They had stopped awhile in their search; now Matthew suggested they move on. He was not ready to give up yet. He said he thought Stubbs might still be at the fair since it was unlikely the young Puritan would leave behind him his few personal possessions, especially the visionary pamphlet with its incriminating annotations and drawings.

This brought to Joan's mind Esmera's prophecy, and she took the opportunity to tell Matthew all that had transpired that morning and how the wise woman's words had been verified by the wine seller's death. Matthew listened attentively as they walked, but when she had concluded and a long silence had mediated between them, she was forced to ask him outright what he thought now, now that proof was before him like a fallen tree on the road of his cynicism.

"She was lucky," he said simply, not taking his eyes off of the booths, the strange faces, the night sky barren of stars and, as yet, moon.

"Lucky! A most marvelous luck indeed to have guessed with such accuracy. Why, see, husband, she *described* the dead man."

"Only in general terms," he reminded her. "She never saw his face."

"But the knife! The knife! She described it. And she warned us against prolonging our stay here, which means the death she perceived in her vision was somehow connected to us, and so Jack Talbot's death was, for Stubbs had also murdered the puppet master near our very town."

"I admit that touching upon that matter, the woman spoke truly," he said.

"Fiddlesticks! Spoke truly!" She sighed with disgust.

Her husband moved on; Joan hurried to keep up. How obstinate he was! How impervious to reason! How he rankled her with his masculine hardheadedness! Why was he being so difficult when the evidence was so plain? Esmera was no fraud, but a genuine seer, endowed with marvelous capacity. "She warned us of danger to *ourselves*, Matthew!"

"And that's another thing," he said, stopping and turning to face her at last. "She was most insistent on that point, the danger to us rather than to the others."

"She was indeed," Joan admitted, failing to catch his drift. "Suspiciously so."

Then she wanted to know what he meant by so prolonging that word *suspiciously*, as though the word had twice its syllables and each must be savored in discourse. Or did he simply mean to tantalize her by suggesting he knew something that she did not? With her husband in this cranky humor that too was possible.

"We've not been harmed, you and I—that's a fact. Now tell me, then, if this woman came to you with such a warning for your safety and mine, why did she not tell the wine seller about *his* danger, for since he's dead he was obviously more in need of her wisdom than we? The poor fellow died with nary a word from her, a word that might have saved his life."

But Joan was ready for this argument too. "As far as we know she might have warned him and he failed to heed her and so he died when he might have saved himself." She said this pointedly and waited for her husband's response.

"The greengrocer Pullyver was at her tent, wasn't he? You said you saw him in his new doublet, coming out of the tent where he had had conference with the woman. Esmera should have warned *him*, since he was as near to the dead man as you or I. But only you were warned. Why, I'd like to know? It's as though you were culled out like a ripe plum from a limb full of many fruit. I swear it, Joan, this Esmera of yours is up to something. Mark my words."

Now it was Joan's turn to walk ahead. She was weary of quarreling with her husband. She pretended to be wholly preoccupied with the passing scene, the faces that—shadowy and distorted in the weak, uncertain torchlight—were like mummers' masks. Matthew followed, but neither talked of Esmera again. The unresolved dispute hung heavy on them both.

Then she heard herself and Matthew hailed from somewhere ahead and presently she could distinguish the rest of the search party, who, earlier having been sent abroad in pairs, had now reassembled and bore the look of weariness and defeat on their faces.

Grotwell motioned the Stocks to join the group, which then turned into a quiet alley.

"Well, what luck, Mr. Stock?" asked Grotwell, somewhat perfunctorily, for it was obvious that the Stocks had also failed to find Stubbs.

"None," answered Matthew.

"I once saw a fellow that might have been he," Chapman offered. The tall, gangling scrivener was clearly excited by his noctural adventure and seemed anxious to have the approval of the others.

"A thousand or more could have been he, but weren't," remarked Francis Crisp dryly.

"Nay, ten thousand," Pullyver added.

After this response, Chapman looked abashed and said nothing. Then there was some talk about what was to be done next and whether the pursuit of the bearward's helper was worth the while since all of Smithfield had been searched thrice over and the hour of curfew was at hand. It was agreed by all present that the little band of hardy searchers had done its best, under the circumstances, and Grotwell suggested they should all make for home since his own watch was done and his relief soon to appear. They were in the midst of leave-taking when they heard Ursula's voice. She was coming down the lane toward them, dragging Rose Dibble behind her. The girl's swollen eyes and bleeding lip gave evidence that the pig-woman had already commenced to exact her promised vengeance, contrary to the Justice's command.

"Here, my masters, is the slender baggage you seek, she that is so great with the murderer of Jack Talbot," Ursula declared. "Here is the lice-ridden blackbird, this deal of lies and infamies, this pinch-boned, addlepated whorelet."

Grotwell interrupted Ursula's litany of abuse to demand when and where the girl had been discovered and whether Stubbs had been with her. He did not seem to care that Rose had been beaten or that Ursula had defied the Justice's orders.

"I found her in the street, like a common drab," Ursula said. "No, Stubbs weren't with her. If he was, I would have dragged the miserable wretch by his privy member, yes, and wrapped it around his neck and hanged him with it. 'Where's the scum?' I shouted at her ear. 'Tell me or it's your present death!' But she wouldn't talk, though I threatened, yes, and beat upon her too, as you can plainly see. With my pig pan I threatened her. 'You'll talk now, young strumpet,' says I, and dragged her around until I found you here everyone."

"Won't talk, will she?" said Grotwell. "I'll make her talk."

"All she'll say is that he's innocent, this Stubbs fellow. Fancy that, sirs. Innocent!" Ursula spat the word as though it fouled her mouth. "All she babbles is nonsense."

"What sort of nonsense?" Matthew asked, looking at the silent, quaking girl.

"Why, such nonsense as the boy was not to blame for what was done, that it was God's will that the wine seller die, and that he, meaning this wretch Stubbs, was no more guilty of the death than she, but is as innocent as a lamb. Innocent as a lamb, my royal arse!" Ursula exclaimed with a dry, throaty laugh and a rapture of sarcasm. "Which is to say no less than the both of them are as guilty as hell. Oh, I tell you, sirs, she knows where the young puke lurks."

"This young man of yours has killed Jack Talbot," Grotwell said accusingly. "Stabbed him dead as a doornail. And before that he murdered Simon Plover, late of the parish and former helper to Mr. Babcock here, and before that another poor fellow named Fitzhenry."

"Fitzhugh," corrected Matthew.

"Fitzhugh, then," said Grotwell. "He's dead, whatever his name may be. All in cold blood, the three of them. Now, what do you say about that, mistress fishface? Will you tell us where Stubbs is? By God, if you don't—"

Here Joan intervened, to Grotwell's great displeasure, to protest his abuse of a girl whose complicity in the murders as far as she was concerned was far from being proved. "If you speak less threateningly to her," Joan suggested calmly but firmly, "we may find out something and get home to bed this night after all."

"Very well, Mrs. Stock," Grotwell conceded. "Maybe I should allow *you* to question her."

"May I ask her a question or two?" asked Matthew, inserting himself between the sergeant and Joan. Grotwell said that he might, but complained that it was shameful how the law must be hamstrung by the meddling of those who were not even citizens of the town, no matter what friends these same persons might have in high places.

Matthew ignored the sergeant's scurrilous tone and asked Rose how she was so sure Gabriel Stubbs was innocent. He said he agreed with the sergeant that the evidence was plain, and Grotwell showed the frightened girl the very warrant for Stubbs's arrest that Justice Baynard had signed within the hour.

But the sight of the document had no effect on Rose, who could not read a word. She did endeavor to answer Matthew's questions, but with great difficulty, for she was obviously terrified by the men around her. "He told me he was *innocent*," she said. Whereupon the men laughed outright and Ursula fell into another tirade of abuse.

But Joan did not laugh and neither did Matthew. Joan's heart ached for pity—pity for the swollen, bloody lip and bruised eye that marred the otherwise lovely face.

"*He* told you?" asked Grotwell with a sneer. "Well, now, gentles, doesn't that prove she knows *where* Stubbs is hiding? Damn the villain's innocence or guilt. We want to know where he is and you, girl, will tell us or the consequences will be dreadful. Your employer's beating will be only the beginning of your miseries. I charge you now, Rose Dibble, in the Queen's name, to reveal his place of concealment or be as guilty of these murders as Stubbs himself."

This dreadful threat with its reference to the Queen and promise of more physical abuse sent the girl into even greater paroxysms of terror. She began to babble incoherently about angels and devils, God and commandments, obedience and disobedience, and like language. Grotwell said the girl had been listening to too many sermons and that the practice had made her as mad as Stubbs.

Witnessing such confusion in the girl's speech, Joan feared the sergeant might be right. Had a religious lunacy infected Rose too? But to the others present, and especially to Ursula, all Rose's talk of God and angels was only a ruse to affect innocence where there was none.

"Satan himself can speak godly if he chooses," observed Pullyver, as though he were as familiar with the subject as with his leeks and turnips, cabbages and pears.

The scrivener agreed, but the two bearwards said that the beating had knocked her brains awry and hence her confusion and they were in favor of letting her go, for they thought there was no real evidence against her, and that surely her present insanity mitigated her crimes, whatever they were.

"Insanity is no mitigation," declared Pullyver with stolid conviction.

"Indeed it is not," Grotwell agreed. "A cabbage head may hang as well as a scholar. There's precedent for it."

Matthew took the bearwards' view and began to speak on the girl's behalf, while Ursula screamed, "She's lying, lying in her teeth."

Then Joan prevailed upon Grotwell to allow her to ask a few questions. She said she thought the interrogation was much too violent and wanted a woman's subtler touch. Ursula let out a great derisive guffaw but then shut up with the others to hear what questions Joan would put to Rose and with what success.

Joan approached Rose and pulled her away from the officers, who had been holding her tightly as though any moment the slim girl would spring from their clutches and dash off into the darkness. Joan smiled reassuringly at the quaking girl.

"I've a daughter of about your years," Joan said. "You and she are of about the same stature too and might be sisters by your face. Now tell me, if Gabriel is as innocent as you declare and he evidently claims, surely he would wish to say as much to the sergeant here, who wants nothing more than to find out the truth. Isn't that right, sergeant?"

Joan cast a glance at Grotwell, who was smirking at her with such insolence that she would have gladly borrowed Ursula's pig pan and remodeled his head with it. Grotwell said in a wheedling voice, "Oh yes, Mrs. Stock. The truth and nothing more."

Joan turned to the girl again. "Wouldn't Gabriel want us to know he was innocent?" she continued. "If Gabriel tells us he is innocent of the wine seller's death, then we will know for a surety. Even as you do now. You do want us to know, don't you?"

Rose nodded her head but still did not speak. She had stopped trembling and looked trustingly at Joan.

"Please tell us," Joan prompted again.

Finally Rose spoke, haltingly and in a barely audible voice. "All should know, even as I. He will explain. Explain as he did to me. Come, I'll show you where he is. He'll tell you everything that happened and why. You'll see. As innocent as a lamb. It's all God's work, every whit. He's at Jack's booth. I left him hiding there. He wanted me to find out how things stood at the bear garden, whether he was accused and sought or not suspected at all. I never discovered until Ursula found me, for when I went to the pit there was no one there save the bear."

"I think she's lying," Grotwell said when Rose had finished her statement. "Why should he be hiding in the dead man's booth? Why, it's a ridiculous place to conceal himself."

"Not so ridiculous," Joan said. "No one thought to look there, it would seem."

"It is the last place we would think to look," Matthew added.

Pullyver and Chapman and the two bearwards all said they thought the girl was telling the truth, on this matter at least, and all were eager to look for Stubbs in the wine seller's booth.

"Well, it won't hurt to look," Grotwell conceded.

Joan went forward to put her arms around Rose, defying the officers to interfere. She felt a sinking in her own heart now that Rose had confessed Stubbs's hiding place. It seemed somehow sinful to take advantage of one so vulnerable to honeyed words. But honey had done it in a way that all Ursula's violence of body and word had not. Rose had surrendered her secret, and as far as Joan could tell by her expression, Rose imagined she had done Stubbs a favor in doing so.

"Well, bring her along," Grotwell said to his men. "If she is telling the truth, the young devil is ours. In the wine seller's booth, is he? All right then, damn me but the lad's got his nerve *if* he is there. You've got to give him credit for that, madman or no."

The curfew hour had come and the booths of Bartholomew Fair were closing one by one, until it was quite dark and the fair looked like a deserted city whose inhabitants had long ago fled some pestilence. The raucous music of the day had dwindled into a few isolated good-nights and the whine of scavaging dogs and cats in the alleys. Through these now, Grotwell led the way, torch aloft, stopping at a sufficient distance from the wine seller's booth so as not to betray the presence of himself or his band. Skeptical before, Grotwell now talked sanguinely about capturing Stubbs and began to sketch out a plan of attack. He committed Rose into the Stocks' care. The rest were to go on ahead, Babcock and Crisp to circle the booth and take it from behind, Pullyver and Chapman to proceed quietly to the end of the lane and prevent an attempted escape in that direction. To Grotwell and his two officers was to go the honor of invading the booth directly, with the specific instruction of the sergeant that Stubbs was to be taken, dead or alive, and if dead all the better. "Stubbs is a killer, remember that," Grotwell said, handing the torch to Matthew. "Here, Mr. Stock, you take the torch. We don't need light to advertise our presence."

With the prospect of violence in the offing, Joan was happy to remain in her husband's company, away from the immediate danger. Yet she was still afraid. The street was so dark and quiet now; the booths so forbidding. Matthew also seemed nervous, as did the other men—all save the sergeant, who was used to such bloody encounters, she supposed. The poor scrivener looked as though any minute he would be sick in the street, so pale he seemed by torchlight.

Grotwell then motioned the men into place and Joan watched, her heart in her throat, her arm around Rose Dibble's shoulder, as the men went off. Rose also watched, praying aloud for the fugitive. Joan saw the shadows that were the sergeant and his two men steal inside the distant booth and then heard a hoarse cry of alarm. It was Grotwell's voice, she thought. Then there was more shouting and curses too and garbled replies from somewhere behind the booth. She heard the sound of splintering wood, as though the invaders were tearing down the booth to get to Stubbs.

All during this commotion Matthew and Joan held their breaths, but almost as quickly as the action commenced it was over, or so it seemed. They were soon coming back, all of the men. They were quarreling and cursing and Grotwell's complaints were the loudest and most bitter. The attack had failed. Stubbs had not been found in the booth. He had either escaped in what now seemed—to Joan at least—a ridiculously inept attempt to trap him, or long before, warned by Rose or by his own instincts to flee. Where had he gone? God only knew, and maybe the Devil too.

"Damnation!" cried Grotwell bitterly. "I'm cursed if that filthy rogue didn't slip by us all."

"Or was never there," said Francis Crisp. "I saw no man."

"It was no fault of mine," protested Pullyver, who was out of breath but for no apparent reason since both he and Chapman had remained at a safe distance during the assault. Grotwell's officers blamed each other. The one said the other was clumsy of foot and gave warning to the fugitive, who hearing the noise stole from the back of the tent through a hole in the canvas. The officer accused of this retorted that it was his companion, rather, who signaled the alarm by crying out like an idiot. "Which cry would have raised the dead man, much more his murderer."

They two argued about this while Francis Crisp and Ned Babcock insisted that they had seen no one in the dark.

"We'll never find him now," said Grotwell. "Not in this gloom. Besides, he knows we're after him. He's been warned good, he has, slippery devil." He turned to Rose. "Now, mistress," he said sternly, taking the torch again from Matthew and thrusting it forward so that it came close to singeing the girl's hair, "we may have lost your confederate, but we have you and we shall carry you forthwith to Justice Baynard, who will deal with you as you deserve."

Joan protested the arrest of Rose, who had done nothing wrong that she could see, but Matthew pointed out that Rose was now in greater risk than before, for surely Stubbs would reason that she had been the one who had led them all to his hiding place and thus betrayed him. But Rose denied that Gabriel Stubbs would harm her. "He's an angel, an angel of God," she repeated, while the sergeant's men laughed outright.

"O poor fool," Grotwell murmured in disgust. "Take her off," he said to his men. Then Grotwell wished Matthew and Joan good-night and the same to the bearwards and Chapman and Pullyver. He thanked them all for their efforts, unsuccessful as they had been. After he and his men had gone, Pullyver said to Babcock, "It seems you are ever beset with bad luck, friend Ned. Surely this new incident of death augurs an uncertain future at the least. Once it is bruited about that you harbored a maniacal Puritan in your midst, your reputation will stink, stink worse that Smithfield. You best sell while you can, Ned, while you can. Why, look you now, I'll buy you out—we'll settle the score."

"I'll not sell," Babcock said resolutely.

"Well said," remarked Francis, who seemed more alarmed by this talk of selling the bear garden than he had been in confronting a dangerous fugitive.

"Samson's been exonerated," Babcock said. "You heard the Justice say as much. And I am not to blame for the boy's fanatical religiosity. Besides, we'll all turn a tidy profit yet—even more perhaps."

Chapman said he thought it was well past the hour to be discussing business, but Pullyver argued it was the best of times, especially in light of recent events and the great likelihood of there being more trouble ahead. An argument ensued between the greengrocer and the two bearwards, during which voices were raised and slanders were exchanged to the point that Joan was disgusted with the lot of them and wanted nothing more than to return to the inn and a comfortable bed.

But Matthew was somehow dragged into the discussion and he lingered. Finally, Joan interrupted to borrow the torch and left the men arguing in the dark while she walked over to the booth to see the damage wrought by Grotwell's invasion.

She climbed over the debris and entered the wine seller's private quarters. Inside she saw a wooden chest overturned and all its contents strewn about, several large malmsey butts still upright, and a clutter of smaller casks all topsy-turvy but unbroken. There was a strong odor of sweet malmsey and she supposed in the fracas some had been spilled and had since seeped down into the straw to give joy to the lice, mites, and other small creatures crawling therein. The canvas back of the booth had been rent, and she wondered if this had been done by the sergeant and his men or by the fleeing Stubbs. There was no other evidence around to suggest that during the earlier part of the evening the booth had been the hiding place of a murderer or that Grotwell's raucous intrusion had done any other good but to dispel the lingering ghost of Jack Talbot.

# · 17 ·

Matthew and Joan returned to the inn, both too weary from the night's adventure to speak further of the murder or lament the loss of supper. Clutching Matthew's arm for security, Joan was aware of their vulnerability in the black night, in the strange city. In her brain a discordant company of conflicting interpretations, suppositions, and theories struggled with one another for preeminence, like unruly guests at a feast.

Arriving at the inn, they found the door fast and the house apparently asleep. Matthew was forced to stand before the door crying out for the host and pounding until at length the host came, wiping sleep from his eyes and looking quite absurd in a nightshirt that came to mid-shank of his bare, hairy legs and slipperless feet. Recognizing Matthew as the clothier of Chelmsford, he said, "You're wanted, Mr. Stock. Master Clerk of the Fair, Justice Baynard, and other gentlemen of note await your return this half hour or more. They sent me to bed, sir, but the rest are in the Lion."

Mathew thanked the host for the message and exchanged glances with Joan to indicate he was as perplexed by this summons as she, although she supposed it certainly must have something to do with the Bartholomew Fair murders.

"The gentlemen said you must come straightway," the host said, eyeing Matthew with a mixture of curiosity and envy that he should be connected in some way to the distinguished persons awaiting him. The host provided Matthew and Joan with candles and wished them good-night.

While Matthew went to the Lion to fulfill his appointment, Joan went sleepily upstairs to their chamber. Holding one candle aloft, she inspected the unfamiliar interior, feeling the heavy weight of depression she always experienced when faced with the prospect of a night's sleep in a house not her own, in a bed not her own. No cheery fire had been laid in the grate to welcome her with its bright licks of flame and smoky smell and cracks and snaps. None had been needed in this dry, hot month. The casement had been left open to air the room. She closed the casement, lighted the larger candle at the bedside, extinguished the smaller, then went to make fast the door. Now more than ever it seemed prudent. She would let Matthew in when he was finished with his meeting and only after he had identified himself as he and not some other.

She made ready for bed, thinking about Stubbs, remembering him as she had first viewed him, shirtless and with his rickety, odoriferous wheelbarrow. A handsome, well-shaped young man, his limp notwithstanding—of poor condition but goodly manners, soft, pleasing voice, clear eye, ready smile. Who would have thought him to be what he was, a monster of sorts, vicious and deadly, wearing his godliness as a concealment. She had not suspected him of being a Puritan at all, much less one driven by dreams and visions. Yet the evidence he was guilty was incontrovertible. What a strange world it was, and what even stranger persons dwelt in it.

And how dreadful madness was too. She had known a madman once, years before when she was a child. A scatterbrain with rheumy eyes and lantern jaw. Yet harmless. The man thought himself a bird. He would flap his arms and cry out shrilly like a lapwing to the delight of the neighborhood children, of whom Joan had been one, amazed and amused as the others by his curious deviation from rational behavior. As though the mind didn't know the difference between man and bird. He had run around the fields, this loony, skipping and gamboling, leaping suddenly upward on legs of amazing springiness, raising his arms in the attitude of flight, splaying his fingers, crying shrilly. His name had been Stephen, she remembered as she had not in years. Stephen Cribbage, the madman of Chelmsford. His aging mother kept him at home, where he cut wood, gathered acorns to make bread, and harvested wild radishes in their season. In midsummer he found berries and tried to fly.

But if Stephen Cribbage had dreams and visions, he did not report them. Content to be a bird when the humor struck him, he had done no murders.

And therefore Stubbs's madness, equally as unfathomable to her understanding, was of a different sort, not the simple derangement people spent good money to see among the mindsick at Bethlem Hospital. Stubbs's madness was the stuff of nightmares.

Joan said her prayers and climbed into the bed, but she did not extinguish the candle at her bedside. With herself alone for company, she had no relish for the greater darkness without it. Besides, she wanted to remain awake—both to let Matthew in when he and the gentlemen were done and to discover what business had kept him from her. She wondered who these other gentlemen of note were the host had spoken of. But in time, rubbing these same thoughts raw, she succumbed to a fitful sleep, and in her sleep she dreamed of Esmera, who clutched Joan's wrists with her strong hands, pressed her long, strangely beautiful face into Joan's, and whispered of catastrophes to come.

The Lion was not a bedchamber but a well-furnished parlor used for private suppers and other meetings of the inn's more wealthy clientele. The room took its name from a large faded tapestry that hung on one wall and depicted the king of beasts surrounded by a flock of lambs and other innocuous creatures who showed no fear of it. The scene symbolized the period of Christ's reign spoken of in the Scriptures, when lamb and lion should be bedfellows and all the world at peace. This image of holy promise had thus been the witness of many considerably less holy festivities, some of them downright sordid, but of these Matthew knew only by hearsay.

When Matthew had come to the door, even before knocking

he could hear from within the sound of a familiar voice and he waited a moment until he placed it in his memory. Grotwell let him in, but it was not Grotwell's voice Matthew had heard.

"Come in, Mr. Stock of Chelmsford. You're right welcome among us," said Sir Robert Cecil.

Despite the great social gulf that separated them, the two men who now greeted each other knew each other well. Matthew had served the Queen's Principal Secretary before, once in the discovery of a particularly sinister and pernicious piece of espionage involving a London jeweler who cared more for Spanish gold than for his country, a discovery that would hardly have been made had it not been for Matthew—and for Joan too, to give her the credit due her. Matthew was surprised to see Cecil here. Her Majesty's Secretary was seated in a large, straight-backed chair that underscored his own diminutive stature, so that he vaguely resembled a child with a middle-aged man's sallow cheeks and baggy eyes. The thought passed quickly through Matthew's mind that were it not for the accident of birth by which Cecil was a great man's son and not some common laborer's, this little man might have ended up among the freaks of Bartholomew Fair, for many, and especially his enemies, ridiculed him for being no bigger than a dwarf.

Forming a semicircle around Cecil were the Clerk, the Justice, and Cecil's secretary, John Wynn, a tall, dark man of about thirty with spectacles and notebook. An oil lamp burned smokily on the table so that the features of the tapestry could be dimly perceived. Cecil came to the matter at hand at once.

"The sergeant here has just finishing apprising us of the night's adventure—or misadventure, as the case seem to be," Cecil said. Cecil spoke slowly and with a quick glance at the sergeant.

"I thought it best to inform Sir Robert of the murders," the Justice said.

"And you were well-advised to do so," Cecil said, keeping his eyes fixed on Matthew. "It's a crying shame the fellow escaped you, but what's done is done. We are now on the horns of a dilemma. The Queen, God bless her, is resolute in her purpose to visit the fair, despite a recent indisposition that has kept her two days in bed this very week. She has expressly forbidden any elaborate preparations for her visit. She prefers to mingle, as she calls it, with her subjects. To take them by surprise with less than the usual pageantry. Oh, she will be guarded, of course. She will be welcomed by the Lord Mayor and the Aldermen, the Clerk here, and other officials of the fair. These then will conduct her about, after which she returns to my house on the Strand for supper. Now, however, I am told that a murderer is at large in Smithfield, and the sergeant here says that you have implicated the man in an even earlier death in Chelmsford."

Matthew said that it was all true and briefly recounted the circumstances of the puppet master's murder. "Can not the Queen's visit be prevented until the murderer is taken?" Matthew asked at the conclusion of his recital.

"If you mean by 'prevented' cancelled, it can be and certainly will, if wisdom dictates. That cancellation would hardly be pleasing to Her Majesty, whose mind is set on her coming. She is, however, so fearful of assassination these days that the very whisper of danger will bring an end to her plans, but she will hardly be pleased that a murderer remains at large, having been identified by name, or that her anticipated pleasures have been denied her. She is not a woman to brook disappointment. It would all look very bad for the Clerk here; worse for the Justice, who might have captured Stubbs earlier. Also bad for me, I must confess it, for she may determine that I knew of the danger sometime before giving her warning of it. You can see, then, Mr. Stock, what a bind we all are in."

Matthew could see indeed, although what his own role in the matter was eluded him. He had no official capacity in Smithfield. He had merely been helping a friend.

"What is to be done, then, Sir Robert?" asked the Justice, breaking a moment's awkward silence and wearing a chastened expression.

Cecil, turning his head upward to the Justice, said, "Very simple, Mr. Justice. The murderer must be taken *before* Her Majesty's visit."

Matthew thought he saw Justice Baynard wince; certainly Cecil's words made Grotwell, standing by the door, squirm.

"We should have called the hue and cry at first," the Justice said, staring pointedly at the Clerk, who had persuaded him against it.

"You agreed not to," returned the Clerk defensively, casting a look of appeal at Cecil. "I'm not responsible for the maintenance of order in Smithfield."

"Then you should not have stuck your nose into my business," replied the Justice curtly, "but suffered me to do what I would."

Cecil held up a hand to stay this dispute, which threatened to grow hotter. "Peace," he said, "the both of you. Squabbling about who's to blame will do no good now. What's done is done. Blame may fall on all our shoulders later. For the present, let's see what good may come of our mistakes. I understand our Clerk's desire to save the fair's profits and avoid panic. And the Justice's willingness to comply. Hindsight has proved foresight a fool in this case, but who can know the future? On the other hand, the Queen must be protected, even from the very rumor of trouble."

Cecil paused and looked up again at the Justice. "Mr. Justice, you are to instruct the sergeant here to round up all who know Gabriel Stubbs by sight. Make deputies of the lot of them but, save for those who already know of his treachery, inform none of why he must be apprehended. Take the man dead or alive. If you cannot apprehend him, at least you may be able to determine that he has fled and presents therefore no danger. Afflicted as he is with religious madness, who knows what his ultimate design may be? The very sight of Her Majesty may inflame his mind to new treachery, for she has done much of late to rankle the more rigorous sort of Puritan."

Baynard said he would do everything that Cecil ordered. He

turned to Grotwell and declared, "See that Sir Robert's instructions are carried out."

Grotwell said he would do it, though it cost him his life.

"We hope matters won't press to that extremity," remarked Cecil dryly.

Cecil dismissed the Justice, the Clerk, and the sergeant, indicating at the same time that Matthew should remain. When the other men had gone, Cecil invited Matthew to sit down in a chair opposite him and began to speak in a more familiar manner. "I can speak with greater candor now, Matthew. It is most important that the Queen follow through with her plan to visit the fair tomorrow. Her visit has been well-advertised, not only among the commons but among the foreign visitors of the City, who will be as curious to glimpse the Queen as are her subjects. She's old and, it grieves me to say it, infirm.

"You well know how rumor every day proclaims her imminent death and how such rumors instill in the multitude fears and anxieties of which the Queen's enemies, here and abroad, may make good use. Now a public demonstration of her vigor would be a great advantage to the public peace and certain diplomatic negotiations now in progress. Seeing her move about in her wonted manner, drinking and eating with her subjects, would inspire confidence that she is Queen still, although aged and worn as nature has disposed. A cancellation at this late date, no matter how justified, would give the opposite impression—that she is in decline; that she is changeful and moody and takes no delight in her own people, keeps not her promises and is two legs and an arm in her grave. No, a cancellation would be most inadvisable. The tale of a murderer of such grotesque sort as this would not be credited. Yet the Queen must not be exposed to danger."

Here Cecil paused, took a deep breath. His voice fell to a confidential whisper. "Matthew, my friend, it is twelve of the clock if I marked the last toll of Paul's correctly. By this same hour of the morning the Queen will leave Whitehall for

Smithfield. Before that hour I must say yea or nay to the enterprise. Help me in good conscience to say *yea.*"

Matthew was about to ask just how he was to assist, but Cecil anticipated the question. He raised an open palm to suggest that Matthew do nothing but listen until he was finished. "By that same hour, twelve of the morning, I expect you to have unraveled all this."

"Unraveled, sir, but—"

"Nay, hear me out and mark me well. You are not as this Grotwell, a man whose wit is in his brawn and strength in his club. In times past you have served me well, yes, and England too. I have more than once mentioned it to the Queen and were I in position now to reveal to her these matters, she would surely commission you as I am about to do."

"What exactly would you have me do, Sir Robert?"

"Marry, this. I have looked at this pamphlet given me of Justice Baynard." Here Cecil paused and took the pamphlet that his personal secretary, John Wynn, had been holding the while. "It makes interesting reading, I'll say that much for it, what little I have had time and energy to peruse at this late hour. The author, Foxworth, is learned. The numerous exempla of satanic possession are not without a certain persuasiveness if one's theological interests run in that direction. But even a good book may prove dangerous in the hands of the wrong person. As thus it is in the present case. Now, as I say, I have perused the pamphlet to catch its drift. You, Matthew, must search out its eddies and currents, its treacherous backwaters. Sound its depths, paying particular attention to these copious notes in the margin, which the Justice tells me are the very work of Gabriel Stubbs."

"They are his work, sir," Matthew said. "For we found his pen and inkhorn in his pack and Francis Crisp the bearward will swear that they are Stubbs's."

"Very well, then," Cecil went on. "Even a madman works by some method, if we can only find it out. And if there be a method here, study may make it known. I would do the work myself, were there not pressing business at court that requires my immediate and constant supervision. So to you I leave this onerous duty, with my prayers for your success. If there is a method to this Stubbs's madness, find it out. Before noon tomorrow, Matthew, before noon."

Cecil frowned, but not at Matthew, at a thought in his mind rather, a deep meditation. Behind him John Wynn stood at attention, his eyelids drooping for the lateness of the hour. "I have read enough of the pamphlet and Stubbs's comment to discern in him one who reads with a literal mind. If an allegory is employed, he takes it a thing he might encounter rounding a corner. He reckons not symbols, but sees hard matter in mists and vapors, poetic flourishes and parables. Damn him if he wouldn't trip over a sonnet, if his interest in poetry were as great as his study of the Scriptures. But that's all one. What is important is that you absorb, somehow, his peculiar notions. Read the book carefully. Where does his thinking lead?"

"But I'm no scholar, sir—" Matthew protested.

"All the better for this work," Cecil answered. "You'll not be distracted by what's irrelevant to the present purpose. Mark what kind of Puritan he is, this Stubbs, for some, as you know, are so earnest in their cause that they would make water on Christ's tomb to show their contempt for relics and would rather tweak the Pope's nose than find a ready admission to heaven. Oh, they are a strange breed, indeed, and have given Her Majesty much grief. Worse than Catholics, she calls them; and I confess, while I'm no Papist, I must concur in her condemnation.

"Here, for example, is this Gabriel Stubbs, a simple bearward's helper (and God knows what before), who feels called upon by the Divine Being to pluck down enormities in Smithfield. Well, he's not the first of his sect to decry Bartholomew pig, scorn cakes and ale, and think himself a judge in Israel. The innocent pleasures of some are the Sodom and Gomorrah of others, eh, Matthew?"

Cecil's face darkened again, having been momentarily brightened perhaps by the thought of the young Puritan assaulting the pig sellers and gingerbread sellers of the fair. "Well, thanks be to God we are not sinners of that sort, but love good food, good wine, and, yes, pray to heaven too."

Cecil laughed pleasantly. He handed the pamphlet to Matthew. "Justice Baynard's a wise fellow and the Clerk's no fool either. They'll give what help you may need. I have told them of the confidence I place in you and reaffirm that confidence now. Yet twelve hours, Matthew, no more. If the murderer is not taken by then, the Queen's visit must be stayed—with what repercussions I have already outlined. She does have her heart set on this appearance, thinking it may well be the last Bartholomew Fair of her mortality. God forbid that it should be so, and yet she is mortal like the rest of us. Even queens owe God a death. She has a round-wombed woman's yearning for the greasy succulence of Bartholomew pig. Don't disappoint her on that score either."

Matthew promised solemnly that he would do all that Cecil had asked. He would try to discern Stubbs's plan. He would prevent another murder. He would assure the Queen of her bite of pig and her afternoon among her adoring subjects. He pledged fully and honestly himself, but in his heart he asked: How can this be done?

If Cecil perceived Matthew's self-doubt, he made no sign. A smile of easy assurance returned to his face and he climbed nimbly out of the chair. John Wynn, hearing his master's movement, now came fully awake.

"Good-night, Mr. Stock, and Godspeed you. Both to your room and to the solution of this mystery," Cecil said.

Matthew shook the great man's hand and wished him goodnight too. Then he went out and John Wynn closed the door behind him. For a moment Matthew stood in the corridor, lost in a maze of thoughts. He had never entered a room occupied by Sir Robert Cecil but he found himself quite undone by the little man's presence, which filled the area around him, despite his diminutive stature. The power of the man's intellect, the depth of his devotion to the Queen, and the cunning by which he maintained his place as Elizabeth's most trusted adviser were evident in every word that passed from his lips. Matthew felt honored that Cecil had so readily taken him into his confidence, and yet he felt such a burden of responsibility—both to Cecil and the Queen—that he wondered if he could bear it long enough to travel the twenty yards and flight of stairs to where Joan waited, eager, he was sure, to learn all that had happened in his absence. Surely Cecil expected too much of a simple clothier and constable of a country town. Wasn't the study of Gabriel Stubbs's pamphlet the work of a university man, a learned divine? Or at least of someone schooled in the subtleties of codes and ciphers?

Still groggy from sleep, holding the candle aloft to confirm that it was indeed her husband at the door, Joan greeted Matthew with an embrace and kiss.

"In good time," she said. "I must have fallen asleep. What hour is it?"

"Past midnight now."

"God save us. What was the business of utmost importance whereof the host spoke?"

While Matthew made ready for bed, he told Joan in whose company he had been. She was surprised. Cecil here? In Smithfield, at the Hand and Shears? Joan, lying in bed again, her head propped up on the bolster, listened intently. Then she said, "The great Sir Robert Cecil. While I slept!"

Matthew told her about Cecil's instructions, how Matthew was to unravel it all, Stubbs's plot, whatever it was. "If we can anticipate his next move—"

"The next move of a lunatic?" she said.

"Sir Robert thinks the man works according to logic. I am to turn scholar, study the pamphlet itself, and ferret out his method."

"Method? A most murderous raving method to stab and desecrate as Gabriel Stubbs has done," she said.

"And babbling of Satan," he muttered.

"Of Satan?"

"The author of the pamphlet, Richard Foxworth, says that Satan adopts many disguises—like a stage player. In these he appears among the wicked and sometimes among the righteous too. In his scribblings in the margins of this same pamphlet, Stubbs wrote of how he had seen Satan in one form or another, many times."

"In dreams and visions undoubtedly," she said.

He slipped into bed at her side. "In waking, rather. As he walked. The puppet master must have been such a one, at least to Stubbs's crazed mind."

"And Jack Talbot and Simon Plover too?" she asked.

"So Stubbs may have supposed," Matthew said.

Joan had seen the wine seller, alive and well. He had seemed a companionable sort, not a bad-looking man, although his complexion was somewhat mottled and his beard untrimmed. Certainly he was no devil incarnate. Who would be next?

Matthew jabbed and poked the bolster, shaping it to his liking, shifted his body in the bed until he was comfortable. The chamber was stuffy and overly warm; exhaustion was a blessing, since the mattress left something to be desired too.

"What are you going to do?" she asked.

"Sleep, that's what."

"Sleep, yes," she murmured.

"My feet are sore beyond belief from all that walking," he said. "I have twelve good hours yet, according to Sir Robert. Twelve hours before the Queen visits the fair or is informed that a maniac is loose and her chief minister and other servants have been unable to apprehend him and provide for her security. Still I am determined to sleep through a quarter of the time. Nothing can be done until morning. I'm much too tired to read now. Let the perverse treatise of Foxworth go hang."

He rolled over on his side; the bed quivered as his body molded itself into the mattress.

"We'll study the work together," Joan said. She blew out the candle.

# · 18 ·

By the first shaft of gray light, Joan and Matthew took turns reading from Richard Foxworth's dreary treatise. From time to time one of them would pause to remark upon a passage of the text, a point of doctrine, or a comment of Stubbs's, penned into the margin in the young Puritan's small, crabbed hand. Their examination confirmed Matthew's earlier impression that Stubbs, if not a trained scholar, was at least that way inclined. Stubbs had totally absorbed the learned divine's thoughts, accepted unquestioningly his arguments, even gone beyond him in carrying Foxworth's doctrines to their logical conclusion. And so at the moment—in Joan's hands now, for her turn had come—she held the creature of two distempered brains, Stubbs's and his mentor's, and a single hysterical vision of satanic evil and infiltration into the normal courses of life.

But here was mind-numbing work indeed, this close study of a document of increasing repulsiveness, and Joan was aware that despite the seriousness of their purpose her husband's attention had flagged. He was half-listening, and sometimes dozing, for during the night both husband and wife had slept fitfully. Duty had now depressed her husband's spirits, and he lay sprawled upon the bed, half-dressed, in an attitude of quiet resignation to his failure.

But then her eye fell upon something on the much besmirched page. She ceased to read aloud and reread the lines to herself.

"Why have you stopped reading?" he asked from the bed, his eyes closed. "Is there something there?"

"A clue at last," she said.

She read the lines—a part of a larger passage—again, slowly

and with emphasis. Then she read the whole text of which the line was a part, the seventeenth chapter of the Book of Revelation. It was one of Foxworth's favorites, and it spoke of a Great Whore with whom the kings of the earth had committed fornication. It spoke of scarlet raiment, gold and precious stones, and a golden cup. This same Whore had drunk from the cup the blood of the saints. She had become drunken with the blood of the saints. "The saints," Joan said. "Mark *that*, Matthew. Do the sanctified brethren not commonly refer to themselves as *saints*? This same Whore has drunk their blood. She is their enemy, Gabriel Stubbs's enemy, and he hers."

"And so?" he said, prompting her on. She had his attention now. He was sitting up in bed, his head thrust forward.

Joan now read the comment Stubbs had wedged into the margin of the same page in his tiny handwriting: "*A goodly image of our most prideful Queen, this scarlet whore, yet she too God will judge.*"

"Certain it is that God will judge—us all," Matthew said when Joan had finished reading and looked up at him for his response. "Vengeance is mine. Judge not lest ye be judged. He's orthodox on that point of doctrine. But the rest is gross slander. Yes and treason too, since it is written against the Queen."

"I'faith it *is* treason," Joan declared with equal conviction, her eyes falling again to the page. "But see, here's more. Here a Scripture is cited."

"No marvel that, the pamphlet is full of it," Matthew said. "Haven't we read enough? Stubbs has convicted himself with his own words. Had he drawn no other blood than a flea's and written such words he would go to his hanging and no jury would have thought twice of it. Surely this man is a danger to Her Majesty."

"John, chapter and verse," she said. "That alone."

"Which chapter and verse?"

"Chapter eleven, verse fifty."

Matthew didn't recognize the text, nor did Joan. "It probably isn't important," he said. "If it were, Stubbs would have written it out. He's capable of infinite pains in such matters. His treasonous slanders are enough evidence for me."

Matthew had found where he put his shoes the night before and was now bent over tying the laces.

"But the verse may be important too," she protested. "The rest of it was. We must find a Bible."

He looked up and made a wry face. "What? Here in Smithfield? As well look for a virgin in the great Turk's harem."

"Matthew!"

He sighed; he was eager to send word of this fresh discovery to Sir Robert. He looked at Joan. Well, what did another quarter of an hour matter since the news would be bad and the time was ample for the warning?

"I'll go ask the host," he said doubtfully. He went downstairs and found the host, who was enjoying his breakfast in the great room of the inn. Matthew felt foolish asking the man for a Bible. Where did he think he was, in church? Or at one of the universities where books were as common as beggars, or at the bookstalls at Paul's where they lay stacked like cordwood? Besides, the host did not look the sort of fellow that would own a Bible.

The host looked up from his rasher of bacon, seemed perplexed for a moment by the strangeness of Matthew's question, and then answered, "A Bible, Mr. Stock? Holy Writ, you mean? Well, no, sir. I have none, nor prayerbook either. None is provided, sir," he said, as though Matthew had asked for clean linen or a second chamber pot. "But there is a learned man residing here. A man of the church. He might own a Bible, sir. Yes, and have it with him too."

The host told Matthew where this clergyman could be found and Matthew apologized to the host for the interruption of his breakfast.

Matthew went to the room where the clergyman was and knocked. His summons was answered by a thin young man of middle height with sallow complexion and spectacles resting precariously on the bridge of his small nose. Matthew introduced himself and asked the man if he had a Bible in his keeping.

The clergyman said he owned a Bible of course, but did not have it with him. It was with his other possessions, sent on ahead by carter a week before to a church he was presently to serve in Sussex. He apologized profusely that he could not be of service but offered spiritual counsel if that was what Matthew wanted. He also said he had a prayerbook and was reading it at the very moment Matthew knocked upon his door.

Matthew decided not to be too explicit about his motives. "A wager, sir, as to a certain biblical verse, nothing more."

The clergyman laughed. He was a good sort who was not above a wager himself when the mood struck him. "I've got a good memory for verses. Try me, sir."

"The Gospel of John. The eleventh chapter of the same and the fiftieth verse."

The clergyman thought for a moment, then smiled with satisfaction. "Ah, yes. The words of Caiaphas the high priest. 'Nor consider that it is expedient for us, that one man should die for the people, and that the whole nation perish not.'"

"You're sure?" Matthew asked, somewhat skeptical at the readiness with which the young clergyman had fetched the passage forth from his memory.

"Absolutely," replied the clergyman. "My memory, I assure you, is excellent for such things. When at Oxford I preached once a sermon on the very text, which was much praised. A bookseller there wanted me to print it. He assured me it would sell very well."

"I'm not sure I understand the verse," Matthew said, somewhat cautiously, for he hoped his ignorance of Scripture would not breed a tedious sermon.

The clergyman invited Matthew to sit down in the plainly furnished room and offered him a cup of wine. For the next quarter of an hour the clergyman discoursed upon the text in question, much to Matthew's discomfort, for he wanted to get back to Joan but as he listened, the meaning of the Gospel text became clearer.

"The wicked Caiaphas prophesies of the Lord's sacrifice, quite despite himself and in the darkness of ignorance, for he himself was an unbeliever—a Jew of obdurate heart. Yet he understood the truth of this proposition, that it is better for one man to perish than a whole nation suffer in unbelief."

"I suppose the same might be argued of a woman," Matthew said.

"What, sir?" exclaimed the clergyman, sitting erect in his chair and regarding Matthew suspiciously, as though he had just advanced a novel heresy.

"The principle would hold, would it not?" Matthew continued. "For a woman—say, a woman of authority—to die would be preferable to the death of thousands, and perhaps more?"

The clergyman considered the proposition, making a thoughtful face. He removed his eyeglasses and dangled them at the end of his fingers. "Why, I suppose it would," he answered at length. "Logic would dictate it, since the distinction between male and female is beside the point, which point pertains rather to the good of many as opposed to that of one alone."

The clergyman now warmed to this new theme, but Matthew was afraid to delay further his return to Joan. He hastily thanked the man for his information and was at such pains to get back to his own room and reveal to Joan what he had now concluded concerning Stubbs's motives that he nearly broke his neck bounding up the stairs.

"So," she declared triumphantly when he had told her all. "The pieces fit."

"They do indeed," he said, still breathing heavily from his climb. "I must send word to Sir Robert at once. There is no reason for further delay. This verse and Stubbs's comment in the margin lend substance to his own surmise—that it is the Queen herself for whom Stubbs lurks. She must on no account come to Smithfield."

Matthew was about to arrange for such a message when a rapid knocking was heard at the door. Matthew opened it and saw one of Grotwell's officers standing there. The man's expression was excited.

"What is it?" Matthew asked.

"Another murder, Mr. Stock. The sergeant says you are to come straightway."

"Come where—to whom?" Joan asked, coming up behind Matthew and peering suspiciously at the young officer.

"To the bear garden in the fair," the man said.

"Who is dead?" Matthew asked, almost fearing to learn.

"It's the bearward himself, sir."

"Which?" Joan asked with sinking heart. "Mr. Crisp or Mr. Babcock?"

"Mr. Babcock it is. He's been done in, like the others, and it is a dreadful sight to behold."

# · 19 ·

Shocked and grieved at the news of his friend's death, Matthew did not, however, proceed at once to the bear garden as he was inclined, but first secured paper and pen to compose a message to Cecil. Babcock, he realized, was now beyond help, his soul in heaven, but the Queen remained in jeopardy.

He wrote quickly and awkwardly, informing Cecil of the bearward's murder, inferring from the fact that Stubbs was still at large, and conveying as best he could the sum of Stubbs's slanders and threats against the Queen. He did not repeat the slanders word for word, but couched them in milder language, for God forbid the very phrases of the young Puritan, so grossly treasonous that they fouled the lips to utter them, might have been construed as his own.

He tried to make it perfectly clear that the danger to the Queen persisted, and he hoped in his heart that Cecil would be moved to call off the royal visit. But he made, himself, no such recommendation. That would not have been his place.

Matthew sent the message by the host's boy, whom the host declared was as faithful in such office as the Queen's courier and fleeter of foot through the London streets. Then he and Joan left at once for the bear garden.

A crudely lettered notice, chalked on a plank and fixed on the gate of the bear garden, announced that the morning baiting had been canceled. Matthew and Joan went directly to Samson's tent. Pullyver, Chapman, and Babcock's dour daughter, Juliet, were already there. So were Francis Crisp and the sergeant's man who had brought word of the death. They were standing silently, turned away from the body that Crisp had found, crumpled in his nightshirt, inside of Samson's cage. To

Matthew, Francis explained that his former partner had spent the night with the bear, there being no other watchman. The dead man now lay outside the cage; Crisp had pulled him out. Babcock's face had been so abused by Stubbs's knife as to be almost unrecognizable. It was a sight to chill an executioner's blood.

The body had been discovered with the poniard protruding from the wounds made in the dead man's back. The weapon had since been removed and now lay next to the body.

While Matthew listened to Francis Crisp's sobbing account of the discovery of his friend and partner, Joan quietly took in as much as she could of the reactions of the others present. Pullyver was comforting Juliet, who was dry-eyed but obviously distressed—if not by her father's death, at least by the sheer horror of it. Chapman appeared to be sick and kept rubbing his lips with a handkerchief. His face was white and glistened with sweat. Grotwell's man stood with his hands folded behind his back like a guard at rest, since he was not himself empowered to investigate. Upon Matthew and Joan's entering, he had informed them that Grotwell and others of the watch had immediately commenced a new search of the neighborhood in the hope of apprehending the murderer while his trail was fresh.

Matthew was kneeling down beside the body, his eyes avoiding the dead man's face. He saw the poniard and picked it up. "J.F.," he said.

"What's that, sir?" asked Grotwell's man, concerned that the clothier of Chelmsford might be tampering with evidence.

"J.F. Those were the initials of the dead puppet master. James Fitzhugh. It's Fitzhugh's blade all right. Stubbs's blade too."

Francis Crisp, tearful and wringing his hands, explained again how he found the body. He said that Babcock had volunteered to spend the night in the tent. "Had I been here, I would have been the dead man," the bearward remarked grimly. Someone had to watch the bear, feed him in the morning.

"What hour was he fed?" Matthew asked, rising.

"At sunrise or thereabouts," Francis Crisp said. "Samson is marvelously punctual in such matters." Crisp glanced at the bear, who was dozing inside his cage, indifferent to the horror a few feet beyond and the human grief and confusion around him.

"Ned's being in his nightshirt," Matthew theorized, "suggests he was killed while he slept. Then dragged into the cage. Stubbs had handled the animal before. He'd have no fear for himself. He probably thought the bear would finish poor Ned. Thank God he was wrong on that score at least. Curious, though, that he left his weapon behind."

Joan thought this was curious indeed. She said nothing but she thought her husband's interpretation of events was problematical at best. Why hadn't Stubbs taken the weapon he had used in the three previous murders and that all evidence indicated he was yet to use in killing the Queen? There was something that didn't fit. She stooped to pick up the poniard, which Matthew had placed on the ground again, holding her revulsion in check for the slender blade was still red with Babcock's blood. She saw for herself the initials carved in the handle, crudely carved but distinct. *J.F.* James Fitzhugh. What other evidence was needed to tie the Chelmsford murder with that of the bearward and both to the murderous instincts of Gabriel Stubbs?

She noticed that the initials seemed freshly carved in the handle. The grooves were white and clean. She called this fact to Matthew's attention.

"The puppet master may have come by the blade only recently himself. Remember, Joan, he's but a week dead. What are you thinking?"

"Oh, an idle thought, husband, nothing more," she said, unsure of what she was thinking but sure that she was not about to reveal her suspicions to the present company.

At this moment Juliet Beauchamp announced that she had seen enough, and Pullyver offered to accompany her home.

Chapman said he would go too, but Matthew reminded both men that their aid was needed in identifying Stubbs. He felt sure that upon Grotwell's return yet another search would be organized. He stopped short of telling them why the apprehension of the young Puritan was so important.

"He'll kill us all," Chapman reflected gloomily. "We that never did him any harm at all."

Francis Crisp said that Ned Babcock was as good and honest a soul as ever lived and that he hoped to give Gabriel Stubbs adequate reward for his bloody work the first chance he got. He hoped that the others present felt likewise.

"We all mourn Ned's death," Pullyver said impatiently. "But these searches are really a matter for the sergeant and his men. We're citizens, not constables."

Grotwell now returned; with him were about a dozen men, some dressed in ordinary clothes and wearing the ragged expressions of men dragged from alehouses and brothels for the occasion. "He's gone to ground again, damn his soul," Grotwell said, telling the men at his back to remain outside the tent.

Matthew asked Grotwell if the Clerk and the Justice had been informed of the new murder. Grotwell said they had been informed and that Justice Baynard was to come presently to view the body. It was for this reason alone that it had not been removed from where it was found. Joan asked about Rose Dibble and was told she had been released from custody an hour earlier. Grotwell was obviously displeased by this development. He said the Justice had found nothing to charge her with, at least not at present. His expression suggested he thought the Justice's move a foolish one. He said the girl had probably returned to her employer's booth.

"That may be the worse for her," Joan said. "Pray the pig-woman does not lay the blame for the new atrocity at the girl's door, or we may still have murder in Smithfield."

Grotwell asked if Matthew would join them on their rounds of the fair since he knew Stubbs by sight. Matthew said that he would but first wanted to speak to the dead man's investors. He asked Pullyver what would happen to the bear garden now that Ned Babcock was dead.

"The rules of the partnership are clear on that point," the greengrocer said smugly, shifting to a lawyer's cant. "At either partner's demise, the said partnership is dissolved, terminated, held for nought. The investors may then come forward to secure what is rightfully theirs, which is precisely what Mr. Chapman and I intend to do. Samson, the bear garden, and all goods and appurtenances are at our disposal."

"But what of Mr. Babcock's daughter?" Joan interrupted to ask, looking at the quiet girl with sudden sympathy. "Will she be left without means?"

"Hardly," replied Pullyver, casting a proprietary glance in Juliet's direction. "She has consented to become my wife. After a decent interval, of course. She will be handsomely provided for, I assure you."

Pullyver smiled and seemed not to care that no flurry of congratulations was extended upon this announcement. Congratulations did not seem appropriate, given the circumstances, the bride-to-be's father sprawled in his gore not a dozen feet away and his killer on the rampage somewhere in the vicinity. Besides, no one seemed to like Pullyver, Joan thought. Not even the woman he was to marry.

At that moment Justice Baynard, resplendent in a new suit purchased for the occasion of the Queen's visit, stepped inside the tent, saw the bearward's body, and uttered an oath of unspeakable vulgarity.

While Matthew and Joan were at the Smithfield bear garden puzzling over the murder of Ned Babcock, Sir Robert Cecil sat at his desk in his fine house of timber and brick on the Strand, puffing on a pipe full of rich, dark tobacco that filled the air of the spacious chamber with a pale blue haze. Before him, unattended, lay a sheaf of papers. There was a letter from the Spanish ambassador complaining about the warlike attitude of certain English sea captains in the Caribbean. There was a recent edict of Parliament touching upon his own family fortunes (and therefore to be studied at length in a lawyerly way, with scrupulous concern for jots and tittles, commas and semicolons). There were also various memoranda and reports of Cecil's European operatives, his eyes and ears in foreign courts. All these documents came under the heading of pressing business, but neither they nor the pleasure of his pipe could distract him from his chief preoccupation: the Queen's visit to Bartholomew Fair and the savagery of Gabriel Stubbs. For but a few hours remained before he must act, and what was he to do?

He considered the alternatives and meditated upon strategies in that methodical way of his. It crossed his mind that he might lie, warn Elizabeth now, and in response to her criticism that she should have been informed before (oh, *much* before!), say that he had only just heard of Stubbs, his madness, his menace to the Royal Majesty of England. That would free Cecil from blame. Perhaps.

But Cecil was not disposed to lie. By nature he was a diplomat who handled administrative problems—to put the present emergency in a cold, objective light—with subtlety and imagination rather than falsehood. Besides, the lie would be easily detected. The Clerk of the Fair, Justice Baynard, the hulking grim-faced sergeant of the watch—all knew that Cecil *knew*. Knew that Cecil had known since St. Bartholomew Eve.

Matthew Stock's message had come to Cecil by the usual route. Once delivered by the host's boy, it had passed through a hierarchy of servants like a hot brand, facilitated in its travel by Cecil's precise and unequivocal instruction to his entire domestic establishment that anything addressed to him, marked "confidential" and "urgent," and by the hand of Matthew Stock of Chelmsford, be brought to him immediately, no matter the hour. And so the message had been handled and received, and it now lay with the other papers, on top of them all, read thrice over and therefore memorized already by Cecil.

*Treason* and *revenge*, Matthew Stock had written, the words standing out boldly. Neither had caused a frisson in this man Cecil—renowned for his dispassion—much less a mundane emotion like fear. Cecil was accustomed to violence of mind, tongue, and hand from his long sojourn in the corridors of power. Matthew Stock's message had thus only confirmed his intuition. So Royal Elizabeth was the madman's target after all. The Queen to be done in, stabbed to death, a royal sacrifice in the very place where Stubbs's Puritan martyrs had been burned for their heresies.

He might have known! Were they not all half-crazed, these sectarians? With their biblical injunctions, sanctified names, and fantastical interpretations and prophecies? With their sermons of three hours' length, their visions, their harangues and wrenchings of the sacred texts of Christendom to suit their mean-spirited ambitions for ecclesiastical power? He granted that some were tractable as subjects, harmless cranks content to assemble together to sing and pray. But there was the lunatic fringe too, who hated Elizabeth because she steered a middle course between the Scylla of Rome and the Charybdis of Geneva. Who spewed her from their mouths because she was neither hot nor cold, at least according to their own pernicious estimate. Who hated the Queen finally and most profoundly because she was a woman. A woman who did not stint to dress according to the world's idea of splendor, a woman who radiated magnificence and encouraged her own cult among courtiers and poets, who called her Cynthia and Diana and Gloriana. Heathen names all—a heathen queen of a heathen court. They hated her because she checked their mighty zeal—detestable word of Puritan cant—and because she was not above sending their saints to prison or exile, should their preaching offend.

He put out his pipe. His head was beginning to ache, perhaps from the tobacco, perhaps from the complexities of his dilemma. He read Matthew Stock's message again, despite the fact he already knew it by heart. He agreed that the slander of the Queen coupled with the threat implied in the Gospel verse was adequate evidence of murderous intent. It was the kind of thing that might be read at Stubbs's trial. If the lunatic were ever apprehended to have one.

He cast a cold eye on the clock. It was half past eight. He had been up and dressed since five, had taken nothing for breakfast. He decided he must have something in his stomach. He would not go to Whitehall fasting.

He could already hear his royal mistress's bitter complaint: "What, Robin, why had you not earlier warned me? Here I am already dressed, the coach at hand, the Lord Mayor of London and other notable citizens positively salivating at the prospect of my coming, and here you stand and tell me I must not come—not come to the fair—because a murderer is afoot and hankers to put a blade in my heart. Is there none among my court I can trust?"

The strident yet beloved voice faded in his imagination. He sighed and turned back to the edict of Parliament, the ambassador's letter, the reports of his spies—all crying out for his attention. But it was no use. He stared listlessly out the open window, the window that looked over the Thames flowing in its solemn majesty. The morning sun shone brightly on the gray-green waters. It was a fine August the twenty-fourth. St. Bartholomew's Day.

He called for his servant and ordered breakfast prepared and finer garments laid out. It would take about an hour to prepare himself. He would go to Whitehall and warn the Queen she must not come, and yet somewhere in the back of his mind he prayed that in the interval the murderer would be apprehended and all would be as before.

# · 21 ·

Joan encountered Rose Dibble by accident. The poor girl was wandering aimlessly through the fair, wearing an expression of hopelessness. When Joan greeted her, Rose flinched at her name. She explained that she had been searching for other employment. She was afraid to go back to Ursula's booth.

But Rose had had no luck. The crowd at Bartholomew Fair was larger than ever. Many had come especially to see the Queen and were already jockeying for positions of vantage along the route Her Majesty was to take. Banners and standards had been erected but hung limp in the still air. A scarlet carpet had been laid and everywhere scarlet-coated guards bearing the royal device could be seen, halberds high.

Matthew had gone off with Grotwell and the others to search anew for Stubbs. Joan had elected to look around for herself. For to her, the search seemed increasingly futile. Stubbs was obviously possessed of animal cunning. If he did not wish to be found, he would not be. It was as simple as that. But the poniard left behind, identifying itself so boldly as to just who had wielded it—that puzzled her. Why had Stubbs not taken it with him? Had he been surprised in the act and fled in confusion? That didn't seem likely either.

It had occurred to her that she might return to the wine seller's booth, where by light of day some evidence, overlooked by the sergeant and his men in the confusion of darkness, might be found. She asked Rose to keep her company, but the girl seemed reluctant.

"Oh, I dare not," she said.

"Come, it's broad daylight. We'll not be alone. See what a

multitude swirls about us. You don't expect Gabriel will be hiding there, do you?"

"No, but—"

"Come, Rose. Your company will be most welcome. Besides, you have nothing else to do."

"But I must dress—dress for the Queen," Rose said. The words spurted forth, as though she had only now remembered the honor conferred upon her of being one of the Smithfield virgins. "The Clerk of the Fair said I must be at the Close and all prepared by twelve o'clock."

"And so you shall," Joan said. "Besides, that is more than three hours off. Jack Talbot's booth is on your way. You'll lose no time by accompanying me. You can well spare the hour."

By day, Jack Talbot's booth seemed more desolate and forsaken than ever in its premature dismantlement since the neighboring booths—both of herb and spice merchants—were doing a steady business. Passersby looked curiously at the wine seller's booth and then went on. Perhaps some had heard about the murder, and if so would shun the place as unlucky or, worse, haunted. But most had not heard, were strangers to the place like Joan, and the abandoned booth with its ruined frontsides aroused only a mild curiosity as to the whereabouts of its owner and the cause of its ruin.

Joan stepped confidently over the rubble. "Come, don't be afraid. Nothing will hurt you here, not now, at least," Joan said, leading Rose by the hand.

They went inside. Everything was as Joan remembered from the night before. The great mess Grotwell and his cohorts had made in trampling about searching for the fugitive was still there, untouched. Joan stepped over the casks and boxes, inhaling the lingering scent of malmsey, more faint now than the night before, when the same scent had the strength of a wine-bibber's breath with two gallon or more of the stuff in his belly. Rose stood quietly while Joan looked around. She set some of the casks upright to have a better view, kicked at the matted straw that covered the floor. Then she saw the poniard. She reached down to pick it up. Rose gasped behind her. "Why, it's Gabriel's knife."

Joan looked at the weapon in her hand, unsheathed it. Its slender blade looked deadly. It was not identical to the one found in Ned Babcock's back, but it was somewhat similar. The haft bore no marks indicating who its owner might be, and Joan wondered if Rose could be mistaken.

But Rose insisted she was not. "It's his, it's his," she cried tearfully. "He's left it behind. But it proves I never lied to the sergeant. He was here. I spoke with him an hour or more. He showed me the knife in your hand, Mrs. Stock. I was so fearful of it he laid it aside. The blade he drew from his shirt was that one. I swear before God, it's true."

Joan searched the girl's face and found nothing but the honest truth in her expression. So this *was* Stubbs's weapon. Had the young Puritan two such blades? Or was the treacherous instrument found in Ned Babcock's back someone else's? Someone who wanted to make it appear Stubbs was the killer?

Joan was considering this intriguing idea when her eye fell on a patch of straw that seemed not only trampled but moist. Still clutching the hasp of the poniard, she knelt down to examine the straw. She had earlier supposed a great quantity of wine must have been spilled during the invasion of the booth and now realized that there were no broken casks in sight. Two large butts in the back parts were upright and apparently unopened. Now this moist straw, confirming that a spillage had occurred the night before, hence the overpowering odor of malmsey. She traced the dimension of the spillage until she came to the upright butts. She knocked on the first of the two and heard the dull thud indicating its fullness. But the second gave a different report: the knock was hollow.

At that moment Joan's investigation was interrupted by the sound of creaking cart wheels outside the booth and the shouts of men's voices calling out to pedestrians to make way for the cart and its load. She heard the rough tread of workmen's boots and a moment after two shabbily dressed men entered and, without asking who Joan and Rose might be, announced that they had come to remove the wine seller's stock, for the man himself was dead by report and the goods were to be put into storage until it could be determined if there were any heirs or outstanding claims. One of the men, a red-faced, muscular type with shirt sleeves rolled up to the elbows, asked Joan's permission to proceed with the work. He said he had come on the orders of the Clerk of the Fair.

"Mr. Rathbone?"

"The very same, ma'am," said the shirt-sleeved man. He nodded to his companion, who was shorter, had thick, curly hair, and wore a dirty jerkin.

"Do as you will," Joan said.

The women stepped aside as the men proceeded with their task, hefting the casks on their shoulders as though they weighed nothing at all and marching forth into the lane to load the same onto the cart, which Joan could see was already piled high with gear of every sort. While the men worked, they commented on the wine seller's inventory, which they obviously envied. They seemed, however, to be honest men, not prone to make a simple job into an occasion for larceny. They saved the malmsey butts for last. Joan asked them what they intended to do with them. The butts were large and would hardly fit upon the cart unless everything were taken off and restowed.

The taller of the men looked puzzled; he had clearly not considered the difficulty Joan now called to his attention. The two men briefly discussed what was to be done. "Ay, they're both as heavy as rock," said the shorter man, looking at the butts and shaking his head. "We shall have to come back for t'other ones," said the taller man, with a sweaty smile of satisfaction that a difficult problem had been solved after all.

Joan regarded the wine butts. Heavy, were they? The both of them? And yet one, she now suddenly remembered, had sounded hollow.

"I would like to see inside that one butt," she said to the taller of the men, who seemed to be chief.

"Why, mistress, will you have a drink? That's a mighty thirst, I warrant," said the short man.

The tall man laughed at the thought. He wiped his mouth and said he was thirsty too. But Joan quelled his merriment with a stern regard.

"I only wish to look inside," she said icily. "Not a drop shall be wasted or drunk, I swear it. I think some of the wine spilled in the booth yesternight, for see how the straw all about is still moist and sticky too. What, will you store spoiled wine, if that's the case, or go to the trouble of hauling an empty or half-filled wine butt to some warehouse?"

The tall man stroked his grizzled chin thoughtfully. He cast an appreciative eye on the slender form of Rose Dibble. The girl was as still as a mouse. "Well," he drawled, "I suppose it will do no good to store ruined malmsey or half-filled butts. I'd be glad too to avoid another trip to Smithfield in this crowd." He looked at the coins Joan had drawn from her purse and that she now held out as an added inducement. "If, on t'other hand, the malmsey is good, sweet, and ample, it could hardly hurt to sample a drop."

"Not a bad suggestion," Joan said, smiling.

The man took the coins and stuffed them in his pocket. "Come, Tom. We'll take the good woman's money for our labors, which is in addition to that we contracted for with the Clerk. Since the laborer is worth the hire, our labor is saved. If the malmsey's good, we'll all be the sounder men for it, for I am near dying of thirst in this weather."

The man called Tom went to fetch a mallet and pry bar from a toolbox in the cart and soon returned, grinning mischievously. He fit the bar in place and struck all around with the mallet until the lid was loose, then he lifted it off. He, Joan, and the tall man all peered inside at the same time.

"Jesus Christ our Lord!" exclaimed the tall man, blinking with amazement.

Aware that behind her Rose was moving forward to join them in inspecting the butt's contents, Joan turned quickly and blocked the girl's vision. She took Rose's shoulders and in a firm, commanding voice, told her to go fetch her husband. "He's somewhere in the fair. With the sergeant and his men. Do try to find him. Bring him here at once."

Confused by Joan's sudden and unaccountable severity of manner and frustrated in her effort to see inside the butt, Rose said that she would go and find Joan's husband. "But what if he will not come, Mrs. Stock? Or cannot come this instant?"

"Tell him he *must*," Joan said. "Tell him I am sick unto death or besieged by thieves. Make up an emergency if you have to. Tell him anything, but bring him here straightway."

Joan watched the girl go off and then turned to the men, who were still staring into the butt.

"Shall we pull the fellow out?" asked Tom, his face as white as a sheet.

"No hurry," said his taller companion before Joan could answer the question herself. "He's as dead as a drowned cat."

Joan did not approach the horrid wine butt for another peek at its appalling contents. Her one glimpse would become a permanent fixture in her imagination, she was sure. Her suspicions had been confirmed. She now understood why the malmsey had been spilled and when. She also knew that Gabriel Stubbs could not have killed Ned Babcock.

# · 22 ·

Later that morning about a dozen persons had gathered in
the great chamber of the Hand and Shears in response to Matthew's summons. This was the room, low-ceilinged and conveniently furnished with benches and stools, that was used during
the days of the fair for the famous Court of Pie-Powders at
which Justice Baynard normally presided. But the Justice, who
was one of the dozen in the chamber, was not holding court at
the moment. The business at hand was not false weights, bad
bread, or some other minor infraction, but murder—murder
not wrought in passion or desperation or madness but in the
cold detachment of reason.

Matthew had chosen the chamber because of its privacy, its
relative quiet from the hubbub of the fair, and its stout oak
door, which could be secured from inside as well as out by lock
and key.

Present also in the room were the other principals in the
Stubbs's matter—Francis Crisp, Ralph Chapman, John
Pullyver, and Juliet Beauchamp. With them were Rose, Ursula,
the pig-woman, and Esmera, the fortune-teller, who had cast
off her usual exotic apparel in favor of a simple plain gown that
made her appear, except for her wine-dark coloring and height,
no more sinister than any other London woman of her age on
holiday in Smithfield. Still others present included the Clerk of
the Fair and Grotwell and two of his men. The sergeant was
sitting in the front of the room next to Francis Crisp. His men
were standing by the door keeping a watchful eye on the assembly.

All of these, most certainly the women among them, had
expressed some bewilderment at the occasion and urgency of

Matthew's summons. But none had refused to come, for Matthew had made it known that he bore Cecil's commission.

Whereupon Grotwell and his men had gone forth through every lane and back street in the neighborhood, rounding up such persons as Matthew had designated and fetching them to the appointed place, informing each in the process that any denial, excuse, or lingering would be regarded as a transgression with grievous consequences. And in that spirit they had come, bewildered, curious, but under penalty of law, and now sat submissively waiting what they were to hear. They voiced no protest when Matthew ordered Grotwell to lock the door behind the lot of them and deliver unto him the key.

Joan found a seat with the others on the hard benches. The persistent rumble of carts and other traffic, the cries of hawkers, and the occasional beat of drums or ringing of bells outside in the street soon faded from her awareness as she focused her attention on Matthew, who had taken his place in the front of the room and now stood, hands on hips in an attitude of authority, facing his little audience like a player on the stage about ready to deliver a soliloquy of some pith and moment.

Matthew began with an announcement, delivered in his typically straightforward manner and without emotion, as though the news touched upon no one present in any meaningful way. He told them Gabriel Stubbs had been found, drowned in a malmsey butt in the very booth in which he had taken refuge the night before.

For a moment there was a silence like the intake of a breath before a sneeze, then an explosion of voices expressing wonder and approval. Wonder that Stubbs was dead, approval that Matthew, or the Justice, or perhaps even the sergeant had somehow brought it about. Those, like Chapman and Pullyver, who had feared for their lives, now sighed for relief and congratulated each other on their escape from danger. Francis Crisp looked pleased that his partner's death had been avenged, and Ursula was as unable to contain her triumph as the bench she sat on was inadequate as a surface for her immense buttocks. She rose to her feet and shook her fist at the floor, booming, "Good riddance to the miserable cur! May he burn in hell."

Esmera sat quiet and expressionless, and Juliet looked grieved as she always did, although it was not clear to Joan, who studied the reactions of the group closely, for whom her grief was intended. Rose, however, seemed truly devastated by the news.

When the group had regained its composure, Pullyver said, "This is very good news indeed, Mr. Stock, but is it for this we have been summoned?"

Matthew said, "No, sir, it is not. Stubbs's death might well have been announced otherwise than I have done it. Fact is, sir, we are here to determine its cause."

"The cause!" exclaimed several voices at once, including Chapman's, who added, "Does it make any difference? It is a godsend to us all, and he who did it may have my thanks and more." Chapman looked about the room as though the perpetrator of the deed would presently raise his hand to receive the applause of them all, but no one rose to claim responsibility for Stubbs's death.

"He did deserve it," said Juliet in a low, steady voice so full of hatred that it sent chills up and down Joan's spine. "For what he did to my father, and to the others."

"And what he might yet have done, Mr. Stock," agreed Justice Baynard. "But tell us, pray, if there is some further mystery requiring light here. Within two hours' time the Queen and her retinue arrive, and Master Clerk and I must be on hand to meet her."

Matthew assured them that his remarks would be brief. He began to pace to and fro in the front of the chamber while he talked. "You have been called here because the true image of these murders wants one or two additional strokes before the likeness is perfect. I beg your patience. Within the hour our business will be concluded to everyone's satisfaction. Except perhaps for one among us. That person will *not* be satisfied."

Matthew stopped in his pacing and studied his audience.

Joan observed that while no one queried Matthew's last cryptic remark, almost every face showed that the remark had been heard, and its promise of some startling revelation taken note of. Bewildered and suspicious glances were exchanged. Ursula grumbled beneath her breath, and an air of nervous expectation now replaced celebration as the dominant mood.

"This Gabriel Stubbs who is now dead," Matthew continued in the same steady voice, "was, as you know, infected in the brain by a religious melancholy of such sort that it led at last to murder and treason. His madness was directed toward this fair itself, which he conceived as Babylon, and even to Her Majesty's own person, for in his lunacy he imagined her the Queen of that wicked city. He murdered a puppet master on the road near Chelmsford within the week, then came here and did likewise to Simon Plover and the wine seller, Jack Talbot, for reasons we may never fathom. Three victims, in sum—victims of Gabriel Stubbs and his madness!"

"You count wrongly, Mr. Stock. Surely you have forgotten my partner, Ned Babcock!" exclaimed Francis Crisp, rising to his feet.

"Yes, Mr. Stock, the lunatic must be given credit for four victims, not three," said the Justice.

"My arithmetic is quite perfect," Matthew replied calmly. "I didn't forget Ned Babcock. The truth is that Gabriel Stubbs did not murder him. He could not have. Stubbs, you see, was by then already dead."

"But his knife was found in my father's back," protested Juliet, her wonted bitterness replaced by an expression of total confusion.

"And his face marked with the claw," added Pullyver. "What can be more certain proof?"

"The weapon used was not Gabriel's, although very like his. The murder was done by someone who wanted it to appear as though Stubbs had done it. Someone who thought that in a chain of beastly crimes, a fourth would not be looked into. That someone stands among you at this moment."

At this there was a clamor of protest, exclamations of surprise, and professions of innocence all around the room, but no one looked prepared to leave now, and even Esmera's inscrutable composure had been replaced by an expression verging on curiosity. Matthew waited for the uproar to die down before proceeding.

"I have brought you here to help me determine who that *someone* may be," Matthew said.

"Is it not possible that Stubbs was killed *after* he had killed the bearward?" the Justice asked.

"That is not possible," said Matthew. "Stubbs was alive when Rose Dibble left him in the wine seller's booth. She declares that to have been about the time the sun set. Eight o'clock in this season. It was some two hours afterward that Sergeant Grotwell and his men surrounded the booth and took it, not finding Stubbs inside. We all supposed that he had escaped. In fact, he had not. He was killed between the hours of eight and ten. First bludgeoned, then drowned. In a malmsey butt, where his body was concealed."

"But how can you be sure the body wasn't put there later than ten?" Pullyver asked.

"My wife entered the booth shortly after it had been stormed. At that time she noticed a strong odor of malmsey."

"I assumed at the time it had been spilled in the scuffle," Joan said.

"Why, I noticed the same odor," declared one of the sergeant's men.

"And I," said Grotwell, "but thought nothing of it. It *was* a wine booth. How else should it smell but of wine?"

"But Rose swears that no wine had been spilled when she was there with Stubbs," Matthew continued, "and since the odor was strong by ten o'clock, it must have been between those hours that Stubbs was killed. Pushing the body into the butt displaced most of the contents."

"I returned to the booth this morning," Joan added. "The

odor was still detectable. But much weaker. Stubbs was killed before ten o'clock."

"So someone did what needed to be done," remarked Francis Crisp, curtly. "What does it matter when he was killed? The Crown is saved the expense of a hanging."

"It matters, friend Francis," Matthew replied, "because whoever killed Gabriel killed Ned Babcock too."

"Pray tell us who the person is, Mr. Stock," asked the Clerk of the Fair somewhat impatiently. "It is nigh unto eleven now."

Matthew ignored the Clerk's remark and went on in his same unhurried pace. "Almost surely one of us who was searching for Stubbs last night found him, killed him, and then kept his death a secret from the rest of us. We should never have known of Stubbs's death at all had it not been that Master Clerk here ordered the removal of Jack Talbot's goods and my wife's suspicions caused the malmsey butt to be opened."

"I gave no such order for removal," protested the Clerk hotly.

"I thought not. The laborers said that they had such an order and were paid in advance for their work. When I asked them to describe the man who had paid them, they grew fearful and confessed that it was no man at all, but a great tun of female flesh."

At this description all eyes were turned to Ursula, who was sweating furiously and cursing beneath her breath. She glared at the Clerk first and then took in the whole room in one sweeping gaze of hostility and contempt.

"Speak, woman. Did you murder Gabriel Stubbs?" the Justice demanded, rising to his feet and walking toward Ursula, his finger pointing at her accusingly.

"I heard her swear to rip out Stubbs's heart on the account of Jack Talbot, who was her friend," said Grotwell.

"Ay, I swore," Ursula said without regret. "I would swear a second time and a third, though I die for swearing it. But I did not kill the imp of Satan. Drowned in malmsey? Why, that's too good for the scum. I would have left his body in the filth of the lane, yea, and bragged about it too. Everyone at Smithfield would have known how Ursula takes her vengeance."

"If you did not murder Stubbs, then why order the men to remove the wine butt in which the body was concealed?" asked the Justice.

Ursula paused before answering, as though deciding whether the question—or indeed any question put to her by the present company—was worth an answer. But slowly it seemed to dawn on her that she was in serious trouble and that no one present either regretted the fact she was charged or was likely to support her innocence. She sighed heavily and said, "The truth was I wanted Jack's goods, the wine. He owed me money, and I had a reasonable claim upon his property. True it is that I paid the louts to carry away Jack's gear. I knew of no bodies in the malmsey butt. What a shame it is for a rat to spoil good wine. I say still whoever did it did God a service, ay, and his country too, and needs a reward, not punishment. Would that I could lay claim to such a reward, my masters."

"The hussy is undoubtedly lying," declared Pullyver. "She killed Stubbs as she threatened and wished to dispose of the evidence."

Others in the room, including the sergeant and his men, echoed the charge, and Grotwell was in the process of ordering the officers to lay hands upon Ursula when Matthew told him to wait. An arrest for murder was premature, he said. "The matter stands that the wine seller's goods were not yours to remove," he said to Ursula. "You used the Clerk's name falsely to cover common theft, and you shall be punished for that. Take her away, sergeant."

Grotwell shrugged and made a face suggesting he was as confused as any other person in the room. One of the officers conducted Ursula out, having first secured the key from Matthew. For once, Ursula did not protest. Relieved to have avoided the more serious charge, she seemed content with the lesser one.

"Is this wisely done, Mr. Stock?" Justice Baynard now asked, his voice heavy with concern. "Given the evidence against the woman, she seems most likely to have taken her vengeance on Stubbs, then stuffed him in the malmsey butt until she could have both butt and boy carried off privately."

Matthew said, "She's no paragon of virtue, that's God's truth. Yet no murderer either. I've made some inquiries which I think Master Clerk will confirm. The sum is that our good Ursula of the pig booth has played such tricks before. Her reputation is fouler than a French jakes. Yet, I repeat, she's no murderer. If she had killed Stubbs, it would have been as she said—out in the open and to the benefit of her reputation as the reigning termagant of Smithfield. No, I have learned that Jack Talbot did owe her a good deal of money. You see, Ursula is wealthier than she appears. Her business is not confined to bad ale and roast pig."

"She's a notorious pimp," added the Clerk with a derisive laugh. "She sells as much punk as pig. She also does a ready business as a moneylender—and at usurious rates! It is likely the wine seller's stock in trade was security for some debt of his. Him dead, she moved quickly to secure what was hers."

"If not Ursula, then who?" Juliet inquired. "Who killed my father?"

"A question I shall presently answer," said Matthew, resuming his pacing. "If as it now appears Stubbs was found and killed before ten o'clock, then it must have been done by one of those searching for him. Only they knew he was a fugitive. Only they knew the method of his madness and were thus able to counterfeit it later. What must have happened was this: someone took him by surprise in is hiding place, struck him upon the head, then drowned him, leaving the body concealed until it could be safely removed."

The sergeant interrupted to say he was very sorry he had overlooked the malmsey butt. "God's truth it is, masters. I thought it contained nothing worse than fifty gallons of wine."

Pullyver said he thought it was a wonder that such a dangerous fugitive had been taken so easily.

"No great wonder," Matthew replied. He nodded in Rose's direction. She seemed still too shocked by the fact and manner of Stubbs's death to follow what had since transpired in the room and sat as if in a trance, her hands limp in her lap and her eyes downcast.

"Rose had left to determine the state of things and he expected her return at any time," Matthew said. "Hearing something astir in the outer booth, he must have supposed it was she returning. He had put his weapon aside earlier. Perhaps he had forgotten he was unarmed. Comes the intruder into the booth and whack! Stubbs is knocked senseless before he is aware. Within minutes he is dead. Drowned. All this could have happened without anyone observing or hearing it, so great was the clamor in the street. Who pays attention to a single cry—if there was time for that? Or the whack of a club or staff? The interior was a private place, although but inches from a boisterous multitude. Afterward the murderer, for such he was, thought quickly. Planned a new murder."

For a moment there was silence in the room, and in that silence Joan studied the intent expressions of those around her. It was as if only now the full significance of her husband's words impressed itself upon them. Someone among them was a murderer.

The noise from the street entered her consciousness but vanished again when Pullyver broke the silence.

"Well, Mr. Stock, it wasn't I who did it."

"Nor I," declared Francis Crisp, a hard edge to his voice. "Although it's God's truth that I would have done it if I could."

"Nor I," said Chapman, his face pale and glistening.

The sergeant and his men also declared they knew nothing of whackings or wine butts. The search of the wine seller's booth, the sergeant protested, had been done in pitch darkness. He had never thought to look in the wine butt for he expected to find the mad Puritan alive, not drowned, and a full wine butt is a bad place for a live man to hide, he said.

Matthew went on, "Had it not been for Ned Babcock's

murder we might never have known *who* killed the boy. Or *why*," Matthew explained when the various protestations of innocence ceased. "In broad daylight I've searched the booth thoroughly. Stubbs's slayer left no tracks there, save Stubbs's true knife, which my wife discovered partially concealed in the straw."

Matthew paused to show his audience the poniard with the bone shaft. He held it high, then placed it before him on the table and continued. "Only Gabriel Stubbs can tell us who his attacker was, and he is silent now. Yet there is one clue. His killer must have been someone acquainted with the method of his own murders. How else know to deface the body, as was done, or drag it inside the cage for the bear to feed upon. Those of us who knew these things kept them between ourselves. The killer of Stubbs therefore must have been one of us. It stands to reason. But it was also someone who wanted Ned Babcock dead."

At this, Esmera, who until now had remained a silent observer of the proceedings, begged to be excused. "I never knew this bearward of whom you speak, or the other victims. I know nothing of these murders."

"Not know?" Matthew exclaimed sarcastically. "I'm very much surprised at your ignorance. Ignorance in one who makes her living by knowing all and seeing it too? Why, what pains you took to warn my wife of the danger she and I stood in— from beasts and knife-wielding murderers. Not know indeed! Sergeant, look to this woman well, for I have not finished with her yet."

Joan blushed at this reference to her own involvement with Esmera but noticed that Pullyver now appeared less composed than before. Juliet too looked nervous.

Matthew went on. "Ned's death has resulted in the dissolution of his partnership with Francis Crisp, the end of what might have been a profitable enterprise. I ask myself, which among you would have desired such an outcome and who therefore would have motive to kill him?"

There were some protests from Pullyver and Chapman, but Matthew dismissed them with a wave of his hand and went on. "I am sorry to say that almost too many of you had such a motive, although in most it was not sufficiently strong—or the result of death brought too much trouble to yourself. Juliet Beauchamp, I begin with you."

"What?" she declared, turning pale and clinging to Pullyver for support. "How can you say I ever wanted my father dead!"

"Easily," Matthew answered, undismayed by the young woman's withering scorn. "You blamed your father for your husband's death. You hated the business he was in, and wished to see it dissolved and your father punished for his lack of remorse."

"He *was* to blame, to blame!" Juliet shouted hysterically, still clinging to Pullyver, as though drawing the strength for her hysteria from his wiry frame.

"I neither excuse nor extenuate his responsibility for your husband's death," Matthew said after Juliet stopped shouting. "I only declare that you had motive, even as you admitted. You deeply resented your father. You wished to see him fail in his business. You held him accountable for your husband's death."

Juliet now seemed more frightened than enraged at Matthew. She stared around her, a pitiful, shaking figure in black, as though seeking a character witness among the present company. Then she said, "You said the murderer also killed Stubbs. Sirs, how could I have done such a thing, being the small woman that I am—hoisted a hale and hearty fellow of twice my weight into a malmsey butt? And how, even with my hatred, have treated my father as he was treated, bludgeoned, stabbed, cruelly scarred?"

For a painful interval her question was answered only by a perplexed silence, as though each one in the room was searching his own conscience to determine the malignity of his motives. Meanwhile Juliet's expression of defiance changed. Panic flickered in her eyes and her lower lip began to tremble. With a loud sob, she hid her face in her hands.

The gesture, pathetic as it was even in so unlikable a person, moved Joan to pity. Pullyver also was moved. He said, "Surely Mrs. Beauchamp speaks reasonably. What daughter could so detest her father? You've set your mousetrap next door to the cat in this instance, Constable Stock. Juliet is too small a woman to heft the likes of Stubbs, especially if he were unconscious and dead weight. She's also too good a woman to murder her father."

Chapman agreed, and Justice Baynard said he thought it a very unlikely thing indeed that Juliet Beauchamp murdered either her father or Gabriel Stubbs. As for Juliet, hearing Pullyver's words, she took her hands from her face and looked at him gratefully.

"Well, I'm inclined to agree with you," Matthew said after a moment's thought. "Unfortunately the same cannot be said for you, Mr. Pullyver."

"What?" protested the greengrocer, flushed of face, trembling with indignation. "How dare you accuse me."

"I dare very easily, sir," Matthew said, frowning. "You did not hate Ned Babcock, but you happily saw him out of business. Not only for such reasons as your future wife may have, but a desire to reap more than you deserved from your investment."

"What do you mean, *more than I deserved?*"

"What I have said," Matthew returned sharply, leveling a steady gaze at the man. "I have examined Ned's records. For all his faults, he was a scrupulous record keeper. It's all in his ledger. His income, his outgo, a summary of his debts. How much he owed to each of you. Also the terms of his agreement for repaying his debt. It's all spelled out."

"As it should be," Pullyver snapped. "Record-keeping's no crime. I was the principal investor. The terms were easy, and he was in a fair way of repaying. On schedule, I might add."

"Indeed, on schedule," Matthew said. "Bearbaiting is a profitable business, as the crowd that flocked to see it may attest. Too profitable for it to remain in the hands of Babcock."

"What do you mean?"

"The terms of your agreement are made plain in your contract with him, a copy of which I found among his papers."

"But as you say, he was in a good way of paying the debt," interjected Chapman. "We would have had our money."

"Yes, but you wanted more than your share," Matthew said sternly. "If the partnership was dissolved—as it might be by agreement of the operators, Babcock and Crisp—then the debt was due and payable. Babcock would have paid off eventually, but you wanted to see the enterprise collapse so you could have the benefit of future profits as sole owner and proprietor."

"*I* never had any such intent," Chapman said, looking askance at the greengrocer, as though wishing to avoid association with him.

Juliet too seemed confused by Matthew's accusations. She said to Pullyver, "I thought it was for me that you endeavored to persuade my father to give over the baiting."

"There's no proof of any of this," said Pullyver.

"Oh, there is proof, sir," replied Matthew calmly. He turned to where the fortune-teller stood and beckoned her to approach. "You have something to add here, don't you?"

Esmera seemed at first disposed to say nothing, then she apparently reconsidered. "He paid me," she said, pointing to the greengrocer, "to warn your wife of great danger to her and you."

Joan was amazed at this revelation, but she realized that Esmera's confession suddenly explained a great deal—the fortune-teller's strange insistence, Pullyver's appearance at her tent, the conspiracy between him and Juliet Beauchamp that she had somehow *felt* without being able to reason it through.

"When my wife first told me of Esmera's warning, I thought it merely a trick to have money of her," Matthew said. "But when the warnings became more insistent and touched upon the both of us, I suspected a more sinister motive. Joan saw Pullyver at Esmera's tent. You, sir, paid her as she claims, to warn us off."

Pullyver laughed derisively. "Now why should I do that, Mr.

Stock? I don't care whether you stay in Smithfield or leave. It's all one to me."

"It's not all one, if our presence strengthened Ned's intent not to dissolve his partnership. You made capital of his fears that Samson would be destroyed and suggested he quit. You pressed the point upon him just last night. I heard you. This young woman," Matthew said, indicating Juliet, "thought it was for her sake you pressed her father, but it was your own greed. When Joan and I arrived in Smithfield and you became aware that we might give some support to Ned's resolve, you decided to frighten us off with the aid of Esmera, your associate."

"He's no associate of mine!" Esmera declared, glaring at the greengrocer.

For a moment all was still in the room while Pullyver bit his lip and glowered all around him. But soon it was evident that the case against him was too strong. "Very well," he said, "I confess that I paid the woman. She gulled a friend of mine. I threatened her with arrest if she did not do as I told her. I meant no harm, however, to Ned Babcock. My sole purpose was to get him to sell out. The business was worth more than he was getting for it. Why, the bearwards of Southwark make a fortune, and here he was, content to show Samson at fairs, refusing to blindfold him out of some overdelicate concern for the bear's dignity. As if animals possessed any such quality."

"But how did you know I consulted Esmera?" Joan interrupted to ask.

"I saw you speak with her the first day of your visit. I remembered your face when we met in the inn that night. I meant you no harm, Mrs. Stock. I only wanted the partnership dissolved. I didn't kill Ned Babcock either, or the boy!"

"We'll see," said Matthew. "You were one of the search party last night; you saw the wine seller's body and therefore knew Stubbs's way of marking his victims."

"But Mr. Chapman was constantly in my company," Pullyver said.

"That's true, Mr. Stock," answered the scrivner. "He was

never out of my sight. We went directly from the tent to the patrol and spent a long evening walking the fair looking for Stubbs. We were together too when at ten o'clock the booth was assaulted by the sergeant and his men."

"And afterward?" Matthew asked the greengrocer.

"Afterward?"

"After the assault on the wine seller's booth. I remember you lingered to discuss business for some time. Then when we bid good-night, where did you go?"

"I went home. To my lodgings."

"And who can serve as witness that you arrived there and remained there during the night?"

"My servant can."

"A servant!" Grotwell laughed. "A fine witness indeed. Servants say what their masters will."

"And you went out again?" asked Matthew.

"At six o'clock in the morning or thereabouts. Chapman came by for me."

"Did he? What hour was that, Mr. Chapman?"

Chapman thought. "It must have been nearly seven o'clock. I heard Paul's toll as I knocked at his door. We were to go to the fair to see the morning baiting."

"In what condition did you find Mr. Pullyver?"

"Condition?"

"Was he dressed and prepared to go with you or no?"

"He was still in his nightshirt," Chapman said. "He looked as though he had just awakened from sleep."

"And since that early hour you never left his side?"

"I waited while he dressed," said Chapman. "We went directly to Smithfield, breakfasted at a booth, and then came to the bear garden, where we learned Mr. Babcock had been murdered."

"What was to prevent Mr. Pullyver from returning to Smithfield under cover of darkness, killing the bearward, and then making fast home to his bed?" asked Justice Baynard, regarding the greengrocer suspiciously.

The Justice's tone seemed quite sufficient for the sergeant, who moved forward as though to seize Pullyver. Matthew ordered him to stop. It was still too soon to talk of charges and arrests, he said. "Besides, Ned Babcock wasn't killed in his sleep, as you all suppose. He was quite awake when he died, already dressed and about his work. If Mr. Chapman tells truly, Mr. Pullyver could not have killed the bearward and therefore did not kill Stubbs either."

"How so, Mr. Stock?" Justice Baynard asked in bewilderment. "Babcock was found in his sleeping garment."

"He was so dressed *after* he was killed; the murderer wanted it to appear that he had died during the night and not in the morning, say, about seven o'clock. Not long before his body was discovered by Francis Crisp."

# · 23 ·

"How can it be that you know exactly *when* my father was murdered?" asked Juliet, her voice rich in incredulity. She had recovered now from her earlier distress and seemed as caught up as the others in Matthew's unfolding disclosure.

"If my wife had not undermined my confidence that Stubbs was the murderer by noting the incongruity of his leaving his weapon behind," Matthew said, "I would never have thought of it myself." He paused and cast an appreciative glance at Joan. She smiled back, and Matthew proceeded, turning his attention again to the dead man's daughter. "Two things puzzled me about your father's death. The first, that Samson had not molested the body." He paused again. Juliet had winced at the phrase; the thought was dreadful. "The second, that the sleeping gown appeared to have been put on him after his death."

Matthew raised his hand to allay the inevitable questions from Juliet, Pullyver, and Crisp on this point and immediately explained. "Even a tame beast, a cat or dog, has been known to gnaw upon his dead master's corpse. According to the cruelty of their nature. But here, wonder of wonders, we are to think that Ned Babcock lay dead in a bloody nightshirt half the night, in the same cage with Samson—a creature, I remind you, practiced in the eating of human flesh—who did nothing more than contemplate his corpse. It's a thing hardly to be credited."

"What do you make of it, Mr. Stock?" asked Justice Baynard.

"Why, sir, I make of it that the bear had either a marvelous respect for the dead or a full stomach."

"A full stomach!" exclaimed Francis Crisp, concerned deeply about anything touching upon his bear.

"What time was the bear normally fed of a morning?" asked Matthew.

"At dawn or shortly thereafter. Samson is very punctual about eating," said Crisp, with pride. "Why, a man can set his clock by the rumble in his stomach. At dawn, Mr. Stock, or very shortly thereafter—or he growls and claws at his cage fiercely."

"There you have it," said Matthew. "Samson didn't touch Ned Babcock because he had already eaten. Babcock was therefore killed after he had fed Samson—at six o'clock or thereabouts, surely no earlier."

"But what if he *had* fed the bear earlier?" suggested Pullyver, still skeptical but obviously relieved that the finger of suspicion had been directed elsewhere.

"Not impossible," said Matthew. "But highly unlikely, given the habits of bear and his master."

"But what about his sleeping garb?" asked Juliet.

"Which brings me to my second point," Matthew said. "We all saw to our sorrow the condition of Ned Babcock's body. The garment he wore was soaked in his blood and yet even I did not notice at first that there were no puncture holes in his shirt. After Stubbs's death was discovered and he ruled out as murderer of Ned Babcock, I had the bloody shirt Ned was wearing fetched. A wondrous weapon it is that makes no holes in cloth—or cloth that repairs itself. I searched Samson's tent again and found Ned's shoes and hose and other coverings for his lower body upon the pallet. But where, I asked, were his lace-fringed shirt and doublet? These were not to be found in the tent. And why? Because he had been wearing the same when he died and the murderer was careful enough in his duties to carry the bloody evidence off and dispose of it. It was a serious error on the murderer's part to forget about the puncture holes. Yet murderers are not always as clever as they think themselves."

"I am more than a little confused by all this reasoning, Mr. Stock," said Chapman. "What exactly is it you're telling us?"

"I'm telling you that Babcock was killed in the early morning, after Ned was dressed and had fed Samson. Not long before Francis Crisp walked in and found his partner's abused body."

"This is truly a wonder, Mr. Stock," said Justice Baynard, who now turned his attention to Francis Crisp. "Am I mistaken in thinking that the finger of suspicion now points to Francis Crisp?"

"At me!" declared Crisp, taken by surprise at the accusation, for he seemed still in a deep contemplation of what Matthew had earlier said about the bear's feeding. He quivered a little and spoke haltingly. "I never . . . killed him. He was dead when I came this morning to the pit. I loved the man like a brother. Oh, I never would have raised a finger against Ned Babcock, no, not on my life."

The much frightened bearward now looked appealingly at Babcock's daughter, but the young woman's expression showed no sign that she had taken the Justice's accusation seriously.

"I believe you, Francis," said Matthew, walking over to him and placing a calming hand on his shoulder. "Whoever killed Ned Babcock knew something of the need to provide himself with an alibi, perhaps, or to place the death as early as possible should the body of Stubbs be discovered before he could dispose of it himself. But he did not know much of the eating habits of bears. As Stubbs did, or as you, Francis, do. No, Francis would not have made this mistake," said Matthew, turning his attention back to the audience as a whole and away from the still nervous bearward. "Besides, Ned's death meant the partnership was dissolved, and all debts due and payable. I doubt Francis wanted *that*."

Crisp looked up at Matthew gratefully and said that he surely did not.

"If not Pullyver or Crisp, then who?" Justice Baynard wanted to know, obviously nettled at having been so easily proved wrong. "The time is short. Can we not come more expeditiously to the conclusion of this business?"

"I grant this inquiry is taking time," Matthew answered mildly, ignoring the implied rebuke. "But the time is well spent. We are ever learning, and that is to the good. Consider

· 214 ·

how terrible a thing it is that an innocent man be accused—why, it's as bad as if the guilty were to go free."

Now Matthew turned to the sergeant, who had been standing all this time following the proceedings with considerable interest, but who was obviously surprised to find himself addressed.

"Mr. Grotwell, when you formed your party to search for Stubbs, which of your fellows of the watch went singly on his mission?"

Grotwell thought for a moment, then said, "None, sir. All were paired. You and your good wife together. Mr. Chapman here and Mr. Pullyver. Then Mr. Babcock, who is dead, and Francis Crisp."

"Have you not forgot *yourself*, sergeant?" asked Matthew.

"Myself? Why, I see I have, sir. Yes, I was alone, sir, there being no partner for my watch. We were an odd number."

"Which worked out most conveniently for you—odd or no."

"I don't know what you mean," Grotwell said with a forced smile. "I never missed company, if that's what you're saying. I often do my rounds alone."

"What I mean, sergeant, is that it was convenient for you to kill Stubbs without a witness. You found him on your rounds, I don't know how or exactly when, but surely before the lot of us gathered again and Rose Dibble discovered Stubbs's hiding place to us all. That was no news to you, his hiding in Talbot's booth, although you feigned surprise and professed your disbelief like an accomplished play actor. *You* found the lad earlier yourself. Found him, bludgeoned him, drowned him. My only question for you is this: had you planned earlier to kill Babcock too, or did that wicked thought leap into your brain the instant you stuffed Gabriel Stubbs head first into the malmsey butt?"

During Matthew's speech, Grotwell's square, stolid face had begun to twitch nervously. Now his hand rested on his own dagger. "That's a filthy lie, and filthy is he who gives it to me," he said menacingly. "I never killed a soul, save in the line of my duty. And why should I want the bearward dead? He was nothing to me, neither friend nor enemy."

"Oh, he was more," Matthew said. "And he did hurt you."

Matthew motioned to the sergeant's men to seize their leader; they hesitated a moment, unsure of their loyalties, then obeyed. Grotwell was grasped from both sides, his arms pinioned behind his back with such force that he winced with pain.

"Prove the lie *if* you can, Stock," said Grotwell between clinched teeth, his eyes fixed on Matthew and full of hatred. "I care not who you know or what you know. A lie is a lie. And damned is he who gives it. *Prove* what you say."

Matthew signaled to Joan and she brought the ledger forward, which she had been holding since before the meeting began. Matthew took the book and began to thumb through the pages.

"Ned Babcock may not have been the businessman Mr. Pullyver would have wanted, but he was a methodical bookkeeper. I have inspected his accounts, you see. Here, for example, is the entry of yesterday. Here Ned recorded the gate—three pounds and some odd pence."

"Why, it was far more if it was a penny," exclaimed Francis Crisp with surprise.

"And so it was, Francis," said Matthew, "for I well remember the sum. We men of commerce always have a ready ear for another man's profits, liking to compare them to our own. It was more indeed. Yet considerably less is recorded."

"Why? I never knew Ned to tamper with accounts. He was most scrupulous indeed," said Crisp.

"Perhaps he wanted to defraud me," said Pullyver defensively.

"I think he owed money elsewhere," said Matthew.

"To whom?"

"To the sergeant here," said Matthew.

"I never had any dealings with the man," Grotwell said.

"You *did* have dealings," Matthew said.

"Again I say, prove it, sir, or shut your mouth," Grotwell said. "What, will you bring the bearward alive again to testify against me?"

"There's no need, sergeant," said Matthew. "The facts speak for themselves."

"What facts?" asked the Justice.

"These. Ned Babcock was paying out the greater part of his share of the profits to *someone*, that's evident. If it were a legitimate debt, he would have made his partner aware of it. He would have recorded it in the ledger. But he left his partner in ignorance and, except for recording the proper sum herein, says nothing here to explain the discrepancy between what was taken in at the gate and what went into his pocket. Now I remind you that Ned Babcock, whatever his other foibles, was scrupulously honest. But this payment to someone has all the marks of extortion."

"Extortion," exclaimed Francis Crisp and Juliet in unison. Now everyone, with the exception of Grotwell, urged Matthew to continue.

"What I mean is that someone had threatened Ned Babcock, someone who knew something that would destroy his fortune. It wasn't you, Mr. Pullyver. You wanted Babcock's business, that is to say, *Samson*. But what Ned feared more than anything was that the bear would be destroyed. He told me so. And why shouldn't he be afraid? Within the year Samson had killed his own son-in-law. I grant it was provoked, and yet on that occasion Samson narrowly escaped condemnation. When a body was found at the muckhill, Ned viewed the remains and knew at once who it was—he recognized the man's hose, for they had once been his own. It was Simon Plover, his former helper. Now if this truth had been understood from the beginning, almost surely Samson would have been impounded, then destroyed."

"Indeed the bear would have been destroyed," Justice Baynard declared. "But it was later discovered that the bear was only an ignorant accessory. Even a man may escape hanging for that."

"At which time Ned Babcock breathed more easily," Matthew continued. "Samson was off the hook for the crime. Before that, however, he was terrified that the dead man's identity would be discovered and Samson's guilt be confirmed. As I say, it was a lucky guess on my part aided by a slip of Ned's tongue that led me to deduce the truth. Yet someone else knew the truth before me."

"You're grasping at straws, Stock," snarled Grotwell, struggling to free himself from the grip of his own men.

"At solid planks, rather," Matthew said. "You knew who the dead man was, Grotwell, for all your threatening and railing at Ned. You recognized him from the patched hose too. As well you might. You had ample opportunity to know him and his hose. You and Plover were boon companions, I have since discovered. You haunted the Smithfield ale houses together and in your office you had thrown him into the stocks often enough, fixing his ankles into the brace."

Matthew paused. The room was quiet. The accused man's eyes were hard stones.

"You went to Babcock privately and told him what you knew. You railed at him in public but in private you promised to keep his secret—for a price. You would take a share of the gate. It can be exactly determined from Babcock's ledger, by subtracting what I and Francis remember the real sum was from the difference recorded here. You see how eloquently dead men speak. Speaks from his very account book, you base devil!"

Grotwell still made no response. He seemed content to wait the charges out.

"Everything would have been well for you but Stubbs was found to be the murderer of Plover. Samson was cleared of blame. Then quite reasonably Ned wanted his money back. What did he do, Grotwell, threaten to tell the Justice here or Master Clerk if you did not return the money? That would have been bad for you. Now the tables were turned. You had to return the money or pay the price—or shut Babcock up for good."

"Lies, all lies," said Grotwell. Suddenly the burly sergeant broke free from his captors and bolted for the door. He shook it violently but it was locked and Matthew had the key. His men, recovered from their surprise, threw themselves at him from behind and wrestled him to the ground. While all in the room watched the struggle, the two officers pummeled the face and body of their former leader. They stopped only when Matthew ordered them to, when Grotwell was bleeding and subdued.

They yanked the sergeant to his feet and shoved him back against the door so that his head banged violently on it. Grotwell made no resistance now. With bloody mouth and eye and broken nose, he gaped at the chamber. He made wheezing sounds as he breathed and clutched his side. His left leg was damp from the codpiece to the knee; he had urinated during the struggle.

"Now will you tell the truth?" demanded Justice Baynard, approaching the man.

"Yes, speak, speak," everyone in the room demanded.

Grotwell was beaten and he knew it. His bloody lip trembled and when he spoke his speech was slurred like a drunken man's. "It's true, what Mr. Stock has said. I knew Simon Plover. We had many a drink together when I wasn't on duty and a few when I was. And I had clamped his ankles in irons enough times for public drunkenness. He had but one pair of hose and foul-smelling they were, so patched as to be naught but patches. I knew those hose like I knew my own face, worse luck for me and him. When I saw the leg—what remained of him— I knew who it was that had been found in the muckhill. I knew Babcock *knew* and I understood his silence well enough. A man wants to keep his living, and a bearward without a bear is in a sorry state of affairs. I told him I would keep his little secret if he would help me to a bit extra."

"A good portion of his takings," added Francis Crisp, outraged.

"Yes, a good portion," answered Grotwell, turning slightly to Crisp. "It was my due. It was either pay me or lose the bear and perhaps face arrest himself. I put it very plain to him. I had the authority. He knew it."

"Then he did want his money back later?"

"Oh, yes, he was most insistent. Told me he had great debts that must be paid and could not afford to allow me to keep what was mine. I told him to go to hell. He told me that he might go to hell indeed, but he would see I went with him. He gave me until the next morn to pay. I resolved to give the money back. Then I found Stubbs, came upon him quite by accident. Not looking for him at all. I was thirsty, wanted a drink and didn't feel like paying for it. I remembered the wine seller's booth and knew there'd be some good stuff there, just waiting to be had. I thought that if I was noticed there no one would pay attention, but think I was just making my customary rounds.

"I came upon the booth just as the girl was slipping out. I put two and two together—guessed I'd come upon Stubbs's hiding place. So in I went and all of a sudden there he was. You should have seen the look on his face. He reached in his shirt, I suppose for the blade, but it was gone. What a surprise. I brought my cudgel down smartly and that was all for him. I was about to spread the alarm, summon my men who I knew were in the neighboring lane and shortly to meet me at the Close. Then it occurred to me what fortune had laid in my way.

"I decided to finish him. He was a murderer, a rotten murderer, and my conscience never bothered me for that. I pried open the top of the malmsey butt and lifted him up, stuck him in head first. He was drowned in a minute, never knowing what had happened to him. So much for his dreams and visions, eh?

"The next morning I went to see Ned Babcock. He was expecting me and, yes, he was dressed. I supposed he had fed the bear but I thought nothing about that. Babcock thought I had come with his money. I told him I had and that I was sorry for having taken it and hoped he would say nothing of our previous agreement. He was very well spoken about the whole matter. I reached into my purse and pulled out the coins he had given me—something less than he had given me, to tell the truth of it, for I had already spent some to pay debts of my own. As I was handing it to him I pretended to drop it, and when he reached down—"

At this Juliet, who had been listening all this time, let out an anguished groan and fell into a swoon. Everyone rushed to her, to see if she was dead.

# · 24 ·

Joan felt a peremptory hand on her right shoulder and knew who it was that touched her as surely as though eyes in the back of her head had confirmed it. Her embarrassment was renewed. Her husband had gone on ahead with Justice Baynard. The two of them walked arm in arm, Baynard putting praise in her husband's ear like a pious worshiper dribbling pennies into the poor box—praise for his cleverness, his resoluteness, the sharpness of his eye and memory.

It was disgusting! Joan was angry at Baynard (pompous ass!), angry with Matthew, angry with herself for being angry with the both of them. What did it matter if Matthew got the credit for unraveling the skein of the Bartholomew Fair murders. Were she and he not one flesh, husband and wife, an indissoluble bond? Was his praise not therefore somehow hers?

Moments before she had decided in her heart that it was not, and she felt at the moment all the umbrage of injured merit, umbrage that now expressed itself as anger with her husband and with the entire race of men, meaning not the species of humankind but the gender of males, great and small. But Esmera, Esmera walking behind her, creeping up behind her, touching her, and in doing so begging that she stay her course! All that was still another offense. She turned on the woman in a fury.

"Now what?" She almost spat the words, blocking the doorway with her arms akimbo, and fixing a gaze of withering contempt on the cunning-woman. "More prophecies to make me look the fool?"

Esmera, seemingly unmoved by this expression of hostility, stared back mildly; slowly a smile crossed her face and seemed to transform her into another person. But it was still Esmera, to Joan at least. Joan knew that as soon as the woman spoke again.

"I pray you be at peace with me, Mrs. Stock. Surely I meant no harm to you. One such as I, forced to live by her wits and talents, must sometimes—"

"Must sometimes take money and make an honest woman a gull," Joan interrupted with all the bitterness she felt.

She hoped the cold, despising glance would reveal to Esmera just how displeased she had been to learn the full scope of the fortune-teller's complicity with Pullyver. Joan was in no forgiving mood. Had the horrid woman not caused her face to burn in the chamber, when Matthew had unraveled the truth of all her dire warnings, revealing them to be nothing but the basest effort at manipulation? Joan's blood boiled as she remembered her meetings with Esmera. Suddenly it all came back and the memory was agonizing to her spirit. She had never known such humiliation.

But the smile did not fade from Esmera's face. Undoubtedly she had been confronted before by outraged clients and knew how to pacify them. Joan was resolved not to be pacified.

"You are a liar and a cheat," Joan said.

"Never a liar, Mrs. Stock," answered Esmera, mildly.

"I say a liar and stand by the word," Joan challenged.

"I told no lies," Esmera repeated.

"None without a good profit." Joan snorted with contempt and turned to follow her husband. But Esmera raised a hand to Joan's arm. "Wait," she pleaded. "Hear me out, for mercy's sake. You misunderstood."

"God's bodkins, I think I understood very well, thank you."

"Oh, no, mistress. Never. If you think I lied for a paltry—"

"And what exactly was the sum?" Joan asked, fixing the woman with her steady gaze of contempt.

"Pullyver is an ass, an ignorant man," Esmera said, no longer smiling. She shook her head as though the greengrocer's stupidity was somehow her responsibility. "He does not understand, neither did the others. But surely *you* can."

"Understand what, for heaven's sake?" Joan demanded, impatient to be on her way, lamenting in her soul the waste of her time, the tarnishing of her reputation.

"Pullyver did not send me to you, save after you had first come to me," Esmera said. "His money didn't give substance to my warning, only turned it to my advantage to reiterate it. Consider, Mrs. Stock. The destinies are a thing apart from our little pettinesses, the base motives that rattle in our brains and that we take to be the cause of action. It is the stars, rather, and the writings of fate imprinted in our palms. That is *destiny*. Your destiny does not depend on Pullyver any more than my warning wanted truth because he paid me to issue it. And remember, Mrs. Stock, my warning *was* truth. Within these few minutes it was confirmed. What did I say? A murderer with a long, pointed blade? Danger to you and yours? Danger you would have escaped completely had you gone home to Chelmsford. See how time has vindicated me!"

"Gone home and been out of Pullyver's way, you mean," Joan said, turning now, but Esmera stayed with her, clutching her arm. Esmera followed Joan out into the street, like old friends meeting at the fair. They merged with the throng moving toward the Close. The sun shone brightly. Everywhere there was noise and color, the day of the saint's feast.

"I must join my husband," Joan said, trying to catch a glimpse of him somewhere up ahead. She did. He was still walking with Baynard. She hurried to catch up, but Esmera dogged her step like an importunate beggar.

"Wasn't it so? Wasn't it so? Everything that I said."

Joan stepped out of the way of the heaviest traffic surging around her.

"Was it not so?" Esmera repeated, looking at Joan out of dark, appealing eyes.

"It was so. It was as you said," Joan conceded, quite despite herself. She would have gladly rid herself of this woman, this woman for whom she had nothing but resentment, and whose companionship now embarrassed her. But the truth was the truth. If not from the stars, then from the plain facts, the natural sequence of causes. "There *was* danger," Joan conceded. "You were right on that score. Now leave me be, I beg you. I *must* join my husband."

The ingratiating smile returned, slowly, like a sunrise. "Mark me well, Mrs. Stock," Esmera said, her voice falling into a secretive whisper Joan was at pains to hear for the racket in the street. "I told no lies. Not then, not now. Look you, I will tell you another fortune—see if it does not come to pass. I don't even need to feel your palm to tell it. Honor awaits you, great employment, gifts of love and substance. Mark my words. May my tongue be cleft like a snake's, may my soul never rest in its grave, if what I say to you does not come to pass. Mark my words."

Joan glared at Esmera suspiciously, but the nape of her neck tingled with a strange excitement at the prophecy. In her heart, belief strove with doubt, desire with memory of her humiliation. Shortly, belief and desire conquered. Without fully wanting to, despising herself a little for uttering it, she asked, "*When* shall these things be? And what honors and employment do you foresee?"

Esmera smiled a new smile, one that could only be interpreted as satisfaction. But Joan's curiosity was strong. Esmera's smile contrasted oddly with the woman's eyes, which seemed to regard something not there, like the wandering pupils of the blind. "All will come in good time," was all Esmera said. That and good-bye.

Joan watched as Esmera moved into the current of the street, became a bobbing, hatless head and then a nothing. The woman had hurried away—as though she were late for some pressing business.

Pressing business. Suddenly Joan remembered the time. Surely the hour was late, surely the great bell of Paul's had already struck its single golden note announcing the Queen's approach and the glorious ceremony Joan was determined not to miss for the world.

But as she hurried to her own destination the woman's words rang in her ears—rang louder than the cannon blasts, the great single note, and the blazonry of trumpets. Honor, reward, great employment. What did it all mean?

Or had she been gulled a second time by the devious woman?

Joan caught up with her husband, but only because he had walked slowly; the crowd made any movement difficult. He was still talking to Baynard, but the subject was no longer the murders.

A platform had been constructed for the dignitaries of the fair, the Clerk and the Stewards, notables of the City, and a retinue of other persons who had managed a position of honor. The platform was crowded, but Joan and Matthew had been assured of a place giving good view of the red carpet stretched out before. Down this carpet the Queen was to come to be greeted by the dignitaries, who would descend from the platform to kneel at her feet. All had been carefully planned. The Queen's way was already indicated by the presence of the royal guard, splendid in their scarlet livery, halberds skyward. On each side, the crowd pressed in for a view, a touch.

Joan had never seen the Queen, although often her image, and she was seized with a powerful excitement that put the gruesome details of the Bartholomew Fair murders quite from her mind. Then in the distance she heard a new blast of trumpets and the furious roll of a drumbeat. All heads in the crowd turned, and those packed on the platform struggled for a view. The crowd began to cheer wildly, even before anything could be seen. "God save Queen Bess! Long life to Her Majesty!"

Joan found herself shouting too, praising Elizabeth, best of queens, marvel of women. The guard was now at attention and had closed ranks, forming a wall between the royal path and the people who pressed in on all sides.

The cheering continued. A dozen or so young white-garbed women could now be seen. These were the virgins of Smithfield, the attendants of the Virgin Queen. They moved slowly down the path, strewing flowers. Following them came the Queen herself. The Queen carried a wand in one hand and with the other she waved to her subjects, nodding graciously and drawing thereby an even greater outpouring of devotion.

Then the procession came to a halt and Joan had full view of Elizabeth. There she stood, like a divinity indeed, hailed on all sides and glorious in crown, wand, and jewels. She was a little taller than Joan had expected but somewhat stooped. Her face was oblong and fair and wrinkled and she wore false red hair. Her nose was a little crooked but not ignoble. The cheering died away. She said, "I thank you, my good people."

"Long live Queen Elizabeth!" returned the assembly in unison, and hats flew into the air.

The officials of the fair descended the platform and knelt before her, while the virgins who had accompanied her now spread around the Queen as though she were a great ruby and they her foil.

Joan recognized Rose among them. She pointed her out to Matthew. "There's Rose," she said.

"So it is," said Matthew. "It's a good sign she's overcome her grief. It's a shame such a pretty one as she should have become so enamored of a madman. Why, look, she's the fairest of the lot of them, her swollen lip notwithstanding."

Joan agreed. Rose was lovely, dressed finely as she was. And yet she noticed no joy in Rose's face. The other girls were smiling, proud of their distinction, their proximity to greatness. Rose seemed grave. Was she still grieving after all?

The Queen's guard had made a wall around her and Joan thought of Stubbs's plan. To kill the Queen. How, she wondered now, had the young Puritan ever thought to penetrate that wall of protection, those stout armed men each of whom would sooner lay down his life than see his royal mistress assaulted?

Yet Rose had penetrated the wall, stood now within the enclosure as the very image of innocence and purity. Rose's beauty had accomplished what her lover's stratagems had not. Rose. Simple, winsome Rose. Rose who loved the handsome lunatic who had confused the Queen of England and the Queen of Babylon and whose belief in her lover's crazed dreams and visions must surely have been as strong as her love, indestructable despite the terrible revelations of his murders. Had it been strong enough to cause her to share not only his delusion but his mission?

In a split second the scene before her was blotted out and replaced by another fetched from her recent memory. In her mind's eye she saw again the great chamber of the inn and her husband standing before them, holding Stubbs's weapon aloft to show the true instrument of death and mutilation. Then Matthew had laid it down on the table in front of him, where it had remained through all the startling disclosures that followed as the primary exhibit of the young Puritan's treachery. For the long anxious hour it had remained inert there in silent witness. Joan remembered it, lying there as her husband had denounced the sergeant for extortion and murder. Then there was the scuffle. Grotwell's futile effort to escape. All eyes were turned to the back of the room. Matthew had left his station, moved quickly to call off Grotwell's men before they killed him. Brutal men only too happy for this opportunity to do violence with impunity. Grotwell's subduing and his subsequent confession had distracted them all. All save one. Again Joan saw the table in her mind, saw it as it had appeared just before Matthew had dismissed them all. It had been bare, the tabletop. The dagger was gone! And who had taken thought of its disappearance then, with congratulations in the air like the whir of birds' wings and great haste to be gone before the Queen should come?

Besides, was not the weapon's owner dead, the mystery solved at last?

Someone, she now realized, had snatched the blade up while

all heads were turned, fixed on the beating Grotwell's men were administering to him with such zeal. That someone had not been so easily distracted, someone for whom the knife remained a relic not of murder but of devotion to a righteous cause. That person had snatched it up and concealed it, borne it from the chamber and kept it still.

The present scene returned. Joan saw Rose. The girl was moving, inching toward the Queen. Her expression was hard. A face not made for grimaces and glowering was twisted almost beyond recognition by malevolent thoughts not her own.

In the same instant, while the Clerk of the Fair was between sentences and the tedium of his address of welcome was beginning to be evident in the restlessness of the crowd and the wavering of the royal attention, Joan made sense of it all—the missing dagger, the evil design of Gabriel Stubbs, the tragic complicity of innocence. Joan screamed to the full extent of her lungs. She screamed again, aware as she did so that she was either proclaiming herself the maddest woman in England or the savior of her monarch from imminent assassination.

Every head turned. Her husband, nearly deafened by the blast, stared in wordless astonishment, his mouth agape. The Queen's guard, uncertain of what this outburst meant, closed around Her Majesty, pointing their halberds toward the officials' stand to ward off the threatening danger.

"The girl, it's the girl!" Joan cried, pointing toward the white-garbed virgins.

Rose had stopped, momentarily distracted by Joan's scream. Now she made a sudden move, shoving aside another of the virgins. But the movement was ill-timed. The guards, fully alerted, noticed the move and intervened, wrestling Rose to the ground. The basket fell and rolled toward Elizabeth's feet, emptying what remained of its contents—a handful of posies and the unsheathed blade with which Rose Dibble had conspired to pierce the heart of Babylon's Queen.

# • *Epilogue* •

It was afternoon. The dog days of August were done. September had brought the benison of cool rains, one of which was even now tapping against the window with gentle insistency.

In the Queen's apartment in Whitehall, for more than an hour they have been conversing, the Queen and her Principal Secretary. Her Majesty was in a merry mood, and Cecil with unerring instinct had matched his own to it. The room filled with her throaty laughter.

"Why, by the Mass, Robin, this is more diverting than any court gossip you've treated me to this twelve months. Pray don't stop now."

Encouraged, Cecil went on, "Well, Your Majesty, this Grotwell—"

"The murderous sergeant—" She leaned forward in the great chair, frail of body but alert of mind.

"The very man. This Grotwell, I say, has been tried, convicted, and hanged. They say he made a good end on the gallows, confessing all and encouraging the youth present to forswear his example."

"As well they might," she agreed, "if they desire to live, and go to heaven too."

"Already he's the subject of five ballads and as many broadsides. The only shame is that he can't enjoy his share of the profits. But here is the best part. As it turns out, this same Grotwell was none other than the grandson of the famous Grotwell or Cartwell—a hangman who was himself hanged with two others for robbery of a booth at Bartholomew Fair in your illustrious father's time. His ancestry was not remembered before his villainy made him notorious."

"The grandson of a thief! And him a murderer too. By God . . . that proves blood will tell. There's a fine sergeant for you! As well have the cat guardian of the milk as entrust a sergeant with such bad blood to keep the peace. I can readily believe the story. But pray, how goes it with this young would-be murderess, Rose Dibble—she who tried to stab me at Bartholomew Fair with half of England there to bear witness to her treachery?"

"She remains at Newgate. Her trial is yet to come."

"Well, hanging is too good for her. She's totally mad, you know. As mad as this Stubbs, whose disciple she was. A mad disciple of a mad sectary fit for a paragraph in the acts and monuments of wickedness. How did she ever think to escape after she'd done it? But perhaps therein lies her madness. Show me one who has no regard for his life and I'll show you a madman or a great fool—and probably both. You know, Robin, I have lived all my life in fear of death. Fear that I would meet my mother's end, my head on the block, the cries of scorn ringing in my ears and ushering me to heaven. Yet even as God has granted me so long a life—"

"And so glorious a reign," he added.

"Don't interrupt! You know I can't abide it. At night I wake in a cold quicksilver sweat, afraid that beyond the curtains of my bed some merciless . . ."

She was falling into a melancholy. The drizzle at the window seemed less friendly than before. A chill settled in the room, in Cecil's bones too.

"Let us not speak of these fears," he said soothingly, "but pray that God spares us such misfortunes."

"I must do something for the clothier and his wife," she said, changing the subject and at the same instant seeming to return to a happier frame of mind. "What would be an appropriate token of gratitude?"

"I cannot deny but that they deserve it, Your Highness."

"What would you recommend—a gift of land, perhaps? A purse of gold?"

"Matthew Stock is a great treasure in himself. A man of most genuine goodness of soul and brave resolve. His appearance belies his cleverness."

"As does yours," she said, smiling mischievously.

He laughed, long used to her taunting. Only from her would he have endured such taunting, not only because she was Queen, but because she was herself, Elizabeth Tudor, a woman of indomitable spirit even in the twilight of her mortality. A sadness fell upon him.

"You praise the husband," she said. "What of the wife? You men are all the same. You think of goodness and bravery as the sole rights of your sex, forgetting these qualities are also woman's. Had this clothier's wife not vented her lungs in Smithfield I might have spilled my blood then and there. And who would you have had to succeed me?" But she did not wait for a response, and he was not eager to give it. The subject was a delicate one to them both.

"I suppose a knighthood would be too much," she conjectured, glancing at him out of the corner of her eye.

"Less deserving men have received one," he answered.

"We shall see. I'll think upon it. What other talents does the man possess?"

"He has a most marvelous tenor voice. He's not a bad clothier."

"England has clothiers in great number and singers too. Write him in Chelmsford. Invite him to London this coming month. Make sure he brings his wife. What's her name?"

"Joan."

"Joan, a good solid name. A thoroughly English name. I'll endure Matthew Stock's singing for his wife's company. Between now and then I'll hit upon a way of rewarding the both of them. And I think I can use their particular talents as well. In a private matter that has caused me much consternation since Michaelmas term."

"A private matter? *Do* let me guess."

She chuckled and said, "Don't bother. You'll find out soon enough." She shut her eyes and leaned her head back on the bolster. It was his signal to depart.

Sir Robert Cecil took his leave, treading silently across the room, the little man who was the greatest man in England because he was principal servant to the greatest woman.